———————— ★ ————————

MC punched the remote, opened her car door, and tossed her duffel bag over to the passenger seat.

Her heart skipped when she heard a shuffling noise. When nothing threatening appeared, she imagined there'd been an animal in the clump of trees near her car. She started to climb into the Nissan—except a hand grabbed her left arm and held her tight.

She gasped and winced in pain. She tried to kick, but she was locked in place, her legs pressed against the bottom edge of the car. Whoever it was reached down and pushed the button to unlock the other doors. Then he opened the back door and pushed her onto the back seat.

———————— ★ ————————

"Superb plotting, likeable characters and enough romance to appeal to fans of that genre turn *The Carbon Murder* into a fabulous crime thriller."

—Harriet Klausner

The Carbon Murder

Camille Minichino

W🌐RLDWIDE®

TORONTO • NEW YORK • LONDON
AMSTERDAM • PARIS • SYDNEY • HAMBURG
STOCKHOLM • ATHENS • TOKYO • MILAN
MADRID • WARSAW • BUDAPEST • AUCKLAND

To Dick Rufer, my husband and
24/7 tech support, the best there is

THE CARBON MURDER

A Worldwide Mystery/March 2005

First published by St. Martin's Press LLC.

ISBN 0-373-26522-0

Printed in U.S.A.

Acknowledgments

My special thanks go to my stepdaughter and equestrian, Claire Thomas, and to Dr. Andrew R. Clark, DVM, MBA, for their information and advice on equestrian matters; to Revere High School science teacher David Eatough, for information on his urban coyote field study; to Inspector Christopher Lux of the Alameda County, California, District Attorney's office, and Robert Rice, Director of the Revere Public Library, for their quick and amazing willingness to answer my questions, often the same ones more than once.

As usual, I drew enormous amounts of information and inspiration from Robert Durkin, my cousin and expert in all things mortuary; and from my cousin Jean Stokowski, constantly available and supportive.

Any misinterpretation of such excellent resources is purely my fault.

Thanks also to the many writers and friends who reviewed the manuscript in progress, in particular: Judy Barnett, Verna Cefalu, Margaret Hamilton, Dr. Eileen Hotte, Jonnie Jacobs, Anna Lipjhart, Maggie Long, Peggy Lucke, Lynn MacDonald, Ann Parker, Sue Stephenson, Karen Streich and Barbara Zulick.

I am most grateful to my wonderful editor, Marcia Markland, who has been with me in one way or another from my first book; and to my patient, remarkable agent, Elaine Koster.

ONE

"Isn't this perfect?" my best friend, Rose Galigani, said. Her newly applied auburn highlights caught the light from the faux Tiffany lamp as she swung her head from me to her daughter, and back.

Girls' Night Out at Tomasso's Restaurant and Coffee Annex on Squire Road in North Revere. A fall evening, a few months after I'd moved out of my apartment in the Galigani Mortuary building and into the house owned by police detective Matt Gennaro, my second boyfriend since the Kennedy Administration.

Rose smiled broadly. "First you come back from California, Gloria, and then MC comes home from Texas. Our own little city is like Capistrano. The sparrows always come back to it."

"Swallows, Mom. It's the swallows that come back to Capistrano." MC orchestrated the melody with her hands. "When the swallows come back to Capistrano, da da da da da dee," she sang. Softly, but still, Rose or I would never have done such a thing in a public place, even at MC's age. Generation Thirty-Something-Years-Old was a more self-confident lot.

My godchild Mary Catherine Galigani, MC to her friends, had returned to the nest after several years in Houston, first as a field chemical engineer for an oil company, and then making a career change to their carbon research facility. *I went from huge hydrocarbons of petroleum to tiny diamondoids,* she'd said in a letter to me. *Imaging roasting petroleum at almost a thousand degrees and getting miniature diamonds for your trouble.* I was eager to have MC to myself to hear more of the research—and why she'd left it to come back home.

She, her mother, and I sat in a red vinyl booth that smelled of oregano from meals past, sharing our thoughts and our innermost secrets. The one I wanted both of them to reveal was how the mother (size six) and the daughter (size four) managed to eat pizza regularly and still look the way they did. They even each had a beer, while I (size undisclosed) nursed a calorie-free espresso.

"I meant *swallows*," Rose said. "And how many times do I have to tell you about the *Mom* part?"

MC laughed. Her short, dark hair fell artfully in front of her face. "Oh, right. *Maaaaaa.*"

Rose gave her daughter a playful nudge. "Don't make fun of your old *ma*."

MC was a much quicker little swallow than I was. It had taken me thirty years to return to my hometown. I'd fled across the country to Berkeley, California, after my fiancé died in a car crash a few months before our wedding. Not until three decades later had I been ready to move on with my life. Or, to come back and face it, was Rose's diagnosis.

Her playful demeanor aside, MC seemed distracted this evening, as if there were more on her mind than our light conversation. While Rose and I covered topics that took in her whole family, MC's gaze wandered to Tomasso's old, cracked, wooden door, then to the tiny dark-glass windows, then to the long weathered bar along the side wall as if she were expecting another guest. I wondered if she missed Texas. Or maybe a particular Texan.

Rose didn't seem to notice MC's preoccupation, and engaged me in a long agenda—how her husband, Frank, would respond to the new mortuary chain that was moving into the North Shore, threatening to buy up all the independents (in unprintable language, Rose predicted); whether MC's older brother John, a journalist, would ever settle down (maybe not until his fifties, like me, I suggested); whether the Galiganis' only grandchild should go to Revere High School or to the new Catholic school (RHS had been good enough for us, Rose and I agreed).

My issues were slight, having to do with redecorating Matt Gennaro's house, and keeping up with my volunteer work in science education. I was on a deadline to come up with a hot technology topic for the second half of the term for the Revere High Science Club. *Call Daniel Endicott, the new science teacher,* I reminded myself silently.

"Did you say redecorate?" I heard Rose ask with great enthusiasm when I tuned back in to her. This was her field. She knew I preferred computer stores to any other, the latest software to a new couch or lamp. "You know I'll be happy to go furniture shopping with you."

"How about choosing the furniture *instead* of me?"

MC picked at her pizza crust, nibbling at a burnt piece. Rose played with her slice, pushing mushrooms around with her fork—the Tomasso waitresses all knew that they should bring Rose a full set of silverware, even if she ordered finger-food. Maybe I was witnessing the Galigani women's secret. Small bites, with long waits in between. I was more inclined to immediately bite off a sector with a two-inch radius.

"Any plans yet, MC?" I asked.

She shook her head, seeming to return from some distant land, perhaps the Southwest. "I'm just glad to be out of Houston. I got tired of the weather, and…other things."

MC told this to us, and, inadvertently, to our waitress, who wore a Tomasso's uniform shirt the color of old marinara sauce. She smiled down on MC, her blond/black beehive hairdo at a precarious angle. Her look said one of two things: *You're home now and we'll take care of you,* or *If I could get out of Revere, I'd never come back.* I couldn't decide which. Either way, she deserved a big tip.

Tomasso's had not adopted the practice, so common in California, of supplying name tags for employees, so I named our waitress myself. In my mind I called her *Josephine,* my mother's name. Josephine Lamerino had never left Revere, either.

Tomasso's was one of Revere's tourist attractions. Visitors who came for the beach and the famous Revere Beach Boulevard also heard about Billy Tomasso the Fourth, who made the best pizza outside of Boston's North End. Old-timers could remember when the restaurant was even better—years ago, when half the facility was devoted to baking Italian bread. Few could pass without succumbing to the fresh yeasty smell and picking up a crusty loaf for supper.

Now half of the building had been turned into a trendy coffee bar—Tomasso's Coffee Annex—serving breakfast pastries in the morning, and Italian desserts the rest of the day. Tiramisu, cannoli, pasticciotti, pignoli, rum cake. I would gladly call any of the selections *dinner.*

On this Tuesday evening, a group of four middle-aged women in various Hawaiian prints posed with a waitress in front of Tomasso's famous coffee vat while a busboy took their photograph. On weekend nights patrons lined up for this shot. The vat, at the far end of the coffee bar, was enormous. A large gold eagle perched at the top of the center section. Highly polished, coppery gold, in three sections, it looked at once like a medieval religious triptych and a futuristic rocker launcher.

Billy kept a bulletin board behind the vat and posted photos, some of famous visitors, like former Boston mayors Curley and Tobin and even a Kennedy or two. Mixed in were postcards from patrons who sent messages to Billy when they returned to their homes in Indiana or Kansas.

Although the vat hadn't been used in my lifetime, I could imagine rich, dark liquid dripping from its elaborate valves.

"An oil refinery," Rose said, as if she'd had the same image as me, except with oil instead of coffee pouring out of the shiny spouts. She wrinkled her nose, and I realized she was still trying to come to terms with an unlikely combination—her lovely, only daughter working as a chemical engineer, surrounded by hard hats and enormous drilling rigs.

A few years ago Rose had toured an oil refinery, humoring MC in her daughter's attempt to share her work world. In her more recent research career MC had been involved in very clean laboratory work, experimenting with the newly discovered diamond fragments that lurked inside crude oil, and she'd also taught a chemistry class at Houston Poly. But Rose hadn't made the adjustment. Besides, to Rose, one science or engineering field was the same as another.

"You should have seen those steel pipes," Rose had said to me. "Miles of them."

"I have seen them," I said.

"Oh, yes. I forgot it's your fault MC is a scientist in the first place." Rose's happy grin always took the edge off comments like that.

I liked to think Rose was right, that MC had been influenced by me, her godmother, now-retired physicist Gloria Lamerino, who'd made MC a tiny white lab coat when she was four years old.

"How did you manage, Aunt G?" MC asked, bringing me to the present, where MC was no longer a toddler. "Working in that huge organization for so many years—there were eight thousand people at the Berkeley lab, right?"

"I only worked with six of them."

Rose and MC laughed, but I knew what MC meant. I had to admit that I'd like getting lost in an army of coworkers, the better to keep my private thoughts and feelings to myself. I thought of other advantages also, however, ones I could share with Rose and MC, and I recited them. "There's a lot to be said for a big organization. You can move around, work on different projects, and still have the same employer, with all your benefits and a permanent office and phone number. And in my day, scientists at the big labs didn't have to worry about bringing in their own funding. We all wrote grant proposals, of course, but even if nothing came through, you knew you could keep working."

"Our tax dollars at work," Rose said.

MC nodded. "Good points. But I think I'm headed for 'small' next time."

Rose finally scooped a forkful of mushrooms from the top of her pizza and ate it. "MC thinks she might want to teach full-time, but those scientists at the Charger Street lab are after her already."

Our waitress, who'd come back to give me a fresh espresso from the coffee bar, heard that remark, too, I noticed. Her narrow, penciled-in eyebrows went up a few degrees of arc, generating tiny, fleshy waves across her forehead. *If you have extra guys after you, send them to me,* her look said.

"A woman named Lorna Frederick left a message for me this

morning," MC said. "She's a project leader at Charger Street. Her name is familiar to me. I think she's an equestrian, like my boyfr…uh, friend…Jake Powers. Do you know her?"

I understood why MC didn't want to talk about an ex-boyfriend. No one in Revere had ever met him, but she'd hinted that it hadn't been a happy breakup.

I shook my head. "I don't think I've ever heard the name." The Charger Street lab, and R&D institution with government funding, was almost as large as the Berkeley University Laboratory in California, where I'd spent my career. Charger Street was technically a division of the Massachusetts University Department of Physics, with its main campus in Boston. I remembered a good laugh when my Berkeley friend, Elaine Cody, a tech editor at BUL, noted that I'd gone from BUL to MUD.

"So I guess you're deciding between research and teaching?" I asked MC.

She nodded. "I'm torn, Aunt G. I loved the one class I taught, but I don't know if I can give up research entirely. And Charger Street is working on very interesting projects, too, some really new carbon nanotechnology, which is like an extension of what I was doing, and what I'm most interested in."

"At least she's out of the oil business," Rose said. "I'd rather tell people my daughter is a teacher, or she's doing research, finding a cure for cancer. And look, she's so famous, they know about her clear across the country."

"Everyone knows everyone in the field, Mom," MC said, smiling at her slip of the tongue, and at her mother's pride in her. "It's all part of doing research, Ma. I met a lot of the Massachusetts people at conferences."

I nodded, knowing how it worked. When I was experimenting with titanium dioxide, I knew every person in the world who had a similar crystal, how powerful their laser was, and how far they'd progressed in characterizing the crystal coefficients.

MC turned to me. "You'll love this, Aunt G. I got involved a little in buckyballs, and that kind of fun stuff, and even had one of my students do a paper on it."

"Buckyballs! Pure carbon!"

While my eyes lit up, Rose rolled hers.

"You two and your science. But let's not forget that the Charger Street lab has been a den of crime lately."

I winced at Rose's reference to my new career as a consultant to the Revere Police Department. Retired from physics—good, clean work, as my father had called it—I'd fallen into police work, helping the RPD with science-related cases. And many of those cases had involved the staff at the Charger Street lab as either vics or perps, in cop talk.

"Speaking of teaching—" Rose said. She paused for our laughter at her creative segue, then went on. "Mrs. Cataldo, your old high school chemistry teacher, was asking for you, MC. I told her you were coming home, and she'd love to see you. She's at the senior care center on Pearce Street."

"We should both visit her," I said to MC. "Although I think she gave you better grades."

"That's because she was only ninety years old, and still sharp, when you had her. By the time my class came along, she was a hundred and fifty and only giving As."

MC had the same smile as her mother, the same high-pitched voice, and I was thrilled to be with them both. Magnificent fall leaves outside and my two favorite women inside.

What could go wrong?

Nothing. Until Rose excused herself to go to the rest room. Once she'd slipped gracefully out of the booth, I hoped MC and I could sneak in a few words about buckyballs.

I pictured the buckyball molecule, made up of sixty carbon atoms, folded over into a soccer-ball shape, one atom on each "corner" of the soccer ball. After reading articles on the new material, I'd spent some time trying to think up a non-sports metaphor for the configuration. Maybe MC had some ideas.

But I knew I had to address more personal matters first.

"Is something wrong, MC? You seem a little distracted." MC pulled her shoulders up, her neck almost disappearing into the ribbing of her gray TEXAS THE LONE STAR STATE sweatshirt. "Or are you just bored with the over-fifty crowd?" I asked, to give her a way out of talking if she needed one.

She leaned over and spoke softly, a catch in her voice. She pulled the sleeves of her sweatshirt down over her hands, further emphasizing her waif-like appearance.

"I guess I need to tell someone. This would be between us, right?"

A nervous wave went through me. "Of course."

"I'm being stalked."

TWO

My FIRST THOUGHT WAS, *It's my fault.* They're not after *her,* they think they're stalking *me.* I'm the one who's made the bad element of the city unhappy. And MC had taken up residence in the apartment I'd abandoned, three floors above the family business, the Galigani Mortuary. As I once did, she lived over a prep room—home of embalming fluids, otherworldly sinks, and the occasional defensive weapon.

"Is someone hanging around the mortuary? Maybe they think I still live there. I've had my share of—"

MC held up her hand to stop me, her eyes frightened, the sparkle of her musical "swallows" performance gone with the last sip of her beer. I knew I should pursue an investigative tack, or say something comforting; I settled for simply not becoming hysterical, which I accomplished by a few deep breaths.

Girls' Night Out was falling apart. I wished Matt were with us. MC and I both needed the levelheaded perspective of law enforcement.

While "Josephine" fussed over slipping the check under a wet glass, I formulated some questions in my mind. How long have you been stalked? What did "they" look like? How close have they come to you? Do they know you know?

Once our waitress left, MC was ready with thoughts of her own. "It has nothing to do with living at the mortuary. I know who it is, and why."

"You've seen him? Her?"

"I just know. It's Jake Powers, my ex-boyfriend."

So, "boyfriend" extended into at least the thirties. Irrelevance always crept in when I was tense.

"The one you left in Houston?"

"Yeah, well, I thought I did. But he was very upset when I left him, and I guess he followed me here."

"Has he been to the apartment? Phoned you? What?"

She shook her head. "Right now he's just hanging around everywhere. My health club in Winthrop, the grocery store, the library. I see this shadow, but I know it's him. He's a small guy. I know it's just a matter of time before he makes himself known. I haven't told Mom anything about this. Or anyone else."

"Good move." I pictured MC's father, Frank, and her two protective older brothers, Robert and John, forming a SWAT team around her. I tapped the table with my unpainted, uneven nails. My nervous thinking exercise—how to get Matt involved without upsetting the rest of our small circle.

MC's perfect carmine fingertips poked out from the ribbing of her sweatshirt as she put her hand on mine. "I'm scared, Aunt G."

I swallowed, suddenly unable to think of her as anything but a little girl. "Come home with me tonight. We'll talk to Matt. He can put a car outside the building at least. They'll catch him lurking and give him—" I racked my brain. "A restraining order."

MC shook her head, tilted it toward the ladies' room. "I don't want everyone to get all excited."

"We don't have to tell anyone." I breathed deeply. "Do you think Jake is dangerous?"

MC lowered her eyes, played with the remnants of her napkin. Not the "whole truth" posture. Should I trust what came next? I wondered.

"He does have a temper. He'd get angry and break some dishes whenever he came home without a ribbon."

"A ribbon?"

"Besides being an excellent chemist, he's a very competitive equestrian."

"He's one of those people who jump over hurdles on a horse?"

The beginning of a smile. "Something like that. They're called fences—made up of poles or plants, or even walls—and there are lots of different configurations that I learned about."

"Not as fascinating as what we can do with the strong bonds

among the carbon atoms in that new material you were working with." A pause for a smile, and then I had to play godmother, responsible for MC's s spiritual, mental and physical well-being. I felt no less liability because MC was now an adult with two perfectly functioning biological parents. "Did Jake ever…take out his anger on you, MC?"

She shook her head, but just barely, eyes cast down once more. Unconvincing. "He was all possessive, and who needs that? He listened in on my phone calls, checked my mail, got jealous of even my nights out with my girlfriends. And if I ever went to lunch with one of the male techs, he'd…"

"So you got along well with the technicians out there?" *Your mother's on the way back,* was what I meant, and MC understood.

WE LEFT TOMASSO'S and headed for our three vehicles, having foisted the leftover pizza on Rose. William, her teenage grandson, was spending the night at her house, so we were sure the food would not see the light of morning.

I gave MC one last look that said, *Please come home with me.* She bit her lip and shook her head, ever so slightly. *No.*

Leaving me no alternative except to follow her home and see what was going on outside my old apartment.

IT SEEMED PERFECTLY NATURAL for me to head for Tuttle Street, around the corner from St. Anthony's Church. I'd loved my mortuary apartment, in spite of its proximity to scenes of mourning and its constant reminder of mortality. Rose and Frank had offered me the apartment on the top floor of their building, temporarily, to make my transition from California smoother.

The apartment above the funeral parlors of Galigani Mortuary had served me well, but it had its drawbacks. The smells, for one. I'd never minded chemical odors in the science buildings of my life, but the noxiousness seemed exaggerated when I was aware that a particular compound was being pumped into—or out of—"clients," as Frank and Robert, his son and partner, called the corpses that arrived regularly at their door.

I'd considered eventually buying a small condo in one of the new high-rises that now lined Revere Beach Boulevard. A balcony overlooking the Atlantic Ocean, with spectacular sunrises for breakfast. A salt-smelling sea breeze. The sounds of seagulls and breaking surf. Memories of my first job, selling cotton candy and then going home with sugar crystals stuck to my eyelashes.

But I'd ended up staying at the mortuary until I moved in with Matt. Why had I chosen the odor of restorative, wound-filling chemicals, the whirring of pumps and saws, over the smells and sounds of Revere Beach? Matt's theory was that, deep down, I couldn't stand the thought of living where in my youth there had been the world's greatest amusement park. Two miles of thrill rides and food stands, a bowling alley, ten-cent prizes, and Sunday bandstand music. All gone by the late seventies, replaced by enormous apartment buildings.

"I think you'd feel like you'd sold out to the developers," he'd said.

He had a point. As if my boycotting a one-bedroom condo with an ocean view would bring back the Cyclone, the biggest roller coaster in the country in its time, or the two colorful merry-go-rounds, which were more at my level of risk-taking.

I arrived at my stakeout just as MC's silver Nissan turned into the garage. She had an easy time with her normal-size car, I noticed. I didn't miss the times when I'd had to maneuver my Cadillac between a hearse on one side and a limo on the other. I was still driving the large, hand-me-down Caddie from the Galigani Mortuary, hard to hide on the narrow, one-way Tuttle Street. At least it was black, I told myself, and MC wouldn't be expecting me to do something so silly as sit outside her building looking for her stalker.

Silly, indeed. I tapped the steering wheel, wondering what in the world I was doing there, parked across the street from a funeral parlor, other than reminiscing about my twin blue glide rockers, which I'd left for MC. I had a feeling that MC was not being completely candid about Jake and their relationship, that he'd been violent to more than MC's dinner dishes, and I wanted to see him for myself.

But I'd forgotten to ask what Jake looked like. Skin coloring?

Facial hair? A limp from horseback riding? And what might he be wearing? "Fine police work," I muttered, half aloud.

And suppose I did see someone suspicious—what would I do? Shake my plump finger at him and tell him to leave my godchild alone, or else?

Like the rest of New England at this time of year, tree-lined Tuttle Street still had a wash of reds and yellows, startling even in the dim light of the streetlamps. Several times as I sat in my car I heard or saw movement, but nothing out of the ordinary. Teenagers hanging on to each other, a kid shooting hoops by the light of an open garage door, an older couple almost jogging. A dog-walker came by—a possible? I wondered if you could rent a dog to blend into an environment where you were stalking someone.

I liked the more ordinary living quarters I had now—the house I shared with Matt on Fernwood Avenue, just west of Broadway. It smelled fine, and looked fine, if not up to Rose's standards. It even came with china and silver, from Matt's ten-year marriage to Teresa, who died of genetic heart disease many years ago.

When the light went on in MC's bedroom, I held my breath, as if listening for a crash or a shot. Nothing. Even so, I imagined different scenarios, none of them attractive. I punched Matt's number into my cell phone so it would take only one button to ring him in case I needed him in a hurry.

RRRRRRRing!

I jumped, and banged my knee on the wheel when my phone rang on its own, making me wish I'd opted for a sweet melody instead of a straight alarm sound. Elaine Cody had programmed her cell phone with the love theme from *Gone with the Wind,* I remembered. I fumbled with the RECEIVE button, all the while glancing around for Jake Powers, of unknown appearance.

"Hi," Matt said. "Is everything all right?"

His gravelly voice always brought a smile to my lips. "Oh, hi. Yes, the phone just startled me."

"Rose called a minute ago, she forgot to check on the time for your shopping trip tomorrow."

I laughed. "I never agreed to go shopping. She wants to redo your entire house."

"It's *our* house, Gloria, so feel free." A pause. "She said you all left Tomasso's almost an hour ago."

"I...uh...had an errand." At eleven o'clock at night?

But he didn't ask what errand, what could be open this late. I knew he'd wait until such time as I wanted to explain. Probably that's why I'd agreed to live with him.

I'd met Matt Gennaro when Rose forced me upon the Revere Police Department as an expert witness in a trial involving a defective TV set. I was charmed by him, immediately comfortable with his scratchy tones and chunky build, like that of all my uncles when I was growing up.

We were now dealing with other people's opinions of our "living arrangement." According to recent demographics for Revere, Matt and I were among the two percent of residents living with "unmarried partners." For Rose and Frank, it seemed natural—and, in Rose's case, about time—for me to move in with Matt after almost two years of "dating." For the West Coast vote, Elaine, who'd been through at least three relationships in that time, heartily agreed.

So what did it matter that my seventy-plus-year-old cousin, Mary Ann, in Worcester, hadn't spoken to me since I called to tell her my new address? Or that Matt's sister, Jean Mottolo, had said something equivalent to "Lots of luck," when we told her our good news.

The dog-walker came by again. At least two creatures had spent a useful half hour or so. Time for a decision. I should either march up to MC's apartment and convince her to come home with me—the silliness of that idea overcame me—or go home.

I ended my stakeout at the mortuary and headed for Fernwood Avenue.

AT ABOUT ELEVEN-THIRTY I joined Matt on the sofa that was one of my contributions to the living room. My blue-gray striped corduroy couch was much newer than his seventies-style plaid affair, and, unlike my rockers, minus the wear and tear of a cross-country trip. But still my furniture looked out of place. It seemed to be shifting around nervously, like a new digital spectrum analyzer trying to fit into an old lab system with analog components.

Matt was in his robe, surrounded by files and newspapers. He gave me a kiss, then a look. The expression he'd used during an entire career of wringing information from suspects, I guessed.

"That look is wasted," I said. "I've already decided to tell you where I've been and why." Little as I had to go on, the slight chance that MC might be in danger upset me enough to contact the police, so to speak.

"I'm listening."

I told Matt about MC's ex-boyfriend, and why I'd taken a detour from Tomasso's. He kindly resisted a scolding about why I'd put myself in danger, or what made me think I could take on someone MC couldn't handle. Neither did he scowl when he learned I had no descriptions—not of the alleged stalker, and not of MC's ex-boyfriend.

"He rides horses," I'd said; then we both laughed. Such useful information. A Texan who rides horses.

"Jake Powers," Matt said, as he wrote in the notebook he kept handy. "I'll check the database, and I'll call the Houston PD. We'll see if he's done anything like this before."

I wondered if "broke china cups and saucers" would show up on the criminal history computer database. "Can you send a car around to the mortuary?"

Matt nodded and punched in a number.

MC was safe. I relaxed.

Too soon.

"Now I have something to tell you," Matt said, pulling a sheet of stationery from a brown envelope. I drew a quick breath as I recognized the logo—a thick cross, like the Red Cross symbol, only black and gray. The logo of Dr. Abeles, Matt's doctor.

"Now, don't worry," he said.

Of course not. I could hardly breathe. "What's wrong?"

"We're not sure. Abeles says this is inconclusive." Matt waved the paper as if it were a police report, like the kind he handled every day, perhaps a B&E or a mugging. "I need a biopsy. My blood test showed a prostate-specific antigen, whatever that is,

at a borderline high level. And there was some abnormal hard-
ness." He flicked his wrist toward his groin with his closed fist.
Not to be too specific.

I blinked, futilely attempting to block a sudden headache.
Frustration pulsed through me in tiny waves. I was frustrated that
I had only the vaguest idea of what an antigen was. That I had
no idea what a good level of it would be. I knew by heart a long
list of physical constants. The fine-structure constant of spec-
troscopy, 1/137. The main transition line of a helium-neon laser,
6328 Angstroms. The ratio of proton mass to electronic mass,
1836. But I didn't know what quantity of blood protein made the
difference between life and death for the man I loved.

Matt seemed to be reading my face. He was the one needing
a biopsy. He was the one who had watched his wife of ten years
die. He shouldn't have to worry about me, I thought.

"Look," he said, showing me the paper he'd received from Dr.
Abeles. "See how INCONCLUSIVE is checked off?" The page looked
like an inventory sheet, or a to-do list. Not an official medical report. "It could just be an enlargement of the gland, not cancerous."

Cancer. He'd put the word out there. I hated hearing "cancer,"
or any form of the word. It was better whispered, or referenced
indirectly. Like in the old days. When my Uncle Mike got cancer, my mother said, "Mike has…" She left the word unspoken,
tilting her head and rolling her eyes up and to the side. Reluc-
tance to utter language she thought vulgar? A prayer to God?
Submission to fate?

I felt pain in my shoulders, my arms, my jaw. "Inconclusive"
was not an encouraging word, not a much better word than "cancer." "Inconclusive" was a term reserved for data of the kind I'd
dealt with in my physics career. It meant the curve didn't follow
the path of a known equation, or that some outlying points pre-
cluded a smoothing algorithm. In a medical report, I wanted yes or
no. No, actually. No foreign body. No unhealthy cells. No cancer.

I tried not to show Matt the depth of my panic. "So when is
the next test?" A simple question.

"I haven't scheduled it yet. I didn't have my calendar with me."

"Your calendar? What could be more important that you

wouldn't schedule it immediately? It's a biopsy, right? How long can that take?" I heard my voice rise in pitch, if not in volume. My hands were folded on my lap, my knuckles white.

Matt pulled me to him. "Don't worry. I almost didn't tell you, since there's nothing—"

"Conclusive." I finished for him. I leaned against his chest, tense, listening to his heart. He was right, I told myself. It could be nothing. Like MC's alleged stalking.

When the phone rang, I hoped it was good news. Not likely at midnight, however, I thought.

But it was, at least, definite.

"It's Berger," Matt said, covering the speaker with his hand as he listened to his partner. "There's a nine-twenty-one at the Galigani Mortuary."

I mentally reviewed my code list, and gasped. MC had called in a prowler.

"Everything's okay," Matt said, when he hung up. "Uniforms were already arriving for canvas, so they picked up the guy and they have him at the station."

I grabbed my purse from the hallway table.

Matt gave me a slight teasing smile. "I suppose you want to go down there with me."

"You drive," I said.

THREE

THE REVERE POLICE DEPARTMENT was one of the beautiful, old, redbrick buildings in the City Hall complex. It belonged to a different century than that of its modern vehicles—a fleet of shiny, white motorcycles, sedans, vans, and new SUVs, all with red, white and blue lettering—lined up in the parking lot and along Pleasant Street. Beautiful as this nearly hundred-year-old building was, a plea for a new facility was in the local news at least once a month, and the vowed priority of past and present city officials.

Matt and I passed through the blue foyer and into the main hallway. The photos that lined the wall were as familiar to me as Matt's stories—Harry, one of the revered horses from the pre-motor vehicle days; young policemen shot in the line of duty; groups of officers in the old uniforms with high helmets like those in English hunting scenes.

Halfway down, where the burnt coffee smell was strongest, George Berger greeted us. Berger was Matt's junior by about twenty years, but his slow, lumbering gait made him seem older.

"I knew you'd come, too, Gloria," he said, pulling a photo out of his wallet. Little Cynthia Berger's deep brown eyes peered at me, her pudgy body and curly dark hair framed by a playroom scene, clearly a backdrop in a mall photo studio. She held a Teddy bear in a choke hold; a giant gold lion lay at her feet. It always amused me when parents gave their children cuddly representations of creatures that would maul them if real.

I forced a smile. "She's getting so big," I said, hoping I didn't sound like a voice-mail recording, which was close to how I felt. I handed the photo back.

"Oh, no. That's your copy," he said.

I managed a happy-sounding thank-you and slipped it into a side compartment of my purse. Matt's partner had come a long way from the days when he resented my work with the RPD. I was sure his conversion had little to do with my competence, but was instead because I'd led him to believe I loved all children, and his daughter in particular. A misleading presentation of myself, but it had worked. He'd come to accept me as a kind of third partner in special cases.

I looked around for MC.

"Mary Catherine's doing the paperwork," Berger said, responding to my questioning gaze. "The guy's in the Orange Room. We're running his ID through the system."

"Jake Powers," I said, with some confidence.

Berger shook his head, flipped some pages in his notebook. "Nope. Name's Wayne Gallen. Chemist at Houston Poly. Says he's a colleague of Mary Catherine. Says he came to warn her about something and that's why he was skulking around the building."

"A warning?" I'd often worried about MC's vulnerability among the drill pipes and rotary bits of her oil company job, but not in a research lab or classroom, and not now that she was home. What kind of danger could a chemical engineer be in, once she was out of fieldwork?

"That's what he claims," Berger said, scratching his fleshy chin with his notepad.

In the next few minutes—thanks to Frank's police scanner— the blue hallway became very crowded with Galiganis in various stages of after-midnight attire. MC's brother John, a reporter for the *Revere Journal,* in thick maroon sweats. Frank and Robert, father-and-son partners at the mortuary, in business casual, as if they might be picking up a client. Rose and daughter-in-law, Karla, in almost-matching navy pantsuits that they could have worn to a Civic Club luncheon. Fifteen-year-old William in respectable jeans and a clean sweatshirt, probably a condition of his being allowed to come along. I was still in my Tomasso's outfit, consisting mostly of black fleece.

I doubted the RPD hosted such a hubbub for a prowler call-in in a normal case. The Galiganis were a key family in the city, their mortuary business and John's newspaper job bringing them in regular contact with Revere's infrastructure. The family even had a divorce lawyer in its ranks—Robert's wife, Karla. Though I liked her, I hoped I'd never need her services.

An inordinate number of uniforms milled around us. I wondered if the phones, radios and keyboards were always this busy in the early morning hours. With the staff thus occupied, it seemed an excellent time for a felony across town.

MC sat against a wall, the center of attention in her extra-large Texas sweatshirt that dwarfed her tiny body. She'd returned from talking to Wayne Gallen, who was still being held in the Orange Room.

Standing in the farthest of three semicircles around her, I caught only snippets of the chatter.

"I heard a car screech away. Wayne thinks it was *them,* these people who are supposedly after me," came from MC.

"Did he get into the building? Did he hurt you?" from Rose, distraught, notwithstanding her crisp white blouse.

"Wayne says he didn't want to lead the others to me, but he thinks he might have done exactly that," from MC.

"What others?" from John, thankfully not taking notes for the *Journal.*

"Did you hear a noise or something?" from Robert.

"Why was the guy sneaking around?" from Karla. "Are you going to press charges?"

"Who is he again? I didn't know you taught at Houston Poly," from someone I couldn't see.

Non sequiturs. I couldn't stand them. I needed a logically laid-out version of the night's events. I forced my way to the front, aware that Matt wasn't in the immediate vicinity. I had a fleeting worry that he might be in a corner somewhere, doubled over in pain.

I scrambled closer to MC. When I brushed past William, the only person in the room shorter than I, I heard him say, "Go, Auntie Glo." At least someone in the group was relaxed.

I leaned over MC, cross-legged on the seat of a wide gray chair. "Mary Catherine…" I said.

She gave me a frown that I read: *Is this really so serious that you have to use my full name?*

"MC," I said, with a smile meant to calm us both. "Can you start from the beginning? What led you to make the call to the police in the first place?"

She took a deep breath and wrapped her hands in her sleeves. She shivered, as if she were chilled to the bone, in spite of the stuffiness of the area. "I was doing laundry in the basement and I heard a noise at the window."

My eyes widened, and MC smiled for the first time. She knew I'd be impressed that she'd use the mortuary laundry room, below street level and immediately adjacent to the prep room—and late at night. I had chosen to cart my clothes to a Laundromat every week rather than deal with the eeriness and deathly odors of the Tuttle Street basement even in the light of day.

"And then?"

"Then I heard a car pull away, really loud. Screeching. And I couldn't tell if the noise at the window was a knocking or a, you know, break-in. And who would be knocking on the basement window of the mortuary at eleven-thirty at night anyway? Plus, with this feeling of being followed lately, I guess I overreacted. I had my cell phone down there with me, so I just called nine-one-one." MC took a sip of water, slowed her breathing. "Wayne's not a bad guy. I met him at Houston Poly when I was teaching that night class. He was a great resource for one of my students who needed material for a term paper. I shouldn't have called the police on him."

I patted her knee. "You did the right thing," I said. "Did he say what exactly he's doing here, following you around?"

She shrugged her shoulders. "Well, I know he likes me. He'd never ask me out though, while I was with Jake. But he said he came to warn me that the research guys at HP are after me." I assumed she meant Houston Poly and not the real HP, the company that made my printer and other peripherals in my home office. "But it's hard to believe anyone's on my case. I never did anything to make Alex Simpson or the guys on his team mad at me, as far as I know."

"Did he give you any details about why they're after you?"

"Supposedly I have some privileged information that came to me through an e-mail I shouldn't have gotten. It could be something about the research, maybe a patent? Not that I'm working with them that much, but I've had a little interaction through Wayne and this student, Mary Roderick, who's doing a term paper on buckyballs."

I'd blocked out the crowd around us until I heard a chorus of "Buckyballs? What are buckyballs?" I thought I also heard "Bocce balls?" and "Bucking broncos?"

Berger's reappearance prevented me from calling everyone to attention and giving a lecture on buckyballs, starting with the original "Bucky," F. Buckminster Fuller, and the geodesic dome, and nanoscale technology—one of the hot items in today's research arena.

"We're going to let him go," Berger said. "No priors, no reason to keep him, since you're not pressing charges. Right, Mary Catherine? Berger raised his bushy, dark eyebrows in a gesture that offered one more chance for MC to request formal police action.

MC shook her head. "He's harmless, really."

For myself, I thought Wayne Gallen ought to be punished simply for upsetting my godchild. I couldn't understand why he didn't knock on her door if he had information—I suppressed "a warning"—to give her.

"We should at least check out your e-mail," I said, swinging my head from MC to Berger. *Before you let him go,* I meant, but Berger had turned and walked away by then.

"I'm sure it's nothing," MC said.

I smiled and nodded. She didn't need to know I'd be nagging her until we had no loose ends.

It took about ten minutes to clear the area outside the station. At one in the morning the breeze from the ocean had taken over, lowering the temperature several degrees. The chill felt more intense after the overheated police station. I suspected the heating system in the old building had only two settings, on high or off completely, with no control in between.

The Galigani clan moved quickly to their cars, but slowly enough for hugs, kisses, and expressions of both relief and concern. Rose had talked her daughter into spending the night with her and Frank on Prospect Avenue, a few blocks from our house, and well across town from the scene of the incident.

Matt, who showed up while we were dispersing, threw his coat over my shoulders as we walked toward his Camry.

My mind was anything but settled. I had the feeling I hadn't heard the last of Wayne Gallen. Or a few other Texans.

ONCE STRAPPED into the front seat, I mulled over the appropriate time to ask Matt for an account of his whereabouts during our ad hoc interview with MC. But a bigger question came up. Instead of heading home, Matt turned left on Broadway and drove toward Chelsea.

"I think Landano's is closed," I said.

Matt smiled. "But they're probably in there baking the cannoli shells right now. I can flash my badge, and…"

I laughed. "You win. Matt, where are we going?"

"Gallen will be released in about fifteen minutes. We're going to beat him home."

"We're going to Houston?"

"Ha." Matt hit the steering wheel to indicate *good one.*

"You pulled his address," I said, then reviewed my own language. When had I switched from "discovered" or "located" to police jargon like "pulled" an address?

Matt made no reference to my migration to his language. "He's registered at the Beach Lodge," he said.

"And you want to make sure he stays home tonight."

Matt nodded. "Covering all bases. Two guys are standing by outside the station. I offered to take the first shift here, and since this is not likely to turn into a wild ride, I figured I'd save myself the trouble of suggesting that I take you home first."

I stretched across the seat, my ample bosom straining the fabric of my seat belt, and gave his rough, dark cheek a kiss, a reward for not banishing me from the action. "Good move."

The gray in Matt's hair, a pattern that nearly matched my own, caught the light of the streetlamps along Broadway, and eventually the bright signs in the motel parking lot, giving him neon-green highlights. I'd always considered Matt the picture of health, if on the chunky side of the insurance stats. He had a lot of well-paced energy, decent upper body strength for a man his age, good coloring. That he looked tired and pale this evening was all in my mind, I told myself, a reaction to hearing his medical report.

He caught me looking at him and covered my hand with his. "You're thinking we could do better than a B-rated motel, aren't you?"

I smiled. The Beach Lodge was a joke among the natives, its name playing a trick on tourists. We'd all seen their brochures that implied an ocean view, whereas in fact the so-called inn was at least two miles from sand and surf. I'd never been inside, but its low rates and dingy exterior didn't inspire confidence about the amenities within.

The parking lot had few cars, not surprising in the off-season. We parked in a corner, facing the entrance, the Camry's taillights toward the intersection of two major arteries, the Revere Beach Parkway and Route 1.

I scanned the area. My second stakeout in one evening.

"I'll bet you know what Wayne Gallen looks like." I realized that's where Matt had been while everyone else was gathered around MC—he'd been checking the stats on Gallen.

He nodded, and smiled. Together we said, "It's what I do.

"Short, thin. A lot like the way MC described her boyfriend to you, which must be why she thought it was Powers hanging around. But Gallen has some facial hair—a long handlebar mustache if you can believe it, and a short beard. All red." Matt massaged his own hairless chin.

Traffic on Route 1 stayed light, and there was not much action at the lodge. We talked, uninterrupted, speculating alternately about Wayne Gallen and about the cost of a new roof on the Fernwood Avenue house, about MC's emergency call and about yet another fund-raiser Rose and Frank wanted us to attend. In the air between us was health talk, as if we had an unspoken agreement to take it up later, when we were face-to-face in a well-lit room.

Matt pulled out the large, heavy-duty department thermos

and poured us cups of coffee. I took a sip, and promised myself a Tomasso's Coffee Annex high-quality double cappuccino at the next possible opportunity.

Then a light dawned. I had a captive audience.

"About buckyballs," I said.

"Oh, no." Matt pressed the palm of his hand to his forehead, but I'd long ago stopped being sensitive to that kind of rebuke.

"Let's start with nanotechnology. A nanometer is one billionths of a meter. That's about a billionth the size of your leg." I reached over and ran my hand along his thigh, to his knee, down his calf. "Well, at least the leg of a tall man."

He laughed. "Do that again. Maybe you'll pique my interest after all."

There was a time when a line like that would have sent a flush across my face, but that was a different, more naive Gloria. I could tell that my cheeks had not turned red, just slightly pink. I pushed on.

"The width of a period at the end of a sentence—that's already about a million nanometers, and buckyballs are only about one nanometer in diameter. Impressed?"

A slight nod from my captive student. "The technical name is buckminsterfullerenes, after Buck—"

"Buckminster Fuller. I get that part."

"Buckyballs are just one molecule among many that make up the science of the very small."

"Nanotechnology."

I nodded. "The original buckyball discoverers were chemists from Houston, as a matter of fact. Most people—most scientists, I mean—give them credit for kicking off the nanotechnology revolution."

"So?"

Matt yawned, a fake one I thought, so I went on. "It started with buckyballs about fifteen years ago, then buckytubes or nanotubes, a sort of cousin to buckyballs a few years later, and now, well, it could lead to nanoscale computers eventually."

"I'm falling asleep. You'd better step it up. Or make that measurement along my leg again."

Too late. A progression of loud noises took over. Tires whipping up gravel, indistinct cheers, and whoops of laughter. A group of young people had arrived in tandem cars, their raucous partying already well under way. The flickering lamps and garish red door of the lodge added to the Halloween atmosphere. A couple of weeks early, but there was no mistaking a large, brown, lumbering bear, no fewer than three witches and two fairies, and a couple in prom attire.

"Whatever happened to curfews on a school night?" I asked.

Back to slouching and coffee. By the time the second RPD shift arrived, I'd slipped in some of the major applications of nanotechnology, explaining how the word was used to describe many types of research where the characteristic dimensions were less than about one thousand nanometers—data storage and gasoline production among the most common. Plus the big market for new, smarter drug delivery systems. Like the kind that might be used for treating prostate cancer.

Michelle Chan, out of uniform, came up to Matt's window and gave us a friendly smile. She waved at me. "Hi, Gloria. We need to get you a badge. You're putting in more hours than my partner. Any action?"

Matt shook his head. "Unless you count the rowdy kids in cheap costumes."

"That's funny. Gallen was released about an hour ago."

We'd been there longer than I thought.

"What about Jaspers and Connors? They pick him up from outside the station?"

Officer Chan shook her head. "Nope. Well, you're off the hook anyway. I'll check it out."

My stomach tensed. Where was Wayne Gallen? How had he evaded the police who were supposedly on his tail?

At least MC was safe at home with her parents. Wasn't she?

I dug my cell phone out of my purse and pushed the numbers for the Galigani residence. Matt raised his eyebrows, tapped his watch, mouthed "two-thirty," and, in the end, threw up his hands. I ignored his elaborate gestures.

Rose picked up on the first ring. I pictured my friend, wrapped in dark green chenille, in her unable-to-sleep spot—her closed-in front porch, in full view of her special roses. "She's fine," Rose whispered. "Tucked in upstairs. The world's fine, Gloria. We should be sleeping. Or shopping."

A laugh, a few more whispered words, like the kind we used to share in the back of the long-gone Revere Theater when we were kids. *Is that Paul with his arm around Carol? Are you going to wear heels or flats to Boston on Saturday?*

I hung up. Rose was right—we should all be sleeping. There was nothing wrong with Wayne Gallen wandering the streets of Revere. The real concerns were the inconclusive cells wandering around Matt's body.

I leaned over to him. I wanted to know if he was in pain, if he was afraid. I wanted to be strong for him, to assure him that I'd take care of him, no matter what.

"Are you all right, Matt?" was all I could manage.

Most of his face was in shadow, but I caught a pinched expression, then a loving one as he turned to me. "I know you're here for me, Gloria. That means everything to me."

As usual, Matt was ahead of me in expressing his feelings, and mine.

He ran his hand down my cheek. "Let's just see what happens with the biopsy."

I smiled. I could be patient—this was like a research project needing more data.

I focused on MC tucked safely in her childhood bed.

FOUR

MC'S HEART RACED. Her breath came in quick bursts as she pumped the pedals of her nephew William's bike. She sped through the quiet streets of Revere at two-thirty in the morning, not sure whether she was headed toward or away from something. A goal or an escape? It could be either. Yes, she wanted to check her e-mails to see if there was anything that would clarify what Wayne was talking about, but she also needed to prove to herself that she wasn't trapped in her old bedroom.

What am I doing wrong? Coming back to Revere was supposed to bring me peace.

MC rode past the bank where she'd deposited her first babysitting check, the dry cleaners that had removed a telling beer stain from her satiny pink prom dress. Past an all-night gas station, past pungent Dumpsters that lined the deserted parking lot of the old corner market where she'd bought endless quantities of junk food. Except for the beach, with its missing boardwalk, the city hadn't changed much since she'd drawn daily hopscotch outlines on the sidewalk.

MC had taken advantage of a middle-of-the-night phone call that kept her mother busy for a few minutes. Probably Aunt G, since the call came in on the family's private line. She'd slipped down the back stairs and out of the house.

MC needed to see her e-mails, and her parents, the last of the Luddites, had no home computer. Anyway, there was no need to upset her family. They were only trying to protect her.

But MC needed action. No more reminiscing in her old bedroom, with its overabundance of nostalgia. Enough staring at the walls that still held her Duran Duran posters. Her mother had turned Robert's room into a sewing area and John's into a den for her father, but had left MC's nest nearly intact.

"My boys have their own bedrooms, in our same zip code," Rose had said. "My daughter needs a place to come home to."

Often enough over the years MC had heard how she still looked like a teenager—small-boned, thin face with a boyish haircut. And flat-chested, MC thought with a grimace. She was sure that was the impression she gave tonight, in her latex pants and her nephew William's shocking blue helmet. MC refrained from curb-jumping; still she knew that if a sleepless Revere resident happened to look out his window, he might think she was a late-night runaway kid tearing through the streets.

She zipped around the corner of Revere Street and Broadway, sailing past Oxford Park and Pomona Street, where her best girlfriends had lived. Annie, Claire, Valery, Joanie. She remembered how they would all give up potato chips and candy for Lent, then eat double helpings of rubbery packaged cupcakes.

MC needed to be in her own apartment, to maintain a semblance of independence, even though her landlords were also her parents. And she couldn't wait another minute to check her e-mail messages for the misdelivered memo, or whatever, that Wayne allegedly crossed the country to warn her about.

She took a deep breath, relaxing her tight hold on the handlebars. At least it wasn't Jake who'd followed her from Texas. MC touched her cheek. It wasn't as though Jake had bruised her or anything. Except her ego. And it was only once or twice that he'd slapped her. Lightly. Still it killed her to lie to Aunt G. She should have told her the truth, but it was too embarrassing. A smart girl from a loving family, salutatorian of her class, a graduate degree in chemical engineering, a great career, and she'd let some jerk knock her around. *Maaaaa* would never have stood for that, nor Aunt G.

She remembered wonderful summers in California when she was little. Aunt G had always treated her like a grown-up, introduced her to scientists and engineers and programmers. Dr. Karen this, and Dr. Annmarie that. A little too obvious—they

might as well have worn signs saying FEMALE SCIENTIST ROLE
MODELS, but MC had loved it. Especially an all-nighter one time
with Dr. Marcia, who'd let her help change spectrometer plates
every half hour through the night, and write the data on gray
graph paper with blue lines.

MC slammed her fist against the handlebar. *Damn.* All those
strong women in her life, plus the gentlest of fathers and brothers, and she'd let them all down. For a loser. Maybe living near
her family again would give her a new start, get her out of the
depression she couldn't shake. She was ninety percent of the way
to being over Jake, ninety percent toward chalking it up as a temporary lapse in judgment.

She pushed ahead on William's bike, deliberately overwork-
ing her calf muscles until they ached.

Wayne Gallen had said the e-mail was incriminating. To
whom? She hadn't looked at her computer since her return. Once
she got serious with her computer, she reasoned, she'd have to
look for a job, and she wasn't ready for that. *Life Plans* was too
big a category to handle, but now she was curious about what
could have driven Wayne across the country. He'd refused to give
her details.

MC slowed down to make the turn onto Tuttle Street. Her plan
was to ride the entire length of the one-way street to check for
strange cars before doubling back and turning into the mortuary
driveway. As if she'd know an enemy car from a friendly one.
Or a stranger from a Tuttle Street resident. She hadn't lived in
the neighborhood long enough to tell the difference.

As she cruised by a new sedan in the shadow of a tree, she
had the impression that there was a person, maybe two, slumped
in the front seat. She tensed, then let out a long breath. Her loud
whoosh cut through the still fall air. Probably a couple of
teenagers making out. She knew what that was like.

But the sedan seemed out of place—the nicest car by far,
among the old hatchbacks and pickups parked in the driveways.
To play it safe, MC rode through the backyards on her return up
the street. If someone were checking everyone who came by, he'd
think she was a guy who disappeared into a house at the end of

the street. She half rode, half walked the bike around the lawns and vegetable gardens, ending up at the storm door at the rear of the mortuary.

MC's hands were clammy, her breath quick, as she dug out her key. She felt as though her body were on alert, sniffing out danger. Like when she heard Jake come through the front door after a few beers with his pals. This time she was in control, she reminded herself. Jake was half a continent away. So why was every hair on her sweaty neck bristling?

She'd stuck a small flashlight in her waistband and used it now to make her way around the mortuary parlors, mercifully empty of laid-out corpses, to the stairway to the upper floors. Quieter than the elevator, just in case...

MC entered her third-floor apartment, keeping the flashlight beam low. She looked out the window, saw the sedan still parked under the tree. No sign of life in the vehicle, however. She must have been mistaken the first time.

Still, she drew her curtains and turned her computer monitor away from the windows. She'd soon find out what Wayne Gallen was talking about, if anything. She had a suspicion that he'd made up the story about the buckyball memo—that really he was simply hot for her, and with Jake out of the picture, saw an opportunity to make his move. Still, it was a long way to come on the off chance...actually, not a chance.

Wayne could be sweet, but he was way too slow for her. He talked slow, walked slow, thought slow. Drove her crazy by constantly caressing that 1890s mustache, rolling the thin curve of red hair between his fingers. Also, to tell the truth, Wayne was kind of creepy. He did little things for her—brought her a bag of corn chips from the vending machine, wiped off her windshield on a rainy day, helped her out at the copy machine if she was overloaded. You couldn't fault a guy for behaving like that, but something about the way he looked at her made her uncomfortable. She'd found herself not wanting to be in the lab when it was just the two of them working late.

MC took a long, cold drink from a bottle of water she'd taken from her neglected, smelly fridge, and maneuvered around a nest of wires to hook up her system. She welcomed the familiar popping sounds as her computer booted up.

CONNECT. CONTACTING HOST. SENDING LOGIN INFORMATION.

MC got up and cracked a window to get rid of the odor let loose when she opened her refrigerator. As soon as she straightened out this memo business, she'd clean up her act and go grocery shopping like a normal woman. Watch *Friends* reruns on TV. Have real friends over for dinner.

RECEIVING MESSAGE 1 OF 25. 2. 3...

She read quickly.

YOU'VE WON A MERCEDES!

Delete.

SEE HEATHER UNZIP!

Delete.

MEET SINGLES LIKE YOU!

Hmm. Maybe I should give this a try. Delete.

Once she'd cleared the spam, MC scanned the list of To/From, mostly messages from human resources. As if she hadn't filled out enough forms before terminating her employment at the oil company and the university. A few posts from students in her night class, mostly ones who had *Incompletes* to work out. She focused on several items from Alex Simpson, the university buckyball project leader, opened each one, read through routine memos on purchases, deadline changes, maintenance schedules, and visiting dignitaries (read *venture capitalists with deep pockets*).

The communications on grant money were also innocuous.

MC already knew the team was forging partnerships with pharmaceutical companies. CRADAS, they were called. Cooperative Research and Development Agreements.

Subject: CRADA milestones
Subject: Tracking sheet for first quarter
Subject: New account numbers

MC sighed. Boring. A reminder of what was waiting for her when she attached herself to another job.

Subject: CRADA personnel
Subject: Interviews with new hires
Subject: Capital equipment budget ·

Then, finally an intriguing subject line. She opened the message.

From: Alexsimpson@hpbp.edu
To: galig@hpbp.edu
Subject: Millions of $ in the offing!

This one sounded like a spam tag line, but the sender was Alex Simpson, so MC opened it.

We've got them hooked. The idea of smart medicines is too good for them to resist. We'll plug the cancer vaccines first. I'm thinking $100 million in funding to start...

MC thought of Alex Simpson, a slick chameleon with as many faces as the number of venture capitalists on his list. He'd don an Italian silk suit for a New York CEO, a cowboy hat and a swagger for a wealthy Oklahoma rancher. He had every restaurant in town on hold until he discovered the favorite cuisine of a moneyed visitor. A Texas accent came and went, as swiftly as the airplanes that carried his potential benefactors. Alex was a master imitator, especially when it suited his purposes.

MC reread the message, hated the offensive tone, as if there weren't human patients at the end of this drug research project. She remembered the promises made in the journal ads. "Smart medicine" meant drugs that go straight to a tumor or diseased organ. KNOCK OUT THE BAD CELLS WHERE THEY LIVE, said the headlines, WHILE LEAVING HEALTHY CELLS ALONE. She'd had enough lab experience to understand the possibilities were there, but she was enough of a realist to know how long it would be before the miracle prescriptions would be in local drugstores. Still, there was nothing new or incriminating in Simpson's message. Just the usual hype.

Another subject line, dated the week she left Houston, caught her eye.

From:Alexsimpson@hpbp.edu
To: galig@hpbp.edu
Subject: Trouble

MC read carefully.

There's good news and bad news. Our contact sees no problem delivering the package, but one unfortunate outcome—the bute that's not bute—might bring trouble.

"Unfortunate outcome." "Trouble." Could be trigger words for something confidential. Or not. "Package" meant illegal drugs in a lot of the movies she'd seen. And there was that movie with Gene Hackman where Tommy Lee Jones was the package.

MC tapped her fingers on the keyboard, lightly, not pressing them down. Making that almost musical sound she liked. "Bute that's not bute." She thought about butane, butyl. Nothing she'd ever worked with. It could even be a misspelling, for all she knew.

If it hadn't been for Wayne Gallen's so-called warning, this note wouldn't be the least bit suspicious. She wished Wayne were around. This time she'd force him to give her details.

MC sighed deeply. *What a life.* Four in the morning and she was sitting on a hand-me-down rocker above a mortuary. Moreover, she now had to ride her nephew's bike across town to get back to her parents' house before they knew she was missing. She'd just waltz down to breakfast in a couple of hours, as if she'd been tucked in all night with the old panda that Robert won for her at Skeeball before the wrecking balls destroyed the amusements on the boulevard.

MC felt the frustration in her jaws, behind her eyes, in the joints of her fingers. She was no wiser than before this wacky bicycle trip, except she'd found an e-mail about some vague "trouble."

She felt younger than William, but older than Mrs. Cataldo, her retired chemistry teacher.

She got up and headed for the door.

For good measure, she looked out the window one more time. The sedan was still there. This time she saw the tiny glow of a cigarette in the front seat.

Her throat constricted, suddenly dry after almost thirty-two ounces of water.

Come off it, she told herself. *No one is watching you.*

FIVE

MATT AND I ENTERED the North Shore Clinic and signed in. We took seats on thinly upholstered chairs, a pattern of greens and blues not found in nature, two of a long line that had been welded together and bolted to the floor, as if an outpatient might be tempted to walk home with a few for her dining room. I tried to keep my breathing shallow, lest I absorb a sickness or an inappropriate medicine, simply by inhaling one of the unpleasant odors that surrounded us. I wished Matt hadn't chosen to see Dr. Abeles during his shift at the clinic, but I figured he preferred being in Everett, his hometown, a few miles from Revere. I felt almost as uncomfortable in a regular doctor's office anyway.

The waiting room was full, serving a long list of doctors with different combinations of letters after their names. No one looked especially ill, but I felt sorry for each and every one.

Matt twisted his body and leaned across the shiny metal connector between our chairs. He stroked my hand. "Everything's going to be fine, Gloria."

An observer would have assumed I was the patient, not Matt; that I was the one waiting for a needle to be inserted into the wall of my rectum.

"Did you make a list of your symptoms?" I asked Matt, suddenly recalling a piece I'd read on-line. "You know, frequent urination could be caused by a benign prostatic hyperplasia." I nearly tripped over the words, so much more complicated than phrases like "nuclear magnetic resonance," or "the alpha particle tunneling effect."

Matt smiled. "You've been doing research. On-line I suppose."
I nodded. I'd spent hours searching out information from the

National Institute of Health, the Mayo Clinic, the National Cancer Institute and the Harvard Medical School Family Health Guide. Any site that seemed reputable. I read comparisons between the side effects of surgery and radiation therapy and tried not to retain the fact that 31,500 men would die of prostate cancer this year.

I'd checked out sites for the latest in hard-science news, objectively, with no hidden agenda. But now, searching the health sites, I had a different approach. I looked for good news only. Unlike other cancers, I read, a man is more likely to die *with* prostrate cancer than *of* it. On average, an American male has about a thirty percent risk of having prostate cancer in his lifetime, but only about a three percent risk of dying of the disease.

Whew.

But statistics have never given me long-lasting comfort. In that three percent was someone's husband, someone's brother, a teacher, a cop.

"Dr. Abeles is ready for you."

Matt let go of my hand and answered the call, the high-pitched voice of a woman whose short peachy smock was strewn with lavender smiley faces, a nice complement to the receptionist whose white smock had an arrangement of unidentifiable pastel animals in human clothing. My mind wandered to the possibility of a new market: grown-up designs for hospital workers' uniforms.

The book I'd brought along was another sign of my shift in interest to the life sciences. I'd picked up a new biography of molecular biologist Rosalind Franklin. Not the best choice, since Franklin died of ovarian cancer at thirty-seven, but I'd heard that the book shed light on Franklin's role in the history-making double-helix model of DNA. The burning question: Did Watson and Crick take advantage of the low status of women at that time and steal her research? For a few minutes, the ongoing debate between methodology (Franklin) and intuition (Watson) kept my mind off the tiny biopsy gun I'd read about, and which Matt was now facing, with only a local anesthetic between him and severe discomfort.

Matt appeared after about a half hour, about twenty-five pages into the Franklin-Watson controversy. Just in time, since I was becoming upset again, this time at the conditions at Cambridge University in the 1950s—only males were allowed in the university dining rooms, and after hours Rosalind Franklin's colleagues went to men-only pubs to brainstorm the direction of the next day's work.

"All set," Matt said, doing a good job of smiling. For my benefit, I was sure. "We'll know in about three days."

Three days—not long at all. Unless you're waiting for a medical report.

DINNER AT HOME was interrupted by several phone calls, all asking how Matt's procedure went. George Berger phoned from the station, plus Rose, Andrea Cabrini—a Charger Street lab technician and my latest attempt at making a friend—and Matt's sister Jean, who was still in denial that Matt and I lived together.

"Is Matt there?" she always asked immediately when I answered the phone. No "Hi, Gloria," or any other gesture toward politeness. I'd tried different responses, from "One moment please," in a detached, telephone-operator-like tone, to "Oh, Jean, it's me, Gloria. How nice to hear from you." The latter usually annoyed her.

Matt thought Jean's aversion to me had nothing to do with me personally, but rather with her devotion to Teresa, his first wife.

"They were like sisters," he'd tell me after each rebuff.

This, of course, only increased my feeling of inadequacy as potential sister material. I'd thought of buttering up her children, but I knew I'd feel guilty playing on the tension between teenagers and their mother.

Elaine Cody was the last to call, her time zone being three hours behind. Elaine and I had held each other's hands through many such trials during our thirty-year friendship in Berkeley, and we continued now to be close, if three thousands miles apart.

"If you need me, I'm there…" I heard the snap of her fingers "…in a minute. I know you have Rose and all your Boston friends."

We both laughed. Elaine knew that "all my Boston friends,"

like all my California friends, could fit into one curtained-off space at the North Shore Clinic. I'd never been very social as an adult, blaming my retreat into graduate work on the death of my fiancé, Al Gravese, right after I finished college. It seemed easier to never again get close enough to anyone you'd miss when they left. Between Elaine's almost yearly change of significant others, and Rose's extended family, I was happy enough, and busy enough, with a couple of friends on each coast.

We hung up after Elaine extracted a promise from me that I'd tell her if I needed her to come to Revere.

I looked across the table, past the large bowl of salad, the linguini in reheated clam sauce, and the bottles of mineral water, to where Matt buttered a thick slice of Italian bread, apparently comfortable on the tubular pillow we'd added to his chair. I couldn't recall making a different decision about letting people into my life, but there he was.

"You look taller," I said, my first attempt at lightening the mood.

He threw back his shoulders and smiled. "Do you like me taller?"

Not fair to give me that look when he couldn't follow through.

FOR THE NEXT COUPLE of hours, it seemed nothing could distract me from the image of Matt's tissue samples on the way to a pathology lab for diagnosis. I hoped the pathologist was more than twenty years old, which was my estimated age of many professionals I'd dealt with recently.

I'd insisted on throwing all the clothes we wore to the clinic into the wash, as if the sign-in pencil-on-a-string, the doorknobs, and the ugly green chairs were all highly contaminated. The late-night sounds of the washing machine soothed me. Swishing soap, clean rinse water pouring into the tub—Matt's system cleansed by a new miracle drug.

George Berger called a second time, close to midnight. Unlike Jean, Berger always greeted me before asking for his partner. I gave Matt the phone, slipped a notebook and pencil onto Matt's lap, and hung on his shoulder to read his scribble.

"A DOA?" he said into the mouthpiece.

Nina Martin, he wrote.

"Where?" he asked.

Rumney, he wrote. The old Rumney Salt Marsh, former home to mutant insect life and multiple tons of North Shore trash. A few years ago, before the marsh restoration project, a body would never have been noticed amid the discarded shopping carts and refrigerator-size boxes.

"Hmm," Matt said to Berger. I drummed my fingers on the back of his chair.

"The Galiganis?" he asked. An alert. More drumming.

"Anything else?" he asked.

GSW, he wrote. Gunshot wounds.

"Evidence?" he asked.

2 BT on vic, he wrote. Two blood types found on the victim. I was pretty good at Matt's special combination of police code and his own shorthand.

PI, he wrote. Principal Investigator? No; wrong context. That was for grant proposals. This must be a Private Investigator, I guessed.

"Whoa," Matt said.

FDA, he wrote. The Food and Drug Administration? The people who put the purple stamps on rump roasts?

"Thanks for keeping me in the loop, Berger," he said.

"Who's Nina Martin and how is a private investigator from the FDA connected to the Galiganis?" This from me before the telephone receiver hit the cradle.

Matt made a *slow down* motion. "Martin was a PI; she had two business cards in her wallet, one for the local FDA office, and one for the Galigani Mortuary, plus a list of names and numbers they're still tracing."

"Hmm." This time from me.

I settled back on my chair and folded my hands in my lap. Ready for information.

Only when Matt grimaced as he shifted in his chair did I remember his tender bottom. I also remembered to worry about his test results, but pushed that aside. I got his pillow and patted his bald spot. That would have to do for now.

I spread my palms, waiting. "Not to rush you," I said.

Matt gave me a silly smile, cleared his throat. It was the *yes, boss* expression he'd recently adopted.

"An engineer from the EPA was with the MTA people out at the marsh. They're the ones who found her," Matt said.

First the FDA, now the Environmental Protection Agency and the Massachusetts Turnpike Authority. Too many agencies, but it made sense, once I thought about it.

The EPA was needed on the marsh restoration project. An unfinished leg of highway, constructed in the 1960s and called "the expressway to nowhere" for years, had been removed, opening the clogged arteries of the marsh to seawater, and providing the ideal laboratory for wetlands study.

The MTA was connected to Boston's Big Dig, the multiyear, multibillion-dollar construction of an underground expressway, under the heart of the city, and said to be the largest construction project in U.S. history.

The link: Roadbed gravel from the restoration of Rumney Marsh—I thought I'd read two hundred thousand cubic yards of it—was being recycled to Big Dig sites.

Matt tapped his notebook on his knee. "They found a female Hispanic, early thirties, multiple gunshot wounds. Fingerprints came back as a PI. Real name Nina Martin, though she had a couple of different IDs on her. Probably dumped there, though it's hard to tell whether or not the marsh is the crime scene."

"More than one ID? I didn't know PIs went undercover."

"Sure, they do it all the time. Claim to be someone else to get information. They don't usually go deep, though, except for the brave ones."

Or the dead ones, I thought. "What do you make of the Galigani connection?"

Matt frowned. "You won't like this. She's from Houston, and MC's name was written on the back of the Galigani Mortuary card."

I sat up, on alert, my senses suddenly sharpened. Our Fernwood Avenue home was much farther away from a main street than my mortuary apartment had been; at midnight, the only sounds were from inside the house. A zipper clacked against the drum of our dryer; my computer hard drive hummed, always at the ready; a soft saxophone tune emanated from the speakers in our living room.

The loudest sounds were of links connecting, in my mind. A murdered private detective from Houston. Did Jake send a PI to snoop on MC? I couldn't entertain the thought that MC herself had done anything wrong, something worth an investigation, not for a nanosecond. But Jake was a different story. Maybe into drugs?

"The FDA investigates drugs, doesn't it?"

"Yes, but not the street kind; that would be DEA. Are you thinking of the ex-boyfriend?"

I nodded. "Or that the people supposedly coming after MC are into drugs."

"Or the FDA number is completely unrelated. Another case entirely that Martin was working on."

"Or Wayne Gallen hired the PI to follow MC around." He was still "at-large" so to speak, in that no one had seen him since he was released from the RPD on Tuesday night. Too confusing right now. "What else do we know?"

Matt skipped over the "we," having adjusted beautifully to my status as his almost-partner. "Two blood types, one hers. So it's possible we're looking for a wounded killer. Stands to reason, as a PI she would have a firearm and some training in self-defense, and probably got in a shot or two. The word is out at hospitals and clinics."

"Is Berger handling the case?"

Matt twisted his wrist in a *half-and-half* motion. "For now, but you can bet Houston PD will be all over this, and the FDA, too, if she was connected to them at all."

"But it's our jurisdiction, isn't it, if she was murdered here?"

"Yes and no. If they think she was killed while on a job out of Houston, they're going to want in on it. Lots of places, cops and PIs work together. She wasn't just an ordinary citizen touring Revere."

"Maybe she was. On vacation, I mean." Not that I believed it.

"You don't believe that," Matt said. My soul mate.

"Someone should find out who hired her and why." Gloria, the master detective.

Matt nodded. "For now Berger is working this, and I can probably get on board by tomorrow."

I frowned.

"What?" he asked. "I'm not going to sit around here and wait."

I'd gotten used to equating DOAs with consulting contracts for me, formal or informal. It was taking less and less time to move from "a person has been murdered" to "let's solve this puzzle." I wasn't sure this was a good thing, but if there was a chance that Nina Martin was linked to any of the Galiganis, I'd have to put off examining my conscience until after I investigated.

I looked at Matt and smiled. "Well, I'm going to *not wait* with you."

SIX

MC WANTED TO STAY IN BED forever. She'd slept badly, waking up often, each time fighting back tears at the image of the young woman's body on the morgue table.

MC had liked Mary Roderick, or Nina Martin, or whatever her real name was. She was older than MC's other students, and seemed to really connect with her. She'd told MC her birth name was Maria Rodriguez, that she'd changed it to Roderick to sound more American, even though she loved her Mexican family and sent them money whenever she could. MC thought of Mary/Maria/Nina's familiar Houston Oilers cap, barely covering her wild, jet-black hair, and how her sparkling dark eyes brought life to the old, badly maintained classroom at Houston Poly.

The police had asked MC to make a secondary ID, since her name was on the Galigani Mortuary card. MC had wanted to go down there anyway. She had to be sure it was really Mary. Maria. Nina. They were saying that the woman must have enrolled in MC's class as part of an undercover job, that she was a private detective, and maybe even worked for the FDA. Very unsettling, when you thought you'd been close to someone, to find out you didn't even know who they really were. Like with Jake, she thought, in some ways.

MC flipped over onto her back and blew out a breath so harsh it hurt her cheeks. *I'm a Galigani*, she told herself. *I grew up around dead bodies; I am not freaked out by death.* An image came to her mind—her father in the prep room downstairs, inserting thin brass wires into the jaws of an old man, to bring his teeth together; shaping his mouth with cotton into a slight smile. She'd been fascinated watching him, not frightened at all.

She'd gotten used to the sound of the hearse in the middle of the night, and the nasty odors that her mother tried valiantly to cover up. *I couldn't have hated them too much,* MC thought, *since I chose a field with its own pukey smells.* She remembered sneaking down to the prep room whenever she could while her father was working on a body. She'd watch him cutting, sewing, stuffing, painting, and weighing things she couldn't identify at the time.

But none of those bodies was real to her. She realized later that her parents deliberately kept her from the basement when she'd known the deceased.

This woman, Nina Martin, had been her student, or at least pretended to be her student, and was way too young to die.

The class MC taught was almost a throwaway at Houston Poly, basic chemistry for liberal arts majors. Most of the students couldn't care less about science, choosing the class of convenience—they needed a science class to graduate, and this one happened to be on a night when they were free.

But Nina, a pre-law student—or so she'd said—had been so conscientious, seeming truly turned on by state-of-the-art chemistry, especially nanotechnology.

MC pushed herself into an upright position on her bed, Aunt G's bed, really, except that MC had added a little color to the décor, splashing some blue and purple floral pillows here and there over Aunt G's stark bed linens. It was time to move off these pillows. She pulled off her favorite stretch-pants-cum-pajamas, shook out a pair of chinos from a basket in the corner, and selected a white shirt she had actually ironed. This was the best the RPD was going to get. She was due at the police station, to talk about Nina, though she couldn't imagine what she could tell them. She'd racked her brain already trying to figure what Nina was doing in Revere in the first place.

She remembered the day Nina had approached her, early in the semester.

"I'd love to do some extra research, since there's so much going on, right here," Nina had said, sweeping her arm, as fluid as a ballerina's, in the direction of the windowless research facility, the ugliest building on the campus. "I'm especially interested in Buckminster Fuller, and that new molecule named after him—the, uh, what's it called?"

"Buckminsterfullerene—buckyball!"

"Right! I read that buckyballs started the whole carbon nanotech thing. Do you know anyone doing that kind of stuff?"

So MC had put Nina Martin in touch with carbon researcher Wayne Gallen and the nanotechnology team.

And now Nina was dead, and Wayne was MIA. And Wayne had told her "they" were after her. Did "they" murder Nina? MC shuddered, then peeked out her bedroom window, a habit she couldn't shake, even in the middle of the day, ever since she'd first spotted the stalker. That is, Wayne. But maybe not Wayne. Well, at least she hadn't seen the creepy-looking car for a while.

Nina was probably the real target all along, and now I'm safe, she thought.

Maybe one of these days she'd actually enter her house from the front.

SEVEN

ROSE, the unofficial historian of Revere, had Rumney Marsh stories at her fingertips, literally. She held her hand up and drew a map in the air. The middle finger of her right hand was Route 107, also called the Lynn Marsh Road, which split the marsh (the palm of her hand) in two. She pushed her hand closer to me, as if she were asking me to read her future.

"They used to call this the Old Salem Turnpike," she told me. "Remember how they'd find wrecked cars there with their motors running?" She used the fingers of her left hand as cars. "Oh, no, that's right. You weren't home then."

To Rose, Revere had always been my home, my three decades in California a mere blip in my life. An anomaly, like a summer vacation that stretched out too long or a forced confinement that was finally over. Often, I agreed with her.

We sat on Rose's porch, a mass of white wicker and leafy green plants, screened- and storm-windowed-in. We were waiting for MC to come by after her interview with Matt and George Berger. It had started to drizzle, which Rose hated, but I loved. I felt I was due thirty years of greater-than-normal rainfall once I returned to the East Coast. Easier on the eyes than the almost daily, unfiltered California sun; and setting a perfect mood for the hot coffees we drank. The smell of split pea soup from Rose's Crock-Pot, a few feet away, also said "rainy New England fall day" to me.

I tried to get Rose back on track. "Do you know why the dead woman was carrying your business card?" I asked her.

"Well, apparently she was MC's student in that night class. Of course, MC had no idea she was an undercover investigator."

Rose took a sip of coffee. "I was telling you about all these stories in the *Journal,* about the marsh—John covered a couple of them when he was just starting out. The thieves would steal sports cars from Lynn, Saugus, Everett, you name it, and have demolition derbies out in the marsh, on that unfinished road that went nowhere." She wiggled her right pinkie, west of 107, from her point of view. "And then they'd just abandon the vehicles, motors running and all. Some of the cars were from as far away as Boston."

Rose laughed, always enjoying her own stories as if she were hearing them all for the first time herself. I smiled at her depiction of Boston, about eight miles from Revere, as "far away." By West Coast standards, that could be a quick jaunt to the nearest supermarket.

"How interesting," I said. "So, do you think this Nina Martin could have been coming to Revere to visit MC?"

Rose shrugged. "That could be it. But MC doesn't think so. She thinks the woman would have given her some notice, not just showed up. I guess they're looking into other relatives or—who knows. She was undercover, after all." She pulled up the collar of her rust-colored coat-sweater—perfectly matching the highlights in her hair—whether because of a chill or as an illustration of clandestine work, I couldn't tell.

More significant was Rose's nonchalance about a dead Texan in her hometown, a few days after a live Texan had scared her daughter enough to make a 911 call.

Either Rose was avoiding an unpleasant possibility, or I was paranoid about MC's safety.

"THAT'S THE SECOND TIME this week I've been in the police station," MC said. She rolled her shoulders counterclockwise and back, and rotated her neck from side to side, as if to undo the stress of the meetings. She sat on the small wicker footstool at her mother's feet, the one I was sure would crack under my weight, but seemed not to be aware MC had landed. She looked very young, very vulnerable.

I remembered summer visits from MC, the first when she was

just past her tenth birthday, her first solo plane trip. I loved taking her to the lab—she'd squealed in delight at the Berkeley University Lab cap I'd bought her, with B-U-L in bright yellow letters. We cooked macaroni and cheese for dinner, got take-out pizza, stayed up as long as she wanted to, and rode in my Jeep to San Francisco and Santa Cruz to do what I desperately hoped were "kid activities."

"My daughter's giving you competition, Gloria, with all the time she's spending with the RPD." Rose moved a few strands of MC's short, deep brown hair from one side to the other. "I don't understand the crooked parts girls wear these days," she said, with a seriousness that made it sound like a metaphor for life.

"I kind of like hanging around the police station," I said with a smile, then a sigh, as the remark led me straight to worrying about Matt's test results. I'd almost stayed home, in case the doctor called, but I knew they'd get in touch with Matt directly, no matter where he was, and probably not before the weekend was over.

"So how did the interview go?" I asked MC.

In other words, *I'm dying to hear everything.* Rumney Marsh was on the same side of town as the Charger Street lab. Maybe scientists were involved. Maybe someone needed tutoring on buckyballs.

MC rubbed her arms, as if she were chilly, and in the next minute Rose left the porch and came back with a sweater, a tight-knit beige one with tiny off-white flowers along the ribbing, thus preserving her daughter's put-together chino-and-white look. MC gave her mother an adoring glance that warmed me more than my plum-colored wool vest did.

Finally, MC started in, letting out a rush of words. "I guess I wasn't much help—they told me more than I could tell them. Nina was *not* a pre-law student, and she was *not* working nights as a waitress to pay for school, and she was *not* writing any paper on the geodesic dome. She'd asked me for an extension because her mother was sick, who now I know was *not* in Mexico," MC jerked her head to the side at each *"not,"* frowning as if she'd been betrayed, which in a way was true. "Nina's family is middle-class; her mother and father are both dentists in San Diego. Not even her grandparents are in Mexico anymore. She's about as Mexican as I am Italian."

Rose looked at her, seeming uncertain whether that was good or bad.

We ran through the obvious questions, interspersed with tenuously related anecdotes or trivia tidbits from Rose. No, Nina had never mentioned having relatives in Boston that she might be visiting. (Robert and Frank were going to a conference in Boston; they might give a paper on independent funeral homes versus chains.) Yes, Nina would have told MC ahead of time if she were going to fly out to see her. (The Logan reconstruction project was behind schedule.) No, Nina gave no indication that she needed to talk to MC about schoolwork, or anything else. (William's school band would be playing at the North Shore games on Thanksgiving.)

I felt uncomfortable putting MC through yet another interview, but she seemed willing enough to talk. Once or twice I had the feeling MC didn't want to remind her mother how close she was to a "situation," as Matt might call it. Neither did I.

The rain continued falling at a slow rate as the streetlights came on. Up and down Prospect Avenue, all the cars looked highly polished, every leaf glistened, shiny patterns played on fences and on the Galiganis' special rosebushes. Tiny lamps sat on small tables in the back corners of the porch, creating an intimate setting that would be impossible to read in. "It's for atmosphere," Rose had said often. "You're supposed to be musing, not reading."

Rose adjusted the lamp shades as she made her way to the kitchen, where she'd prepare dinner for ten, though she was expecting only five. Matt and I would join MC and her parents. Like my own mother, Rose claimed you never knew who might drop in, and God forbid there wasn't enough food.

MC moved to the chair her mother had used, and pulled her legs up under her—a position my always-chubby body would have had trouble with even in kindergarten.

Alone at last. *But start slowly,* I told myself.

"How did you like teaching?" I asked MC.

"I liked it enough to want to do more, but maybe something more advanced. These students were all…"

"Poets," I said, and she laughed. "I taught a class called 'Physics for Poets' for several years. It's frustrating, because you know most of the students don't want to be there."

She nodded. "On the other hand, there's this great opportunity to change someone's view of science. So you try to make it fun."

"Did you do the banana trick?" I asked.

MC rolled back in laughter. "How did you know?"

Together we mimicked immersing a banana into a vessel of liquid nitrogen, pulling it out, stiff as a board, then cracking it in half by slamming in onto a desk or chair in the classroom.

"I used a hammer," MC said, seeming embarrassed that she'd succumbed to the gimmick.

I'd always wondered if students learned anything from the tricks science teachers came up with to make the subject seem more fun than the amusements that used to line Revere Beach Boulevard. If nothing else, I figured, it showed we had a playful side.

Sharing science teaching anecdotes with MC was fun, but I needed to talk about the recently deceased Nina Martin.

"Had you been in touch with Nina at all since you came back to Revere?" I asked.

She shrugged, apparently not surprised that I'd changed the topic. "Just an e-mail or two. I glanced at them when I went through the list the other night for the first time, but I haven't read hers closely. They seemed to be about her *Incomplete,* and could wait. I have till the end of the year to post the grades." She threw her hands up. "Not that she'll be getting a grade." MC paused to catch her breath. "I'm sure I would have noticed, *Hey, Ms. Galigani, I'm coming up to Revere to visit.*"

"Well, Nina obviously had some intention of contacting you, MC, or she wouldn't have been carrying the Galigani card. Do you even remember giving it to her?"

She nodded. "Vaguely. She said something about keeping a file on all her teachers, for potential casework when she was in law school, and she'd like to be able to contact me after I left

Houston." MC banged her fists together. I saw sadness mixed with frustration. "She sure fooled everyone."

Except for her killer, I thought.

"Have you had a chance to look at all your e-mails, MC?" My way of asking if she had any clue what Wayne Gallen had been warning her about, and whether Nina's murder might be connected to it.

MC nodded. "I went through them all. I didn't find anything in Alex Simpson's e-mails that would explain what Wayne was talking about, if that's what you mean."

That's what I meant. "I was thinking—"

"Would you be willing to look at them yourself, Aunt G?"

"My, what a good idea," I said, feigning surprise.

I loved it when MC smiled.

EIGHT

THE MOST ENTERTAINING dinner table stories always came from Frank Galigani, professional mortician, Rose's high school sweetheart, and husband of many decades. As usual, the contrast between Rose's elegant place settings and Frank's work environment was striking. A soft, cloth runner in autumn hues on the one hand, and the bare, steel-gray embalming table on the other. Cheerful flower arrangements on mahogany surfaces in their home on Prospect Avenue, somber gladioli in stately baskets down on Tuttle Street.

Frank had the same all-Italian look as Matt, only thinner. And neater. Matt's body did not accommodate "dapper" any more than mine did, but Frank always looked perfectly groomed and ready to represent families in mourning, to stand a confident sentinel in a shadowy parlor, to console the grieving with style and grace.

You knew Frank would take care of you and your deceased in the most dignified manner. You knew Matt would be willing to walk through garbage and murky marsh waters to find evidence that would solve a crime perpetrated on you or your family. I loved them both.

This evening's story came as soon as we'd all sat down to Rose's idea of casual dining for a rainy fall evening. Matching place mats and napkins, and a cornucopia centerpiece that seemed designed for Thanksgiving, but, in fact, would be dwarfed by what she had in mind for that day.

Frank served from one end of the table, placing a small, stuffed Cornish hen on each platter. We helped ourselves to gravy, biscuits, green beans, and yellow squash for color, Rose said. We'd already enjoyed small china cups of split pea soup.

"There I am, in the prep room, ready to dress Sonny Lucca's boy." Frank had started his story, with no break in his meticulous serving technique.

"A shame, really, a young boy—he died in that eight-car pileup on One-A." An interruption from Rose, and we knew that Frank wouldn't mind. He waited a respectful amount of time before continuing.

"I push the casket up close to the table, so I can move him after he's dressed. I hate those hydraulic lifts; I like to move my clients myself. I pick up the jacket from the side chair, and I make a slit up the back as usual, and I arrange the arms, and the jacket's way too big." A grin made its way across Frank's face; he could hardly keep from laughing before the punch line. MC, sitting next to her father, put her elbows on the table, on either side of her plate. I thought I saw a grin on her face, too, before she buried her head in her hands. It seemed we had all guessed where the story was headed, but we let Frank have his moment.

"The sleeves are so long, they cover the kid's hands." By now, Frank had dropped the serving tools and used his hands to illustrate various points. "I figure maybe Sonny sent one of his own jackets by mistake. But the next thing I know, Mikey comes down—you know Mikey Vitale, who helps me out sometimes. He was upstairs in the office, on his way to some fancy shindig in his new suit." Frank had a wide smile, ready to erupt in laughter. "'Where's my jacket?' Mikey asks me."

"Oh, no," Rose said, leading a chorus of such exclamations. "You cut up Mikey's jacket!"

"Well, at least *this* story's not a gross-out," MC said.

"As if you never had your own messy stories, sweetheart," Frank said. He patted her arm, and earned the same adoring glance MC had given her mother a while before.

OUR FERNWOOD AVENUE home looked a bit dismal after the festive dinner at Rose's, but neither Matt nor I was willing to put the time into making it anything more than extremely comfortable for us. I remembered a quote attributed to Buckminster Fuller, something like, "Homes should be thought of as service equipment, not as monuments." Besides the couch and coffee table layout in the center of the room, the living room was big enough to accommodate a reading area at one end. We'd arranged two easy chairs and footstools at a slight angle, nearly facing each other, and shared news or ideas across the space.

"McConachie is playing at Jazz Too next weekend," Matt, the avid jazz fan, might say, scanning the entertainment section of the *Boston Globe*.

"Let's plan on it. Look here, there's a new book on string theory by James Bryer, that BU physicist we heard last year."

"Sounds good. Want a coffee?"

"Sure. I'll find those cookies Rose packed up for us."

If married life—not that the phrase had come up—was like this, no wonder people flocked to it.

This evening's banter included police matters, however. Matt brought me up to date on the Nina Martin murder—it looked like the body had been dumped in the marsh postmortem, and there was a kind of standoff between the Houston PD, the FDA, and the RPD.

"The FDA won't tell us why PI Martin had one of their cards until we share our forensics, and...you know the rest."

"Toddlers will be toddlers," I said, and Matt nodded.

"There's a sit-down with us and them on Monday that might get some cooperation on both sides."

"How about Wayne Gallen?" I asked him.

"He hasn't shown up yet, at home or at work in Houston."

"And he never went back to the Beach Lodge once he left the station?"

Matt shook his head. "No reason to put a lot of effort into finding him, either," he said. "Gallen's hardly a suspect in Nina's murder just because he also happened to be in town from Houston. Nothing else connects him to that crime."

"Except the fact that he acted suspiciously with respect to MC," I added. "And he did know Nina in Houston. I assume there's no word from the hospitals about a gunshot victim showing up?"

"Nope." Matt wiggled around to read his vibrating pager. "Berger," he said.

I turned down the CD player—I was tired of jamming wood-winds anyway—and gave him a pleading look.

"I know, the speakerphone." Matt punched in the number and switched on the system so I could hear the conversation.

Berger's speaker voice was hard to understand, but it was better than my standing over Matt's shoulder trying to read his notes.

"The good news is we got the shooter," Berger said, his voice sounding muffled. "A pharmacy over in Chelsea called in response to our bulletin. Told us a guy phoned and said he sliced himself with a piece of broken glass, and he wants hydrogen peroxide, antiseptic cream, tape, bandages, extra-strength pain-killer." Matt and I gave each other a thumbs-up. "And here's the clincher—the guy asks for forceps. Says there's a piece of glass in his hand, he has to catch a plane, doesn't have time to go to the ER, et cetera, et cetera, and he wants the package to be delivered to the Beach Lodge."

"Where Gallen stayed."

"Yeah. 'Course there's not exactly a hundred places to hole up around here. Anyway, by the time we got there the guy was out cold, bleeding like crazy."

Good girl, Nina, I thought.

"The other good news is that we found two weapons in the room. One is most likely the gun used on the PI woman, the other probably her gun, which he must have kept after dumping the body. We have to wait for ballistics, but it looks like the right ball-park all around."

PI woman? Would Berger have said PI man? Never mind, I told myself, *that battle's for another day.*

"Could have been shot by a third party who killed the PI, planted the gun, and so on." Matt made twirls in the air as he spoke, as if he were reciting a formula he was very familiar with, but which needed reviewing. "Or, he shot the PI, and someone else shot him using her gun. Handy that her gun was right there, don't you think?" Matt's tone was more telling than asking, as he continued his elaborate hand gestures. "Won't know till we talk to him. Where is he now?"

"Oh, that's the bad news."

"He's DOA," Matt said, with a click of his tongue.

"Right."

Bad news for sure. I'd been hoping for a wellspring of information from a killer in custody, some connections that might also solve MC's problem, though I seemed to be the only one who thought there was anything to worry about in that regard.

"Any ID?" Matt asked.

"Yep. An ex-con, Rusty Forman, from—three guesses, the first two don't count."

Leave it to George Berger to pull up a corny expression from the fifties.

"Houston," Matt and I said together.

NINE

SUNDAY MORNING. Still raining, and still twenty-four hours before there was a chance we'd hear from Matt's doctor. It had been a while since I'd been to church for anything other than a wedding or a funeral, and I gave it some thought. I pictured myself kneeling to pray, opening my missal—where was it? Had I seen it when I was packing for the move to Matt's house?—singing a hymn, standing for the Gospel. Then came the hard part. I heard the priest's homily as clearly as I had when I was in Confirmation prep classes. As they were then, the words were meaningless to me, and I mentally left the church again.

Rose was still practicing the faith. On the most recent Holy Day of Obligation, August 15, the Feast of the Assumption of Our Lady, I'd called their house, and Frank told me she was at mass.

"She goes for all of us," he'd said lightly.

Later, I'd chatted with Rose about how likely it was that the body of Mary, the Mother of Jesus, had been assumed into heaven, not subject to the deterioration process every other human body underwent.

"And why not just pray wherever you are?" I'd asked her, continuing our Why I Am (or Am Not) Still A Roman Catholic debate.

"Because God lives at St. Anthony's," she'd said with a grin. End of discussion. At times I envied her faith.

The mortuary was just down the street from St. Anthony's Church, so I'd had a daily reminder when I lived there of the choices I made regarding religion. I always came to the same conclusion—I couldn't pretend. Some days I felt I knew what it meant to pray, and others I didn't. Some days I believed there was an all-loving God in heaven who knew each hair of our head, and other days I imagined random gaseous events set in motion and left to the laws of science. There was no use trying to package that into religious observance. Blame it on Sister Pauline, I thought, who never could answer my logic questions when I was ten.

"Maybe they counted the loaves of bread and the fishes wrong to begin with, and that's why there seemed to be more at the end," I'd said, earning no holy card that week.

Surely there was no hope for me now.

Matt, another fallen-away Catholic, as we were officially called by Holy Mother Church, was spending Sunday morning at his office to make up for his hours on the tubular pillow in our living room. He was being productive, while I was home, too distracted to do anything useful.

I grunted and paced the thirty-foot expanse that included the living room and dining room, picking up a piece of lint here and there, ignoring the dust gathering in the corners of the hardwood floors. When the bottom level produced nothing inspiring, I climbed the stairs to the old guest room that was now my office. I looked with distaste at the pile of notes I'd accumulated for my next Revere High Science Club lecture, on crystallography, which had been my specialty in graduate school and for many years after.

The rain beat down on the roof, spilling out of the gutters, sweeping an idea into my head. The Science Club. I shelved the old notes. Another time. I couldn't very well storm the clinic for medical information on Matt, but I could face the other, distracting loose end.

I pushed the phone buttons and tapped my fingers on my desk during the fewer than ten seconds I had to wait for the pickup. I couldn't remember a time when I'd been less patient. "MC. I'm so glad you're home. I'm preparing a lecture on buckyballs for Revere High, and wondered if you could help me out. We could go for coffee and—"

MC laughed. "Aunt G, this is MC. Who are you trying to kid?"

"Busted," I said.

MC AND I SAT ACROSS from each other at Tomasso's Coffee Annex, at a table barely big enough for two espresso cups. We'd forced ourselves to make room for their pastry also, however, a maple scone for MC, a cannoli for me. We finished at the cashier's desk just before a large influx of people who I guessed had come from St. Anthony's Church, a few blocks away.

I knew MC had made yet another trip to the morgue to see if by any chance she'd be able to tell the police something about the ex-con who'd apparently murdered Nina. I'd been hoping she might recognized him from work, from teaching, even from her local supermarket in Houston.

"Nuh-uh," MC said, looking down at her drink, stirring nothing into her espresso. "I've never seen this Rusty Forman before."

I searched her face. I didn't like the lack of eye contact.

"What do you think is going on, MC?"

"What do you mean?"

"Now it's my turn—who are you trying to kid?" I kept my voice low, since the tables around us were now full, black wrought-iron chairs touching, back to back, throughout the small shop.

MC laughed, but only barely. I wanted to put my arms around her and protect her, as I did on a too-windy ferry ride from San Francisco to Sausalito when she was a little girl.

"If you mean Wayne and Nina and this Rusty, I really don't know."

"But…?"

"It's Jake," she said, finally meeting my gaze. "He's been calling, wants to see me. He's at a big equestrian conference in New Hampshire and wants to stop by on his way back to Texas."

"How bad was it, MC?"

She looked away again, her eyes tearing up. I could see her reflection in the shiny copper vat, only a foot or so away from us. "Bad enough."

"Then why would you even think of seeing him again?" I hoped she wouldn't tell me she loved him. For me, love was a choice, not an inevitable "falling" that you couldn't get up from. But no one had ever accused me of being a romantic, either.

"Habit," she said, and I sighed with relief. Habits can be changed, broken. Well, except for the one about eating cannoli.

"I know what I have to do, Aunt G. Get a life. And I'm working on it. I have an interview at Charger Street lab at the end of the month."

"Wonderful."

"In fact, it's with that Lorna Frederick, the woman I asked you about. She's been recruiting me for the nanotechnology team."

"Would you be working directly with her?"

"It's not clear. She has one of those jobs out here on the org chart." MC leveled her arm straight out from her shoulder and wiggled her wrist to indicate a vague position outside of line management. "She has a PhD in chemistry and used to do real research, but now she manages programs. I think her title is 'Special Projects.'"

"I have a well-connected technician friend out there. Andrea Cabrini. I'll ask her if she knows her." I made a note on a small pad I carried. "Lorna Frederick," I said, as I wrote the name. It gave me a feeling of productivity, as if I could be a big part of MC's life again.

MC gave me a big smile. "And—you'll be proud of me—I also have an interview at Revere High later in the week. How's that for moving right along?"

I sat back. "That's perfect."

I resisted the temptation to pat the top of her head in approval. I'd save that gesture for Matt.

We ended our coffee klatch, but not before we set a specific time, six o'clock that evening, for me to review MC's e-mails with her, and another date later in the week, when we'd visit old Mrs. Cataldo in the senior center together.

"Science teachers unite!" MC said, and I grinned.

MY CELL PHONE RANG as I was buckling up in front of Tomasso's. I'd planned to stop at Rose and Frank's, to return a stack of platters that had been sent home with me, piled with gourmet leftovers, over the past month or so. Not to go empty-handed, I'd picked up a fall bouquet at a little stand right outside the coffee shop. I knew Rose would be able to call the flowers by name; I just called them yellow and orange.

"Hi," Matt said. "Where are you?"

"Just finished having coffee at Tomasso's with MC. I'm on my way to Rose's."

"Can you meet me at home?"

My chest clutched up. "What is it?"

"I can be there in ten minutes. You?"

"Don't do this, Matt. I'm not one of your suspects. You can't skirt my questions like that."

"You're right. Sorry. My test results are back, and I'd like to see you, okay?"

I pressed my forehead to the steering wheel of my Caddie, grateful I wasn't on the road. My muscles went to a soft paste, like the filling of my cannoli, my skin as flaky and unsubstantial as its crust. "The doctor called you on a Sunday? It must be bad news."

"He's a good guy, that's all. He was at the clinic today, and he knew we'd be waiting. Please just meet me at home."

The flowers on the passenger seat seemed to wilt before my eyes. I started the car and drove toward Fernwood Avenue, slowly and carefully, as if my life depended on it.

TEN

MC FELT AS TIGHT as a helium bond. She needed exercise, but hated running in the rain, which had been continuous for the whole weekend. She dragged her worn navy and neon green mat onto the living room floor, and sat on it, legs crossed. *Breathe.* She leaned forward and placed her arms, elbow to wrist, flat on the mat in front of her, her butt rising in the air in the process. She rocked back and took a deep breath.

She lay on her back and went through the routine. The straight leg raise. A hamstring stretch. A whole-body stretch. Raise, count, breathe in, breathe out, bend, count, breathe in, breathe out.

When she was finished, she lay on the mat and closed her eyes. No babbling brooks; she was never any good at picturing nature in the abstract, but she'd built a stock of images that helped her relax. The Atlantic rushing toward her at Revere Beach. Lake Tahoe, California, where Aunt G had taken her over Christmas vacation one year. She smiled as she remembered the exhilarating skiing lessons Aunt G treated her to, while Aunt G herself read science books in the lodge.

And all her trips to oil refineries as a professional engineer— San Francisco Bay, the Gulf Coast. Who would have guessed thousands of gallons of crude a day were coming out of such exotic locales? The Caribbean. Hawaii.

Oops. Hawaii. Relaxation over. That's where she'd gotten to know Jake Powers. After a few months as casual acquaintances and colleagues around the plant, they'd been sent to Oahu together on a job. The Hawaiian facility had reported problems with the cracking unit, where the larger molecules were broken down into smaller ones, and Jake was the expert on that part of the process.

"I love making little ones out of big ones," he'd said, cracking his knuckles for emphasis.

She'd been so taken with him. Short, dark, and fit, like her father, and a smooth dancer. And the way he handled his horses, gently, but you knew who was in charge. One time he'd ridden right up to her after a practice oxer jump—he'd taught her the name of the jump with width as well as height—and he made Spartan Q, his jumper horse, bow to her. *Cool.* Later he told her the horse's three snorts were really her initials, MCG, which he'd taught Spartan Q. *Very cool.*

Yes, Jake was a real charmer. But a drinker, she eventually admitted. That first night on Oahu, they'd been sipping something pink at a bar, after a twelve-hour shift at the plant, lots of flirting on both sides. Coy glances, fingering each other's bright fuchsia leis, brushing body parts here and there as they twisted on their stools.

Another night they'd been with about twenty people their own age, many of them native Hawaiian plant workers out for a good time after a hard day's work. Jake had picked up a plastic bowl of salty snack food. She could see it clearly, feel the excitement.

"Hey, everybody! Want a lesson in how to convert molecules? Let's pretend these are the heavy hydrocarbons we start out with at the plant." Jake had swayed and grabbed the counter for balance. Then he smashed the bowl with his fist. Nuts, pretzels, cheese sticks, bits of plastic dish flew everywhere, across the counter, on the floor, on the flowery tee she'd bought in the hotel store. "Now they're converted," he'd said, drawing hysterical laughter from the crowd. "We just made gasoline!" Jake loved that he'd made a joke that only the in-crowd at the oil company would get.

How adolescent was she that she'd been impressed by that display? The other guys and girls had encouraged him also, and it ended up with the manager politely asking them all to leave. MC left with Jake. And stayed with him that night.

A few months later, after she'd been the target of his displays more than once, she'd finally called it quits.

Buzzzzzzzz!

The doorbell.

She screwed up her nose. Who could that be? No one just dropped in anymore, and who's going to climb two flights of stairs inside a mortuary building to take an advertising poll? She was glad Aunt G wasn't very tall, either; the peephole was in just the right place.

She closed her left eye, the weaker one, and put her right eye to the lens. Her breath caught. She stepped back, nearly tripping over the runner.

Jake.

"Come on, MC, open up. I know you're in there. I saw you at the window. I haven't bugged you, like you asked. Just let me in for ten minutes." Jake's voice was pleading, almost sweet, and maybe sober. "Okay, nine minutes." A laugh. The charming side of Jake Powers. She knew if she looked out the peephole again, she'd see a bouquet of flowers in his hand.

MC blinked, turned away, as if her thoughts of him in Hawaii, in Houston, in bed, had caused him to appear on her landing. If she could just stop thinking of him, he would go away. She shut her eyes against the images.

Thump. Thump. Buzzzzzzzz!

"What's going on here?" Her brother Robert's voice, from the other side of the door. He must have a Sunday client downstairs.

MC breathed deeply. She heard Jake's voice.

"Hi, I'm Jake Powers, a friend of MC's. I…uh…I guess she can't hear the buzzer." Robert, at five eight or nine, was the tallest in the family, and the most muscular. MC figured Jake, nearly jockey-size, heard the slightly intimidating tone in her brother's voice. "Maybe I should come back later."

MC went back to the door, and opened it. She saw the two men, one carrying flowers for her, the other ready to protect her. Robert was in a suit and tie, indicating he'd just come from claiming a client. Robert's thick neck strained against his dark blue shirt. It would not be out of the question to mistake him for a professional bodyguard. Jake, on the other hand, was dressed as if he'd just come down from the back of a horse.

Jake glanced over at her, tucked the flowers at his waist, and bowed slightly. His most charming posture, that always won her heart. She could let him in just for minute, she thought.

"It's okay, Robert," MC said. She made very brief introductions, her eyes turned away from Robert. "Come on in, Jake."

"I'll be downstairs," Robert said, knocking his knuckles together.

"I have the number," MC said.

ELEVEN

MATT CAME THROUGH the door, generating a smile for my benefit. The attempt made his face look contorted. I buried my head in his shoulder, not wanting him to see my own unhappy expression.

"Hi, honey," he said. I looked up in time to see his tipping an imaginary hat. Our little domestic joke.

I'd gotten home before Matt and put on a pot of coffee, for something to do. I'd looked around the house at what seemed important only a few days ago. A bag of Christmas wrapping paper and tags waiting in the corner, a tattered kitchen curtain that needed to be replaced, a pile of newspapers ready for recycling, a to-do list, a to-call list. Call Daniel Endicott at Revere High for the lecture schedule; call cousin Mary Ann in Worcester for a holiday date. None of it was real.

"Tell me," I said, still in his arms.

"My cancer is a five," he said.

This is no time to be funny, I thought, but I smiled anyway. Matt often teased me about my need for quantizing everything. Give me a number from one to ten, I'd ask him, if I wanted to know his reaction to a concert, or a book, or even a tie I'd bought him.

We walked to the couch, still holding on to each other. "No, really, they give these things a number. It's called grading the cancer."

"A grade? They give cancers a grade?"

"Yeah, they call it the Gleason system. You know, like Jackie?" Matt tries a *va-va-voom,* so comical I had to laugh, as much as I wanted to cry.

I let Matt explain. "It goes from one to five, based on how much the arrangement of cells in the cancerous tissue looks like normal tissue. I'm only repeating what they told me, not that I understand it completely. But one is good, five is not."

I gasped, held my breath. "Five is the worst?"

"No, no. Sorry. I'm a three in one area, and a two in another, so they add them and get a five, which is my total Gleason score. But the five in the total is not bad; it's average." He paused, resting his fingers from the demonstration, and put on another smile. "I thought you'd like all this math, Gloria."

Not in this context. I moved my lips into a weak smile. My hands had become like ice and I pulled them into the sleeves of my turtleneck, a poor imitation of waif-ness.

He held up his hand, wiggled his fingers. "Five for a total is sort of intermediate. I'm your average guy, as we always knew."

I loved him for sparing me his own anguish. I took a deep breath, calmed myself. It was his cancer, after all, and I should be at least as composed as he was.

"So, what's next?" I asked, with a forced calmness. This was a problem, and we would solve it together, as we had so many others.

"Well, it's a Stage-Two; then there's another designation with Ts and letters." Matt pulled a pile of literature out of his briefcase. "I have to digest this information on treatments and come to a decision." He held the leaflets and notebook pages out halfway between us. "A project for us."

I took them from his hands. We sat on the couch for a few more minutes, moved to the bedroom, and did not let go of each other for a long time.

ROSE HAD BEEN ON MY MIND. Playing amateur psychologist, I'd decided that she was repressing feelings of anxiety about MC, whose student had been murdered, and not long after MC herself had felt threatened by a prowler. But I had a hard time concentrating on anything other than Matt's Gleason score, and in the end she called me first, early Monday morning.

As soon as I heard her voice, I thought of MC and a date I hadn't kept. I'd forgotten completely that I'd made a date to be at her apartment at six the night before.

"Jake Powers, MC's ex-boyfriend, stopped by her apartment last night, Gloria," Rose told me. Apparently, MC hadn't missed me, I thought. "We wouldn't even have known, except Robert was working late with Mr. Baroni, and he saw someone go up-stairs. The guy was banging on her door, making a scene in the hallway. MC let him go in, but Robert waited around until he left, about two hours later."

I pictured Robert, slightly taller than his father, and well-built. "It's good that Robert was there," I said, trying to maintain a neutral tone.

"I'm worried about her, Gloria. I hope she doesn't take that guy back. I think he wasn't nice to her in Texas." Rose's voice cracked as she told me, and, strangely, I was glad. Psych 101 again—better that she's acknowledging her concern.

I thought I'd set a good example, and bare my own soul. "I feel so guilty and selfish, Rose. I meant to call you to talk about MC, and instead this…situation with Matt has consumed me." I knew that Matt and Frank had talked the evening before, and that Rose would understand what the "situation" was.

"Well, I feel selfish, too, and useless. What you and Matt must be going through!"

So we had a deal, born of decades of friendship, that we would allow each other our momentary self-centeredness. Nothing a shared cannoli wouldn't fix, I decided, and offered to take a box over to Prospect Avenue.

"Just come," she said. "The cannoli are already here. That's why I called."

It felt like old times, except for the layer of worry that seemed always present since I'd heard Matt's test results. I tucked him in for one of his naps, no longer rare since his illness, and headed over to Rose's.

WE SAT ON ROSE'S PORCH, squinting at the first bit of sunlight in several days. Rose's collection of glass vases caught the light and I traced the rays with an invisible protractor. Reflection, refraction, diffraction, diffusion—the beauty of geometric optics.

Rose always broke into a stream of stories when she was

overwrought, and having her daughter under any kind of stress qualified for that condition. I let her tell me incidents I'd heard dozens of times, many of them from the early days of the Galigani business, when the whole family lived in the mortuary building. Their residence took up the top floor and the one below, which now housed offices for Rose and her assistant, Martha. Frank's idea was to introduce all the children to the trade, but Rose set limits. She'd never let them see anyone they had known while the client was "being prepared" in the basement, as she called it.

"One time MC sneaked down to the prep room," Rose said, "because she'd heard that her girlfriend Joanie Della Russo's grandmother was a client. She was about five at the time." At the last telling, MC had been closer to seven, but I didn't correct her. "Frank was weighing something, uh, messy, for some reason, when he saw MC out of the corner of his eye. So he swooped down on MC and put her in the pan of the other scale. She laughed and laughed, swinging in that scale. Can you imagine? Any other kid would have been scared to death, but not MC."

Rose recited this anecdote with more pride than usual.

"MC will be fine, Rose. She'll find an interesting job, settle down. She's very strong, and she'll get through all this." I felt I was simply articulating the point of Rose's story.

Rose nodded. "Even when we moved here she'd still go to the mortuary after school sometimes and beg her father to show her 'something smelly,' she'd say." Rose glanced around at the objects of art on her porch, and I wondered what she saw, if not ray optics. Colors, and shapes, I thought. Memories, too, probably. "John—our top-notch journalist—was never, never interested in what went on down there, but I was amazed when MC didn't follow Frank and Robert into the business."

"Well, she just chose a different smelly profession," I said.

"And maybe journalism has its own smells," she said, with her delightful laugh.

MC STOPPED BY BEFORE I left Rose's. I had a couple of minutes with her while Rose prepared a new pot of coffee.

"I'm so sorry I forgot about our date last night. Matt came home with his test results, and—"

MC shook her head. "Not to worry, Aunt G, I know you have a lot on your mind. I really hope Matt will be fine, and I bet he will be." She lowered her eyes. "And anyway, I had some company. I'm sure my mother told you."

I nodded. I paused for a moment, then decided I had to ask. "MC, did you tell Jake he could stop in Revere to visit you?"

"He was on his way back from the New Hampshire Equestrian Expo, and he stopped by, that's all," she told me, a hint of defensiveness in her voice.

I knew what computer expos and scientific-equipment expos were like, but I had a hard time imagining an expo or a demo about horses. Were they on display in booths? Did the booths have giveaways like the pens and periodic-table coasters given out at science expos? I must have given a visible sign of confusion, because MC went on to clarify.

"They have seminars on all kinds of topics, like rider conditioning, breeding, different styles of saddles, equine medicines, that kind of thing. Jake's a specialist in composting and manure management techniques. His chemistry comes in handy for his hobby that way."

I didn't think I wanted to know more details, and besides, MC had not answered my question. "I'm asking if you agreed to a visit."

MC looked sheepish. "Well, I thought I'd told him no."

I guessed MC had said something like "I'd rather you wouldn't," which Jake would take as eighty percent no, twenty percent yes; well worth a shot.

I knew how that worked.

My fiancé, Al Gravese, had never physically battered me, but he'd pressed his will on me in such a way that I did what he wanted—even when I thought I'd insisted otherwise.

"Wanna go play cards with Mike and Angie tonight?" he'd ask, in his peculiar uneducated accent, phoning me in the middle of the day.

"I'd rather go to the movies," I'd answer.

"Angie likes you a lot."

"I don't like poker. I don't know how to play well. I might go to a movie with Grace instead." *Might.* There was that eighty-twenty.

"You don't want to go to a movie with that *stunata*. I'll pick you up at six o'clock. You'll have a good time."

Having had the same kind of subtly coercive relationship with my mother, who told me what my favorite color was, I'd been ripe for the picking by Al Gravese. I shook away the memory.

"MC, it's none of my business," I said. "But—"

"You're right, Aunt G. It isn't." MC stood and walked away. I thought I heard a weak, "I'm sorry."

I WAS DISTRAUGHT over the first tension, ever, between MC and me. I was convinced her mood had to do with more than a drop-in from her ex-boyfriend. Nina Martin's murder, for one thing. Two murders, really, if you counted that of the hit man. And too many Texans making life miserable for MC.

I had to go to work.

Back at my computer, with Matt at the office—for a couple of hours only, he promised—I started to tabulate the information I had, but the table quickly degenerated into just a string of events. Wayne Gallen shows up; Nina Martin shows up, dead; Rusty Forman shows up, dead; Jake Powers shows up. Wayne is now missing. Was that reason enough to blame Wayne for Nina's murder? Was he connected to Rusty Forman?

The string method got me nowhere. I opened a computer drawing program and doodled with a new pattern. A star, with MC at the center, and spokes for Wayne, Nina, Rusty, Jake. All Houstonites, I noted, if that was a word. The design looked western, like something out of a Lone Star State Chamber of Commerce brochure.

Were all these Texans in Revere specifically to see MC? It seemed to have started with Wayne, who said he'd come to warn MC of a threat from Alex Simpson, the buckyball researcher. Jake appeared to be seeking only MC's affection, but I didn't believe in pure motives.

I added a spoke with a question mark, to indicate the possible *AS and the bad guys* who were after MC, the ones who allegedly sped off when Wayne showed up. As far as I knew, Alex Simpson had never been seen in Revere, but I left his initials on the chart anyway.

Nina had a Galigani business card in her pocket but had made no attempt to contact MC. *Murdered before contacting?* I wrote. I still hadn't heard what leads the list of telephone numbers in Nina's pocket had brought. I made a note to check on it with Matt. It was tough doing police work when you weren't a cop. If I were a cop in Houston, for example, I could knock on Alex Simpson's door and ask him to explain every e-mail he wrote this year. If I had any authority at all, I could phone the local FDA office and get an interview with whoever Nina's contact was. I could open her office files and find out who hired her in the first place.

I knew the real cops probably considered the cases closed, but not me. Nina Martin enrolled in MC's class for a reason, and that reason could be connected to her murder. In my mind, therefore, MC was still vulnerable.

The days were getting shorter, and even at four in the afternoon, the light was fading. I switched on a new halogen floor lamp, one of the few items I'd purchased for the Fernwood Avenue home. I'd fixed up one of the extra bedrooms with my computer desk and file cabinets, not bothering to change the bold paisley area rug that hid most of the hardwood floor. I thought how we buy things with the idea that we'll live long enough to use them, that they will "die," or wear out, before we do. We don't plan on our lives being interrupted by disasters. Or by a Stage-II cancer.

I swallowed hard, and went back to work on my star.

Only Rusty's motive for traveling across the country seemed clear: To murder Nina. But if Wayne was right, Rusty might also have had MC on his list, and whoever hired him would still be after her.

I tapped my keyboard. Why was all this happening in Revere? Was it just because MC had returned to Revere, or was there something else going on in Revere, even before MC got back?

I looked at my star. Probably because I was thinking of the

Wild West, I'd drawn little filled-in circles at the ends of the spokes, like the rivets on a western shirt, or the logo for some Bar Star Ranch. All at once the circles looked like atoms. Carbon atoms. Buckyballs. Not sixty atoms like a real buckyball molecule, but close enough. Except for Rusty Forman, all the Texans had buckyballs in common.

Now it was easy. Where were the buckyballs in Revere? I asked myself. At the Charger Street lab. And who at the Charger Street lab had been trying to break into this star? I smiled at my cleverness. Lorna Frederick, I answered. Lorna Frederick, who kept calling MC for an interview.

It made so much sense to me, I picked up the phone to share my insight with the real police.

"I have something," I said to Matt.

"Lorna Frederick," he said.

I dropped my shoulders, slumped in my chair, swept by a mixture of disappointment at not being first and excitement at the verification of my star calculation.

"Right." Too weak, I knew, but I couldn't take it back.

I heard the wonderful Matt-laugh. "You don't like sharing the triumph?"

"Of course I do."

"Isn't there something like this in science, where two people in different parts of the world invent the same thing at the same time?"

I resisted the temptation to explain the difference between scientific discovery and technological invention.

"Lorna Frederick was on Nina's telephone list?" I asked.

"Right. Only one of many, but for some strange reason, I thought I'd take this one to follow up on. I'm going out to Charger Street in the morning. Interested in a consulting job?"

"Does Revere have a beach?"

TWELVE

THAT EVENING MATT AND I took a walk along Revere Beach Boulevard. I loved the shapes of the pavilion and bandstand rooftops, some trapezoidal, others with a parabolic cross-section. They were a deep green color during the day, and darkened as the light faded. Beautiful geometric patterns emerged, sandwiched between the gray sky above the ocean and the now almost completely barren trees on the road in front.

The old-fashioned streetlights came on as we strolled from Revere Street to Beach Street. We were surprised at the low traffic flow along the boulevard.

"Everyone's home watching *Monday Night Football*," Matt said.

"Finally, a redeeming feature," I said.

An amiable laugh. Matt cared as little as I did about organized sports, denying that it was because he didn't make the team in high school. When the debating coach gets as much stipend and attention as the soccer coach, maybe our educational system won't be an embarrassment, was our sweeping, collective opinion. All the world's problems had simple solutions on a stroll by the ocean.

The evening was peaceful, the weather mild, and we agreed to keep our conversation equally serene. No talk of disease, diagnosis, or treatment, though I'd revisited all my health-related bookmarks. No talk of buckyballs, though I'd given myself a crash course from Internet sources, to update myself. Not even a strategy session on our next day's meeting with Lorna Frederick.

We cut down a side street to Ocean Avenue, which ran behind the boulevard, where we'd parked Matt's Camry. We'd covered about a mile and a quarter in all. I wanted to stretch out distance and time, to keep my senses full of the salt-air smells and the sound of the surf, to block out the real-life space-time coordinates that would throw us back into the universe of murder and disease—both too close to home.

Matt started the car, rolled into the northbound lane. "We've got some challenges ahead," he said, as if he'd been in touch with my soul. "And, lucky us, we get to work on them together."

"Lucky us," I said. Lucky me.

I THOUGHT I'D WALKED into a catalog for horse owners—Lorna Frederick's office was teeming with images of horses. Posters of horses; horse sculptures; horse designs on her wastebasket, pencil holder, and lamp shade; photographs of herself with horses and on horses. In one framed snapshot, Lorna, who looked about thirty-five or forty—too old to be jumping over fences in my opinion—was wearing a fitted black jacket and helmet and white pants. I was sure there was a special name for the pants. The word "jodhpurs" came to mind, but that might be those bright, silk outfits that racing jockeys wore, I thought.

Lorna, in person, wore a striking blue knit dress, utterly out of sync with the ranch-like atmosphere of her office. Over her shoulders she'd hung a shawl, or a stole, or at least a large piece of fabric in blues and purples. When she stood to greet us, the beaded fringes on the ends clanked against her telephone. I'd seen such arrays on models in magazine ads, but never on anyone I knew, and certainly not on anyone working in a laboratory. It looked as practical as a prom dress at a rodeo. But what did I know about rodeos? I asked myself. Amazing how I was being carried away lately by images of the Wild West. Texas, big as it was, was forcing its way into my world.

I found myself wishing we could arrest Lorna for fashion violation, to get her outfit off the streets. But in the less-than-perfect world Matt and I were in, we introduced ourselves and began the slow process of gleaning information.

"Sit down. Make yourselves comfortable," Lorna said from behind her desk, with a flare to match her outfit. Her face was pinched together vertically, too small for her body; her light hair, many shades of blond, was short and curled unnaturally at the edges. "It's not every day I get a visit from Revere's finest. My secretary neglected to say what brings you here, but you are welcome to my humble office."

Humble, indeed.

Matt, in the brown suit he wore every Tuesday, nodded his thanks and pointed to the display case of ribbons on the wall behind her desk. Blue, red, yellow, white, all with gold letters spelling something I couldn't make out. I'd seen the raw materials when I'd reluctantly accompanied Rose to a party-supply store one time, and wondered how you could tell which ones were legitimate.

"Very impressive," Matt said. There was no way Lorna could know that the police detective in front of her was afraid of large animals, horses in particular. I'd found this out through George Berger. Matt and I had sat with him and his wife at a department party, and he'd related an anecdote about how the rookie Matt Gennaro had refused to mount a police horse for a Veteran's Day parade. He'd been able to make a deal with his captain, that he'd close at least three cold cases that week if they'd let him off parade duty. He'd closed four. Matt held a smug smile through the telling of the story.

"It's department legend," Berger said, when I asked him how he knew this, since he was much younger and couldn't have known Matt in his early years with RPD.

Lorna sat down and picked up a photo from her desk, herself on a speckled gray-and-black horse. "This is Degas, my Appaloosa, one of my favorites. He's won me one ribbon after another. Not many people realize Edgar Degas painted and sculpted horses as well as ballerinas." Lorna leaned back, steepled her fingers. "I've been a horsewoman since I was eight years old. Cleaned stalls in exchange for lessons, and now I own more horses than my first instructor at Sunset Ranch did."

How nice for you, I thought.

"Impressive," Matt said again, as if he had limited vocabulary when it came to equestrian prowess.

My eyes strayed to a large whiteboard on the side wall, its tray filled with erasers and thick markers in as many colors as the ribbons Lorna had won. I could tell she had left real science and engineering far behind. The board was filled with organizational charts, budget items with dollar amounts, timelines, and acronyms for funding sponsors. My eyes landed on *DoD*. Leave it to the Department of Defense to use a lowercase O, so that every scientist had to tell her or his editors it wasn't a typo. DOE, DARPA, NRC. The Department of Energy, Defense Advanced Research Projects Agency, Nuclear Regulatory Commission. A few nongovernment names, some of which were pharmaceutical companies I recognized, were on the board also, with question marks next to them. Not committed, I assumed. There wasn't an equation or a force diagram in sight.

"Interesting that you didn't choose horse-raising as a career," Matt said.

I wondered if horses were actually raised, like children, or chickens and sheep. My mind wandered in search of a more appropriate word, but neither Matt nor Lorna seemed hampered by the word choice. Lorna told us how her father, a rancher, had convinced her that the best strategy was for her to get an education in a field where she could make enough money to afford the luxury of competitive riding.

"No money in these competitions?" Matt asked, glancing at the showcase, as if to ask the worth of dozens of satiny ribbons.

Lorna shook her head and shrugged her shoulders, almost losing her scarf/shawl. "Not much, at least not in the local shows. There's decent money in the bigger jumping competitions, sometimes as much as a hundred thousand dollars, but that would be split up among the top placings. Canada has a famous event, maybe close to a half million in prizes, but on the average it's much less than that. Most people are in it for the sport." She smiled, leaned forward, sharing a secret. "Well, for ego, too, I admit. You're always competing for points, which you accumulate toward year-end awards, at a big ceremony." Lorna opened her arms wide, to signify how big, again almost losing her wrap.

Matt nodded, relaxed. I knew he was gearing up, letting Lorna get comfortable. "But you have to make a living somehow," he said, giving a palms-up. Compatriots, both just doing a job. I sat in my navy blue business casual, waiting for a piece of the action. So far, I hadn't done much but smile and nod in appropriate places.

"Right," Lorna said, "so, I came East to study engineering."

"East from…?" Matt asked.

"Galveston," Lorna said, raising the hairs on the back of my head. I wished I knew the distance from Galveston to Houston. In a state the size of Texas, it might be the same as Revere to Portland, Maine, but, still, here was another Texan in Revere. Lorna seemed to enjoy giving her bio. "I majored in chemistry at BU, got involved in materials research when I came here to Charger Street as a summer intern. I came back after I graduated, and I've been here ever since. Do I have to tell you how many years?" This last was said in a coy, flirting way that did not become her.

Matt smiled and gave a page of his notebook a casual flip. "Do you know a Nina Martin?"

I smiled, recognizing Matt's style—chat for a few minutes, let them direct the conversation, then hit them with a quick yes-or-no, black-or-white, do-you-or-don't-you question.

Lorna seemed as taken aback as he'd intended. She cleared her throat and then frowned, as if in confusion, but to my mind, it was a cover-up in advance of a lie.

"Nina…Martin? No." Lorna might have been trying to pronounce a foreign phrase. She licked her lips, rubbed her forehead. Matt kept his eyes locked on her. She fumbled with paper clips in a bowl on her desk. "Oh, wait, I did see something on the news. The woman they found in the marsh?"

Matt nodded. I knew he wouldn't say anything just yet. From the interview handbook, I imagined: Create an awkward silence, hope the suspect will fill it. Not that Lorna Frederick was an official suspect, except for all the connections I'd made on my computer-generated star.

Lorna obliged with stuttering remarks. "Terrible thing. Poor woman." She shook her head in tsk-tsk sympathy. "What makes you ask if I knew her? Is that what brings you here?"

"Do you have any connections with the buckyball team in

Houston?" The Don't Answer Her Question; Ask Another One trick, a polite form of "I'll ask the questions here." I was proud of Matt's glib mention of nanotechnology.

"Yes, I know the people from the program out there, of course. You know how it is with research these days, share and share—"

"Can you think of any reason Nina Martin would be carrying around your telephone number?" Matt asked, cutting in.

Poor Lorna. In the last few minutes she'd straightened out two metal paper clips. Goodbye steepled fingers.

"Well, no. I…uh… She had my phone number? I suppose it could have been a permutation or something." Lorna sat up straight again, as if an idea had suddenly come to her. "Or maybe someone referred her to me. I'm responsible for recruiting people to the project. That must be it."

"Would you mind telling me where you were last Friday, Ms. Frederick?"

His voice so sweet, the detective might have been asking her out for coffee. Which reminded me to look for signs of Lorna's family life. She had so many rings on her fingers—I counted three on each hand, including an enormous silver/turquoise number that must have made it impossible for her to bend that knuckle—I couldn't tell if a wedding ring was among them. I saw only one photo that didn't include horses—Lorna with two men I recognized as local politicians.

Lorna hadn't misinterpreted Matt's question as anything but what it was—a request for an alibi. Her face lost its color; she put her hands on her desk and rolled back in her chair, as if to push herself away from the topic. She bit her lower lip and closed her eyes; I thought she might cry. Then, in the next minute, her eyes widened. I imagined her mind churning, angry that Matt had not been open with her from the beginning. Her nostrils flared, as I imagined her Appaloosa's might. She stood and folded her arms across her chest.

"I rode my horse until ten or ten-thirty, then went home to bed." She cleared her throat, ready to deliver an unpleasant message to an underling. "And now I'm going to ask you to leave."

Matt nodded and closed his notebook, giving no sign he'd noticed her new hostility. "Of course," he said.

The interview was over, and I hadn't done a thing to earn my consultant status. I had to get a word in. "If you have another moment—before we leave, I'd just like to get a sense of what you do here as a project director. Does that mean you have responsibility for funding, or do you also set the research agenda?"

Lorna glared at me, picked up a brochure from a pile on her side table, and handed it to be. "Everything you need to know is in here. Now, I have an important meeting." *Unlike this one,* was the implication. She swept her arm toward the door. "So if you will kindly leave?"

We did.

For now, I thought.

"WHAT DID YOU THINK?" Matt asked, starting our traditional post-interview debriefing. We were in his Camry, headed for lunch at Russo's on Broadway. In my mind, I'd already ordered the specialty of the house, eggplant parmigiana.

"She seemed too tall for horse-riding," I said, only half teasing. I realized I was probably influenced by photos I'd seen of jockeys, who seemed not much bigger than Rose.

Matt laughed. "What do we know from this interview? Friendly with the mayor and Councilman Vega, for one."

"I saw that. Windowless, inside office, not far up the ladder."

"Still, able to maintain a pretty expensive hobby," Matt said. "More like an obsession."

For a moment I wished I had a passion like Lorna's for horses. I tried to imagine myself committed in that way to a sport, or to a craft, like the quilt-making craze I'd noticed among women I'd worked with in California. Rose's current interest was in making glass beads for jewelry and decorative lamps. I'd resisted invitations to join her. Did reading science magazines and biographies count as the hobby Rose insisted I needed? I'd have to pursue that thought another time.

"If she didn't know Nina Martin, she definitely knew something she didn't want to share," Matt said, still on the debriefing track.

"I wish I could have learned more about her work. I'll do some checking."

"Notice anything about her alibi?"

A quiz, I sensed, and concentrated on remembering the exact words Lorna had used. "Nothing unusual, just that she didn't give any names."

Matt waited, giving me more time to come up with the right answer, I guessed. "That's it?"

"I'm afraid so. You're going to have to tell me," I said.

"I asked her what she was doing on Friday. What would you have answered, in her place?"

"Aha." I got his point. "I would have started with being at work, during the day, but Lorna went right to the evening and nighttime hours."

"The report says Martin probably died sometime late Friday night. Of course, it could be nothing."

"But it's interesting." I loved how police minds worked. Maybe that was a hobby.

Matt glanced over at my lap, where I held the brochure Lorna had thrust at me.

"Think you'll get anything from that?" he asked.

"Count on it."

THIRTEEN

MY DESK HAD BECOME a repository of brochures. I'd sent away for paper literature from several pharmaceutical companies, to give myself a break from reading long pages of text on my computer monitor. They all made promises, giving sweeping assurances of a better, cancer-free life for all. Strange how all avenues of thought seemed to lead to Matt's disease.

I read about "smart medicines" that ignore healthy cells and go straight to the cancer cells; vaccines made from a patient's own tumors, to "strike cancer right where it lives"; "small-molecule medicines" that disrupt the signal pathways of cancer cell receptors. All of these miracle cures involved drug delivery systems made possible with nanotechnology, the wave of the future; all designed to zero in on disease, to give families hope. So why wasn't I feeling hopeful?

I opened the pamphlet from Lorna Frederick, a typical three-fold affair, with bullets and clip art highlighting the research agenda. It was hard to distinguish the Charger Street lab brochure from those of commercial enterprises. The lab program had several joint projects with pharmaceutical companies, as I'd noticed on Lorna's whiteboard.

I figured pharmaceutical companies had always promised utopia, but this was a new twist for research laboratories, at least in my experience. In my graduate school days, I was funded by the department I studied and worked in, not by a private, profit-making industry. I worked at my own pace, my only goal to satisfy my dissertation committee and myself. Charger Street scientists, it seemed, didn't have that luxury.

The more I read, the more annoyed I became. *This brochure*

is a funding tool, I reminded myself, meant to draw industrial partners into the work of research, to speed up the technology transfer process. A good thing. But what were the consequences for "pure research"? I wondered how scientists could remain objective with someone standing outside the doors of the lab, waiting not just for data, but for a certain kind of data. The *it's a go* kind of data. It seemed to me the perfect environment to encourage fraud. If my entire budget would stand or fall based on the results of one clinical trial, one set of curves, I might be tempted to skew the data, just a little, just enough to keep my research alive. For the greater good, and all.

If I'd been looking for a reason to justify the fraudulent actions of some scientists, there it was.

I realized what I was most annoyed at was my own ambivalence. I wanted a drug on the market that would completely cure Matt's cancer, but I didn't want science to get dirty producing it.

I hadn't slept well for several nights, and as a result, I dozed off in the middle of an article about tomatoes in a journal from a cancer treatment center. Tomato sauce, it said, if eaten regularly, can reduce the risk of prostate cancer. Tomatoes contain lycopene, which gives them their bright red color, and works as an antioxidant in the body. Tomato sauce—the staple of Matt's youth, and mine.

Matt woke me up, coming through the front door, laden with his heavy briefcase and a bag of groceries. He looked to me like he also needed a nap, as if I could see the cancer cells marching across his lower body, making him tired.

Matt looked at the loose pages of the journal article on my lap.

"Find anything interesting?"

"Yes, you need to eat more cooked tomatoes."

He reached into the grocery bag and pulled out a cluster of deep red tomatoes.

"Lycopene!" I said.

We laughed, but we both knew it was time to get serious about treatment. We'd gone through the options for a Stage-II diagnosis, the first of which was called "watchful waiting," to see if symptoms recurred. For Matt, the primary symptom had been a burning in his urinary tract. We'd read that patients with a low Gleason score have a very small risk of dying of their cancer within fifteen years if their cancer is never treated. Not good enough. Waiting was not high on my list of preferred responses, nor on Matt's.

With a backdrop of a harvest moon outside our bay window, we sat on our couch and talked about excision of the prostrate by irradiation; about the retropubic approach as opposed to the perineal approach to radical prostatectomy; about external and internal radiation therapy.

"I'm getting a lot of solicitations to be part of clinical trials," Matt told me. "I can be a subject for ultrasound surgery or hormone therapy." He pounded his chest. "I'm classified as an OHM, otherwise healthy male."

He smiled; I didn't. Matt, subjected to experimental drugs? For one who loved empiricism, I was surprisingly against it in this case.

"How soon do we need to decide?" I asked him.

He pulled me closer. "See, it's that 'we' that makes all the difference. If I could only get you to use that pronoun when you talk about *our* house."

"You're right. When do we leave *our* house and go to talk to *our* doctor?"

"By the end of the week. Which reminds me, Gloria. There's something else you're not going to want to hear."

My heart sank. What next, Stage III? Had Matt been to the doctor without me? Had more symptoms crept in? The look on my face must have caused Matt to regret his facetiousness, and he rushed to clarify.

"Jean wants to come up over the weekend. She's…worried, I guess, and would like to see me."

A visit from Matt's sister. That's all it was. I was at once relieved that there was no bad medical news, and chagrined that Matt felt he had to apologize for having his own sister as our guest for a couple of days.

"Of course she should see you, Matt. I wish I'd thought of inviting her myself."

I'd last seen Jean at a barbecue at her Cape Cod home over Labor Day weekend. She hadn't bothered to tell me that about fifty clients from her thriving real estate business would also be there, and dressed as if for a wedding. I showed up in beach casual, with a windbreaker over my khakis, carrying a small casserole (for the party of five I expected) that could hardly compete with the catered crab cake dinner. Matt tucked the dish away in the refrigerator, and seemed comfortable in his beach clothes, even joking about the miscommunication. I was less inclined to give Jean the benefit of the doubt. *Let's embarrass that old girlfriend of my brother's,* I imagined her thinking.

None of this meant I shouldn't have thought to invite Jean to visit her brother, and I apologized again to Matt.

He patted my hand. "Not a problem. She'll be here for dinner on Friday, and stay over one night. Petey and Alysse won't be coming, they'll be staying with some friends in Dennisport."

While I wasn't crazy about Matt's teenage niece and nephew, in some way, the children provided a buffer between their mother and me. They seemed to enjoy the science "toys" I gave them, bestowing an evaluation of *cool,* when I demonstrated both transverse and longitudinal wave propagation with a Slinky.

The children's father had died in a boating accident soon after Matt lost his wife. I had to give Jean credit for successful parenting, and for not turning her offspring against me. Or maybe they were simply being teenagers, taking the opposite view of their mother toward their uncle's girlfriend.

My second favorite Jean interaction was the time she and Alysse and Petey came for dinner in my old mortuary apartment. I'd cooked a leg of lamb, with all the trimmings my Betty Crocker cookbook suggested. Petey was allergic to nuts, I learned, including the almonds I'd liberally tossed into the green bean casserole; Alysse had become a vegetarian the day before; and Jean had started a diet that morning, partaking of only two lettuce leaves and a few carrot sticks.

"Whose turn to cook this weekend?" I asked Matt.

"Mine," he said, quick as a cake mix.

FOURTEEN

MC STEPPED OUT OF THE SHOWER, onto the newly re-tiled floor of the health club locker room. She rolled on deodorant, pulled on her sweats, fluffed out her hair, tried not to breathe the heavy hair spray residue in the air. She'd finally found a good personal trainer, Rick Gong, at the Windside Health Club in Winthrop, and she was making progress getting back in shape after a lazy, lazy month or two, letting her mother pamper her. Mom—Ma—was amused, reminding MC that she and her father managed to keep fit without spending a lot of money on monthly dues, or hours and hours on special machines.

"It's a different era," MC had told her parents.

"Yeah, yeah," said her father.

"There was nothing wrong with the old era," said her mother.

MC knew her mother was disappointed that she'd hooked up with Jake again, probably afraid MC would head back to Houston—not that MC had promised Jake anything the other night. Just not to shut him out completely. How her mother found out about Jake's alcohol problem and his temper, she'd never know. She was sure Aunt G wouldn't have told, if only not to upset her best friend. Mother's intuition, she guessed, and wondered if she'd ever experience it. She rubbed her stomach, as if that were where the feeling would lie.

Maybe things would work out, and one day her mother would get to meet Jake and feel his warmth and charm. It wasn't that hard to imagine Jake at a family meal, telling stories the way her father often did. But not right away. He had a lot to prove first.

She walked toward her silver Nissan in the parking lot, taking long strides as Rick had suggested. Much as she loved Girls'

Night Out with Mom and Aunt G, she was glad it had been canceled tonight—she'd needed to start this new gym program. It was time to make a comeback, physically at least.

The Nissan's Texas plates, with the state flag waving in the top right corner, stood out even at a distance. Another thing she'd have to take care of soon. She nearly tripped on a crack in the asphalt; she hated that it got dark so early these days. There were few cars in the Windside lot at six-forty-five, and she pictured every other woman her age eating pot roast at a polished dining room table, with a Hallmark husband, and two well-behaved little kids, a boy and a girl.

Or, as Aunt G would say, picture a woman with a lab of her own, making a difference through science and engineering. She smiled at the sound of Aunt G's voice in her head. She couldn't believe how rude she'd been, when Aunt G was only trying to help. She'd call her tonight and beg forgiveness. She'd chalk it up to stress, which was totally true. She'd set a new date to look at the e-mails, and maybe even cook dinner for Aunt G and Matt for a change. Wayne stalking her, Mary/Nina murdered, Jake showing up. Aunt G would understand and forgive her.

She dug her keys out of the new Red Sox duffel bag Robert had given her to welcome her home.

"Time to forget those Astros," he'd said.

She thought of Robert coming to her rescue the other night, though it turned out to be unnecessary, and uttered a long-distance thank-you to her family. Sure, they could be overbearing at times, but all in all she knew they loved her and wanted the best for her. If only she knew what that was. *Uh-oh. More stress.*

MC took a deep breath of cool, salty air. Maybe she'd get an apartment here in Winthrop once she had a job. It was on the ocean—she'd never leave the ocean again—adjacent to Revere on the south side, but had no Galiganis. Close, but not too close. MC punched the remote, opened her car door, and tossed her duffel bag over to the passenger seat.

Her heart skipped when she heard a shuffling noise. When nothing threatening appeared, she imagined there'd been an animal in the clump of trees near her car. She started to climb into the Nissan—except a hand grabbed her left arm and held her tight.

She gasped and winced in pain. She tried to kick, but she was locked in place, her legs pressed against the bottom edge of the car. Whoever it was reached down and pushed the button to unlock the other doors. Then he opened the back door and pushed her onto the back seat.

"Shh," she heard. "It's just me, MC." A familiar voice.

Wayne Gallen slipped in beside her, and grabbed her arm again.

"Wayne!" MC's heart still beat wildly; she looked in confusion at Wayne's grip.

"I'm sorry if I scared you, MC," he said. He let go of her arm, and patted it gently where he'd held it, as if to restore her body to normal. Wayne Gallen was Texas born and bred, and in his pronounced drawl, MC sounded like *Eee-em Say*. "I didn't mean to hurt you. I just didn't want you to shout out my name or anything."

Inythin. Wayne was starting to annoy her. Harmless as he was, this was the second time he'd caused a panic attack. And he smelled. Not that she was proud of it, but she and her friends had often talked about how Wayne wore the same shirt all week, a clean one only on Mondays. Typical bachelor, they'd said, but Jake was as well-groomed as her own father, even when he lived alone.

MC's breathing finally slowed down. "What's going on, Wayne? Where have you been?" She rubbed her arm through her sweatshirt, then massaged her lower calf where the metal ridge of the Nissan had dug in.

Wayne turned to face her, his knees now on the floor of the car, surrounded by empty water bottles and magazines on their way to recycling.

"Come away with me, MC."

MC gave him an incredulous look. "What? What are you talking about?"

She really wanted to ask, "Are you crazy?" but forced something less offensive out of her mouth, not to be too rude, and just in case he *had* gone off the deep end. Wayne Gallen was a good chemist, everyone agreed, but also a little strange. Although he must have earned the same good salary as all the other program chemists, he lived in a trailer park outside town, brought his own lunch every day in what looked like the same paper sack, and gave no visible sign of spending his money elsewhere. And his long, red handlebar mustache alone was enough to qualify him as weird, MC thought.

She'd always known Wayne had a crush on her. Now and then he'd ask MC how things were going with Jake, as if hoping she'd say, "I'm through with Jake. Let's you and me party!"

"Can we start from the beginning, Wayne? Where have you been since you left the police station last week?"

"I've been hiding out, you might say."

"Why?" MC heard herself ask *whaa?* In the whiny sound of her own come-and-go Texas accent. She swallowed, as if to get the drawl out of her mouth.

"MC, you got to trust me. I did not kill that girl, but I don't want to be answering to these Back East police."

"You mean Mary Roderick, uh, Nina Martin? Wayne, they caught the guy who shot her. And now he's dead, too. There's nothing to hide from."

"You don't know the whole story, MC."

"Then tell me."

"I can't tell you now. You're in enough trouble as it is, but believe me, this is how it has to be. I tried to warn you last week."

MC clicked her tongue, frustrated. That e-mail thing again.

"I checked, Wayne. There's nothing in my e-mails to—"

"You're not safe here. We need to disappear, get a new start, MC." Wayne grabbed her hand. Kneeling, holding her hand, he looked like he was going to propose. A pitiful sight.

Wayne kissed MC's hand. She shrank back. From the bit of moonlight that reached to the interior of the Nissan she caught a glimpse of his eyes. A creepy gray-green color, watery, darting around the parking lot as he talked. He wore a silly Dallas Cowboys cap, embroidered with a cartoon horse in football gear.

"I've always loved you, MC. From the first day you brought your students into our lab. Remember that field trip sort of thing you did?"

An SUV with enormous tires and a bar of lights across its roof turned into the lot. She considered trying to get their attention, but the vehicle did a quick U-turn and drove off. It was okay, she told herself. Wayne might be a smitten cowboy, but he was also a scientist; she could reason with him.

"Wayne—"

"I know Jake is in the area," Wayne said.

How do you know that? MC felt the panic return. She tried to remember self-defense moves. Wayne was strong, but small-built, like Jake; she ought to be able to get away from him. She blew out a breath and tuned in again to what he was saying.

"You don't want to take Jake back, MC. He doesn't know how to treat you. I bet he treats his horses better. You were right to leave him in the first place."

Suddenly, the Nissan seemed too small for both of them. She felt Wayne's foul breath on her, smelled his sweaty clothes—the tight black jeans and that very ugly brown western-style shirt reeked, even more intensely than when he'd first gotten in. MC was breathing hard, as if she had just finished a run. She tried to gain control of herself, lest she freak Wayne out by her body language, and...who knew what he'd do? The last car besides MC's started up, probably Rick's, since the club closed at seven. The parking lot was not visible from the street, and once Rick left, there was no chance anyone would come around. If she were quick, she might be able to jump out of her car and run screaming to Rick.

She slid over far enough to press down on the door handle. Locked. Wayne must have hit the child-proofing button while he was shoving her in the back seat.

"Not a good idea, MC." Wayne frowned; his voice went down in pitch. He squeezed her hand harder, put his other hand on her thigh.

MC stifled a scream. "I just need some air, Wayne." Not a lie, MC thought she would suffocate in the close quarters. Wayne's breath reeked of garlic or onion, or both. And cigarettes, definitely. Not alcohol, at least, she thought. She was an expert at detecting that.

Wayne smiled, apparently satisfied; he reached across the

seatback and opened the driver's door a crack, still holding her down with his strong grip. She estimated the chances that she could get in a punch or a kick and then fling herself over to the front seat on the driver's side, and out the slightly open door. Slim to none.

MC sat back, tried to look comfortable, and gathered her wits. She summoned a calm voice.

"I need to think about this, Wayne." She forced a smile, counting on the darkness to hide its deceit. "It's a big decision, but you're right, I should definitely not go back to Jake." *Tell them what they want to hear,* she'd learned from women-in-peril movies. She could use a Keanu Reeves or a Colin Farrell right now, to drive in on a motorcycle and save her. And where were her brothers when she needed them?

Wayne seemed to relax. *Could it be this easy?*

"Okay, MC. I can see that." Talking so slowly. Was he on something? "You do care for me, don't you? I can tell. And I would be very, very good to you."

"I know you would, Wayne." MC was amazed at how convincing she sounded. Thinking of movie stars had helped; she'd cast herself in a woman-in-jeopardy role and now she was playing it out. "Where can I reach you?"

"Don't worry about that. I'll find you."

His grin sent a chill through her. *Be Ashley Judd,* she thought. *Jodie Foster. Julia Roberts.* MC reached out with her free hand, ran it over Wayne's stubby cheeks, her brush with his mustache grossing her out.

Wayne leaned into her, kissed her hard, but then abruptly released his hold. He let out a long sigh, left her car, and disappeared into the trees.

MC could hardly move. She looked for a vehicle but couldn't see or hear one. Where had he gone? Then, *why does it matter?* She quickly flipped herself over into the driver's seat, not wanting to step out of her car, even now that she wasn't being held captive.

As soon as she hit the street, she grabbed her bottle of water from the cup holder. She rinsed out her mouth, lowered her window, and spit the taste of Wayne Gallen into the gutter.

FIFTEEN

IT WASN'T LIKE ME to miss deadlines, even self-imposed ones, but my concern for Matt and for MC had pushed my to-call list out of my mind. At seven o'clock on Tuesday evening, it was time to get back on track, I decided.

I looked up the home phone number for Daniel Endicott, the young science teacher and Science Club leader at Revere High, and punched it in. Thanks to Daniel and his enthusiasm, the science curriculum had greatly expanded since my day, giving students electives in astronomy, meteorology and environmental sciences, beside the core subjects and several AP courses.

"We're conducting a study of coyote populations in urban areas," Daniel told me over the phone, prompting me to wonder if there was any end to the Texas influence in Revere. "We're trapping the animals, with humane boxes, of course. We put radio transmitter collars on them so we can track them for up to three years. We're working with a vet—Dr. Timothy Schofield. He's local, so maybe you know him. In fact, he might come to your talk. He's going to do a session for us later on, and he wants to get an idea of how to do it."

I smiled at the idea of a humane trap, and also at the notion that I might know a veterinarian. I'd studiously avoided pets all my life, not wanting any more maintenance chores than those already required for clean clothes and dishes. That I might be a model high school lecturer also added to my amusement.

"Sounds like you have the wildlife topic covered. I'm leaning toward buckyballs at the moment," I told him.

"Cool," he said, sounding like his predecessor and peer, Erin Wong, who was on maternity leave. "I'm a huge fan of Bucky Fuller. Very cool." I decided *cool* was the designated enthusiastic response of people under thirty. I tried to remember what Rose and I would have said at their age; it seemed it would have been a long sentence, correctly constructed. But then, we weren't very cool in those days.

"And, for the second talk, I thought I'd do Maria Telkes."

"Sure."

Not *cool*. I figured he didn't know her. "Hungarian-American, physical chemist. You might have heard of her as the Sun Queen. She designed the first solar-powered house, long before it was fashionable. It went up in 1948 and is still in use, in Dover."

"Dover, Mass.?"

"That's right. I thought your students might relate to her. Telkes started her research when she was in high school, then went to MIT. She has many other solar-power patents—we ought to have your class try to reproduce some of the simpler ones, like her solar oven."

"Cool. I'm all into solar stuff, so I'm surprised I haven't heard of her. By the way, Gloria, did you hear about the dead body in the marsh last week?"

"I certainly did."

"Well, the weird thing is I got my general science students involved in the restoration project. You know, some dumb land debates held up that construction project, so it became, like, one large junkyard. So I got my kids interested in the cleanup. Environmental consciousness and all that. We hauled more than three tons of trash out of there last year. Well, the point is we were there the day before the dead woman turned up. It would have been awful if one of them had stumbled onto a dead body."

Daniel uttered a shuddering noise.

"Awful," I agreed.

"The reason I'm telling you is, maybe you could mention to the class—the parents, really, but the kids will take the info home—that it's not dangerous to be out there. You know, the chances of getting murdered out there are…"

"Very slim, Daniel. I'll be happy to reinforce that, though maybe you want a visiting detective in your class. In fact, you can tell the students the police think the woman was murdered somewhere else and her body dumped there."

"Oh," he said, weakly, and I imagined he was considering whether that made things sound better or worse to the parents.

When we hung up, I put a check mark next to Daniel's name, and wrote *buckyballs and Telkes* in large letters off to the side.

Andrea Cabrini, a technician at Charger Street lab, was next on my list. I'd done better in the last couple of months keeping in touch with her, and not simply using her as a way for me to get into the lab without a badge. Andrea was the kind of person who wouldn't have minded the latter, but I would have. I was glad I'd invited her to lunch last week, when there was no murder on the agenda.

I punched in Andrea's number. She gave me her usual enthusiastic greeting, always making me feel she'd been sitting around hoping I'd call.

"Hi, Gloria. I've been thinking about you." She lowered her voice. "The body in the marsh and all. And I figured you'd need a consultant."

"A consultant to a consultant. You're too good to me," I said.

"I pass by there all the time, when I go to see my aunt in Lynn."

Andrea had come a long way from the days when she would have thought she might be a suspect herself, for just such a drive-by connection. Her "big, beautiful woman" status didn't help her self-confidence, but I thought she was doing better since she'd started dating my old friend, Peter Mastrone.

Gloria, the matchmaker.

"The only thing is, I couldn't see that there was a link to the lab," she said.

"The police didn't release everything, Andrea." I lowered my voice for effect, bringing her into the small inner circle. "It turns out there might be a connection."

"Wow." She whispered, matching the pitch of my clandestine-meeting voice.

How good I'd become at manipulation—I knew Andrea loved being on the inside of police work. Come to think of it, so did I.

"I have some brochures on the buckyball program, but I need some real, technical reports. Can you meet me—"

"You bet. When and where?"

I gave her specifics of what I would like, and we made a date for the next morning. I checked another name off my list.

I made a few other calls, leaving Jean for last. I'd decided I should personally confirm her visit, and make her feel welcome. I'd prepared an "I'm looking forward to having you" line, with a tone to match. *I can do this much for Matt,* I told myself. As luck would have it, I was interrupted in the middle of dialing her Cape Cod number.

MC arrived on our doorstep out of breath, her eyes filled with tears and panic. She flung her keys onto the small table in our entryway, and curled up on the couch, pulling her hands back into the sleeves of her navy blue sweatshirt. Her retreat position.

"I've never been so scared in my life. I didn't know what he was going to do to me. Kidnap me, or…or kill me."

Jake Powers, I thought.

"Wayne Gallen," she said.

Déjà vu—like midnight at the RPD, my thinking of Jake when Wayne was the culprit.

I sat down next to her. Matt, who'd been reading the newspaper while I was phoning, gave MC a glass of water, which she guzzled down too fast, causing her to cough for a few seconds. I waited for the details, flexing my fingers, clenching my jaw. Had he…raped her? I could hardly think the word, and looked for signs that might tell me. MC did not look disheveled or bruised, which brought me some relief.

I let her tell the story, in fits and starts. The parking lot at the Windside in Winthrop, entering her car, keeping her there, wanting her to go away with him, once again telling her she's in danger from someone in Houston.

"I don't know if he's crazy—well, I *do* know he's crazy—but is he *just* crazy or am I really in danger from something?"

My question exactly.

"I didn't know whether to go to the police first, or come here, Aunt G," MC said, addressing me but looking at Matt. "I figured coming here was a little of both."

"You did the right thing," I said, patting her hand. I looked across at Matt for confirmation. He gave a slight nod, as if to say we were half right, that MC should have made an official complaint. Matt was tied into law enforcement protocol in a way that I was not.

"Did he give you any idea where he's staying?" Matt asked.

MC shook her head. "He appeared from nowhere, and then left. I wasn't paying attention to the direction he went. There was no other car in sight, so I don't know how he got there or how he got away."

"I know he hasn't rented a car from any of the local places—we checked, just for closure after we let him go last week," Matt said. "We could check again, see if anything's changed in the last few days." Matt had taken out his notebook. Making this now an official interview?

"What about the car Rusty Forman rented?" I asked, wondering if indeed hit men did rent cars. "Maybe Wayne took that car."

Matt shook his head. "That vehicle was impounded from outside the motel when Forman's body was found. Either it's still in the impound lot, or it was returned to the rental agency, a place at Logan if I remember correctly."

"What should I do?" MC asked, looking like a child, asking a question to which there should be a simple answer. I felt utterly inadequate.

"A PFA," Matt said. "That's about all we can do at the moment."

"Isn't that like a restraining order? Is that it?" I asked, my voice shrill.

"Protection From Abuse, a specific kind of restraining order. Even that's pushing it," Matt said, "since he didn't really threaten her. Right, MC?"

She nodded, shrugged her shoulders. "I guess not," she said, in a weak voice.

"He entered her car and kept her there against her will," I reminded them both.

"Let me get busy on the PFA," Matt said, doing his job.

We have to find him first, to serve him, I thought, but decided not to make a point of it.

AN HOUR LATER, I sat next to MC in my old apartment on Tuttle Street. Matt had insisted on accompanying us. He made some calls from MC's phone, then fell asleep in one of my old glide rockers. I worried about all the extra napping he was doing these days, and hoped it didn't mean his system was breaking down. The cancerous "five" that was always at the back of my mind.

MC had installed her computer on the opposite side of the room from where mine had been, and I felt lopsided. I found myself checking off items in the apartment that were the same as when I'd lived there. The blue-and-white speckled linoleum in the kitchen, a small bookcase I'd brought from California, appliances that were duplicates with Matt's, like the espresso maker and the toaster. I'd left MC my bed, too, and it looked the same, except for colorful pillows that I wouldn't have thought to add.

We sat together in front of her monitor, waiting, after MC clicked on open messages.

It seemed to take forever, though I knew if we clocked it, no more than fifteen seconds would have passed. How quickly we adjust our level of patience to the speed of the digital era, I thought—by the time we get to MC's children's generation, even the Polaroid camera will be in the Smithsonian, if it wasn't there already.

MC scanned through to two e-mails from Mary Roderick, Nina Martin's undercover name. As MC suspected, the correspondence had to do only with the private investigator's term paper for MC's class. She read the first one aloud.

Thanks so much for extending the deadline for my research paper, Ms. Galigani. Dr. Gallen has given me some new references that I want to check out. MR

"Dr. Gallen. Ugh," MC said, giving a shudder. She wiped her hand across her mouth and took a drink of water from a bottle on the desk.

We double-clicked on the second e-mail, dated a couple of days later, and I read aloud this time.

Just to let you know that I left the paper in your office this morning. :=) MR

"A smiley face and all." MC choked up, biting back a swell of tears. I swallowed, feeling the tragedy myself, though I hadn't known the woman. Playing on the keyboard one day, and the next, the police are dragging your body from a marshy grave.

"Well, see, there's no hint that she was headed for Revere," MC said.

"I wonder why she was so conscientious about her homework if her entire student persona was simply an undercover identity," I said. "It's not as if she really needed a grade."

"Not to arouse suspicion," Matt said, from the rocker, apparently awake enough to hear our conversation. I'd noticed he'd been going in and out of a light sleep while we worked. "Undercovers are nothing if not thorough. She probably had a secretary write the paper for her."

MC groaned. "That's annoying."

"Why can't we just find out who hired her to take MC's class?" I asked, straining my neck to make eye contact with Matt. "And then ask the FDA if she was working on anything for them."

"No one at the FDA admits to knowing anything about a case with a Houston PI. Not their procedure to work with civilians, they said."

"What about the card in Nina's pocket?"

Matt shrugged. "Nothing they know about. They're saying she probably met someone in a bar and the guy happened to work for the FDA and gave her his card. There wasn't a particular person's number on it, just the general FDA switchboard number."

"If it was a bar pickup, wouldn't the guy put his own extension? Or give his home number?"

Matt shrugged, as if to ask, *What did he know about bar pickups?* "FDA offered to give us their telephone directory in case any of the other people on Nina's list are their inspectors."

"So the lack of interagency cooperation in the U.S. is not a myth?" MC asked.

"Afraid not. What we might get, though, is something from the Houston PD. They promised to give us transcripts of any interviews."

"I wonder if Wayne Gallen knows about any of this, if it has anything to do with why he thinks MC is in danger."

"I'm in danger from Wayne Gallen himself," MC said, going through the hands-in-sleeves routine.

I looked to Matt for assurance that the PFA would be in effect soon, but he'd fallen asleep again.

MC scrolled up and down her email list. "Here's the only one from Alex that has a reference that's even the slightest bit mysterious."

I peered at the monitor.

From: Alexsimpson@hpbp.edu
To: galig@hpbp.edu
Subject: Trouble
There's good news and bad news. Our contact sees no problem delivering the package, but one unfortunate outcome—the bute that's not bute—might bring trouble.

Hardly that mysterious. Who doesn't have research troubles?
"The only strange word is 'bute.'" Another Texas word?" I asked.
MC laughed. "I don't think so."
"Is it a chemical term?"
MC tapped her fingers together. "Maybe short for butane or butyl, but I've never heard it used that way."
I pointed to the To line. "It's even addressed to you."
MC screwed up her mouth and moved her lips as if she were literally chewing on the matter. "Ah," she said, giving me a

thumbs-up. "It must have been meant for Wayne Gallen. See, the first three letters are the same. I had a mailbox at Houston Poly. If Alex wasn't paying attention and just hit a return after the gal and then clicked on send, it would come to me. I'd be first alphabetically."

"Then later he might be looking at his sent mail and realized what he'd done. Good call, MC."

"Well, at least we know why I received it, maybe. We still don't know what it means."

"Maybe we should just hit reply and ask Alex what he meant."

MC's eyes widened. "You don't want to mess with this guy. He's so two-faced. He'd always make fun of people, like two minutes after they gave him a million dollars."

"Not very nice."

"'Well, sure, y'all,' he'd say. 'Ah will be happy to give you some of mah millions for your most wah-thy research.' That was Alex. He did a pretty good Texas accent, even though he was from the Midwest. He thought the staff was laughing with him, but mostly it was at him."

"How did you get to know Alex so well?"

"Supposedly I was interning, sort of, to learn some research techniques from his group, since I'd been in the field for so long."

"So you don't want to hit reply?"

MC shook her head, apparently not enjoying my teasing. "No, Aunt G."

"I was just kidding anyway."

A quick search of the Internet got us to the Isle of Bute, off Scotland, and Bute County, North Carolina.

I heard Matt's light snore. I studied the fleshy, gentle face of my—my what? POSSLO? Person-of-the-Opposite-Sex-Sharing-Living-Quarters was what the IRS dubbed it a few years ago. As if it mattered right now, I wondered if there were a more up-to-date term. "Partner" sounded like a same-sex arrangement or a business relationship. "Boyfriend" seemed misleading, conjuring up images of sixteen-year-olds.

MC caught my gaze.

"He'll be fine, Aunt G," she said, and reached over to hug me.
I hoped so.

BEFORE WE LEFT the mortuary building, Matt, who claimed to be
completely refreshed from his time-out, checked all the downstairs windows. I knew MC was locked in on the third floor, her
alarm set, but as we pulled away, I had an unsettled feeling. I
scoured the area for Dr. Wayne Gallen, whom I'd still never met.

SIXTEEN

ANDREA CABRINI TOOK ME through a labyrinth of no-frills, un-carpeted, unadorned corridors at the Charger Street lab. As we rounded a corner and entered the area where her cubicle was, I snagged my purse in a nest of wires and coax cables that hung from the ceiling.

"I'll bet you don't miss all this," she said.

"Actually, I do," I said. I unsnarled my purse and brushed a mist of off-white plaster from the strap.

She gave me a strange look. *Wait until you're retired,* I thought.

Unlike medical facilities, which made me nervous, hard-science laboratories always gave me a thrill. I loved the buzzing and humming of motors and power supplies, the permanence of the oversized, marble-patterned log books on the benches, and even the smell of burning electrical insulation—a sign of something gone wrong. As we passed offices and machine shops, I saw piles of boxes yet to be opened. I pictured new optics nestled in Styrofoam molds, a special software package with a three-inch-thick manual, or a tiny chip that would make a big difference on a technician's chassis.

Andrea's cubicle, located in a corner of a large electronics shop room, had some of my favorite posters. One featured Albert Einstein on a bicycle riding through a Southern California campus; another was a collage of the great inventors of the twentieth century—Thomas Edison, William Shockley, the Wright brothers, Philo T. Farnsworth, Guglielmo Marconi. Today I'd brought her two additions to her décor, posters I'd found and bought on-line.

"For balanced gender representation," I said.

Andrea seemed pleased by the new prints—one of Hedy Lamar, 1930s actress and co-inventor of a torpedo guidance system that was two decades before its time; and the other of Mary Brush, who received a patent for the corset in 1825, one of the first women to receive a patent in any field.

Andrea sucked in her breath and waved her hands as if she were tying an elaborate system of boned fabric onto her ample midsection. "They don't make corsets big enough for me," she said with a shy smile.

"Be glad," I said.

Andrea, in her usual wide black pants and colorful tunic, took a seat on a rickety metal stool by her raised bench, leaving me to sit below her in the good chair, a government-issue, once-padded, gray metal number with scratched arms. I thought I saw a smidgen of rouge on her round cheeks and wondered idly if she had a lunch date with Peter. He'd finally stopped trying to reinvent me once he met Andrea. I knew there was a double date in our future, but didn't look forward to it.

My gesture toward dressing up for the lab visit was an appropriate scatter pin from my "science" collection, which Andrea always enjoyed. Today's was a mixed-metal montage of transistors, wires, and diodes Rose had brought me from a crafts fair, part of her campaign to lure me into attending one with her.

"What do you think is the ratio of metals to lace at one of those events?" I'd asked Rose, getting only raised eyebrows in reply.

Andrea patted the top of a pile of papers stacked on the side of the bench. "From the reference room," she said. "All you ever wanted to know about the fullerene-related research team." She sighed, looked up and to the right, as if to connect with a fond dream. "Imagine having a molecule named after you!"

"And it was named Molecule of the Year, by *Science* magazine, a few years ago," I said, as one who kept track of those awards the way Rose knew who won the Oscar for best movie every year.

Andrea and I played around with cabriniene and lamerinoene for a few minutes, choosing the configurations of our own namesake molecules. I was reminded of my equally amusing "science is fun" session with MC a few days before and realized what I missed more than equipment deliveries was the camaraderie and the in-jokes of a research team. Who else would have fun thinking up interesting arrangements of atoms?

We finally got to work and looked through the papers, sifting through grant proposals and monthly reports, all of which had been filed, according to protocol, in the lab's library collection. I read how a new federal initiative that funneled a large budget into nanotechnology had made it possible for Lorna Frederick's team to garner an impressive amount of research money, some of it directed to small-molecule therapies—medicines that were able to distinguish healthy cells from diseased ones.

The proposals started with the thesis that diseases, like cancers or AIDS, should be classified by their molecular composition rather than by their location in the body or their particular symptoms. The nanotech revolution that started with the discovery of buckyballs now gave us hollow tubes that could transport medicines. *Nanotubes.* I pictured a particular "medicine molecule" finding its way directly to the "disease molecule."

By the time Andrea and I were finished, I had nearly filled a yellow-lined pad with notes, references I planned to check online, names of researchers who were co-authors or copied on the reports. I was still in the dark about why the deceased PI Nina Martin might have been in Revere with the Galiganis, the FDA, and Lorna Frederick in her pocket, but I was in awe of the possible medicines of the future.

I ARRIVED HOME, my briefcase full of nano-notes, to find Matt with a new brochure and notes of his own. External Beam Radiation Therapy. Not a science fiction topic, but Matt's choice of treatment.

"I think this is going to be it," he said, waving the thin pamphlet. He handed me a cup of espresso and the booklet.

I sat next to him and leafed through pages of glossy color photographs of the linear accelerator that would generate high-energy X rays and focus them on Matt's body. For many years I'd lived about an hour away from SLAC, the famous linear accelerator at Stanford University in California. To me linear accelerators were the tools of physics—forcing collisions that would break particles apart and reveal their inner structure. Or create little parts that weren't there before the collision, some said.

Now I was forced to remember another use of the accelerators, a tradition begun by E. O. Lawrence himself, inventor of the cyclotron. I recalled reading an anecdote about how he often kept the machine running all night to produce enough radioisotopes for California hospitals. Lawrence's mother was one of the first to benefit, receiving radiation treatments for her uterine cancer. The end of the story made me hopeful—Lawrence's mother was cured and lived another twenty years, into her eighties.

"The treatment is five days a week," Matt said. "It's outpatient, over seven or eight weeks. They take about fifteen minutes, and it's painless."

I breathed deeply, absorbing the information. "Good. When do we begin?" I tried to make it sound like just another item on the scheduling agenda, still wrestling with the right tone to show Matt support, as opposed to needing it myself.

"There's some preliminary work, they call it a simulation, where they pinpoint where the problem is. Check out the centerfold…they're going to make a Styrofoam cast just for me." Matt opened the leaflet, still in my hands, to show me the mold that supports the patient's back, pelvis, and thighs. "I hope they have a big enough piece of material to take care of me. What's that stuff made of anyway?"

"I think it's an extruded polystyrene material. I can check." Not that I was tense, missing facetious questions.

"Come here," Matt said, patting his lap. I hadn't been able to sit on anyone's lap since the age of seven. But the gesture did lighten my mood.

JEAN ARRIVED SOONER than originally planned, before Matt's scheduled simulation appointment with Styrofoam. I'd never gotten around to calling her, but I tried to welcome her warmly. I'd set up the guest room with meticulous detail. I cleared out two dresser drawers and half a closet for her two-night stay; I dusted thoroughly, put fresh flowers on the bed-side table, and pencils and paper by the phone in case she needed to keep her real estate business going. I plugged a hair dryer into her bathroom socket, fluffed the towels, and installed a night-light. Worthy of a four-star rating, I thought. I quickly learned there were five-star arrangements, and I'd fallen short.

"I thought you'd have an extra robe," she said, checking the closet. Strike one, but I rushed to get her one of mine, happily out of the laundry. Too big, she let me know, with a make-do shrug. "And I never use perfumed soap." She used her thumb and middle finger, her pinky sticking up at a forty-five-degree angle to her knuckles, to pick up the bar. I'd paid more for that one bar of soap than for the six-pack of the grocery-store brand I used myself. Nevertheless, strike two.

Jean was ten years younger than Matt and slightly taller than both of us, or it might have been her more slender build that made her seem so. Or her towering personality. Otherwise, she had the same dark, Italian, baggy-eyed look, expertly de-emphasized with makeup Rose would have approved of.

She'd brought photos of her children, even though we'd seen them only a month or so earlier. "We just don't see you as much anymore, Matty," she said, her heavy-lidded eyes drifting in my direction. Nasty Gloria, cheating Jean's children out of their only uncle.

Matt gave her a brotherly smile. "You've always said that, Jean."

My hero.

"Well, you know what I mean, big brother. Delicious dinner. All my favorites," she said, patting her enviably flat stomach, fully aware that Matt had prepared the meal. I was convinced that if she'd seen me line the vegetables next to the beef in the ceramic roasting pan, she would have choked on a parsnip fiber.

Strike three came with coffee after dinner, prompting me to walk off the field.

"I'm not happy that you're still working, Matt, with your… health…and all," Jean said from her post in our best easy chair.

"Not a problem," he told her. "The doctors tell me to do what I feel I can do, and stop when I can't. Pretty simple."

"Well, I know this case you're spending most of your time on involves Gloria's friend, but your health is more important."

"Excuse me," I said. "Which friend are you talking about?" *Just because you don't like me doesn't mean I don't have lots of friends* was my slightly misleading message.

"The undertaker, of course. Isn't it her daughter who's in trouble?"

Jean made the mortuary business, a great service to society in my admittedly biased opinion, sound sordid.

I kept my composure, but barely. "The 'trouble' is that a young woman has been murdered," I said. "And your brother is the RPD's best homicide detective." *Argue with that.*

She sipped the espresso Matt had prepared for her, which she declared the perfect strength. "I thought Matt said he had to rescue a young friend of yours who has some kind of problem."

I couldn't imagine Matt had put it that way. He groaned and shook his head. "Not what I said, Jean."

Jean screwed up her nose, crossed her thin legs in a direction away from me. "I knew what you meant. You wouldn't be out there killing yourself if *she* weren't implicated." A tilt of the head toward me.

"I'm just doing my job. You should know that."

"Well, all I know is, you were always the picture of health, until…recently."

In other words, Teresa would never have let him get cancer.

Matt put his head in his hands.

My head was splitting, my vision clouding from anxiety, tears at the brink of erupting.

In a couple of days, Matt would get measured for a Styrofoam cradle, as if he were a piece of delicate equipment ready for shipping. I wanted desperately for him to have no further stress over my relationship with his sister.

I stood up, brushed my skirt into place. "Why don't I let you two talk," I said. "I just remembered I promised Rose I'd drop over this evening to help her with…" I stumbled. "A project."

MATT WALKED ME TO THE DOOR, kissed me goodbye. "Trust me, it will be different when you get home."

I could hardly wait.

SEVENTEEN

"FRANK'S MOTHER didn't like you at first? How come I never knew that?" I asked Rose.

As I'd expected, Rose had welcomed my surprise visit, pulling out our favorite espresso cups and three kinds of biscotti. We sat in Frank's den, the coziest room in the house, with dark paneling and brown leather furniture, while he was fast asleep upstairs. Frank had had to make an early pickup that morning, Rose told me, since Robert was at a casket show out of state. Horse shows, casket shows—no end to the uses of large convention halls I'd assumed were only for the different branches of the American Institute of Physics.

"You knew how my mother-in-law slighted me at every turn. I complained constantly at the time—you just forgot." Rose shook her head slightly, probably thinking, correctly, how hopeless I was at history. "Don't you remember when I'd whine about how the family would stop playing cards as soon as I showed up? That's just one example. All the Galiganis—Frank's parents, Rico, Muffy, all the brothers—they'd be playing poker in the back room of the old house on Oxford Park. I'd come in and old lady Galigani, God rest her, would say, 'Hokay, boys, there's a-no-mo tonight.' And then she'd say to Frank, 'How longa she be he'?' Meaning me."

Rose's parody of our old relatives' dialects brought back memories of our immigrant parents and grandparents, all deceased, and I finally did remember the tension with her in-laws in the early days.

"The issue of the flowers," I said, smiling.

Rose nodded and laughed. "Frank would bring me these

lovely bouquets he'd put together from the sprays around the caskets." She moved her hands gracefully, forming a bouquet in the air. "And Ma Galigani thought it was a sin. It was stealing from the dead, she'd say, and she thought I put him up to it. I was a near occasion of sin, as we said in those days. Me, a temptress!"

"But eventually Mrs. Galigani loved you, Rose, like the daughter she'd always wanted. How did you finally win her over?"

I was ready to take notes. If Rose could bring around a stubborn old Italian mother-in-law, surely I could do the same with an educated, professional woman who was my peer.

I'd always thought Realtors had to have excellent people skills, and that they'd be logical in their communications. Certainly they had to know a combination of mathematics and finance that eluded me. The one time I bought a house, my condo in Berkeley, I felt completely at the mercy of my real estate agent, who talked glibly about fixed rates, points, balloon payments, equity. And I gave up on trying to understand the distribution of mortgage payments toward principal and interest. A payment should be a payment, I thought, the way subtraction usually worked. Real estate arithmetic was more economics than pure mathematics, I decided, and left it to my broker.

Rose reached over and picked a lemon biscotti crumb from my knit skirt. "I think when his mother saw how happy Frank and I were, it helped, but really she didn't come around until I got pregnant with Robert."

"Uh-oh," I said, mentally closing my imaginary notebook. "That's not going to work."

We had a good laugh over that, making up stories for me to tell Jean.

"Tell her that her only brother is going to give her a new niece or nephew," Rose said.

"I could say I've been irritable lately because I'm in the first semester."

"Trimester."

"Oh, thanks."

"Say her brother wants to make an honest woman out of you, and would she be the godmother."

"I could say it was fertility drugs, and we're having quints."

We let the single-concept joke run its course, nearly doubled over much of the time.

How to turn a bad evening into a great one—leave the trouble spot and run to your best friend.

MATT JOINED ME for an early breakfast of coffee and toast and told me he'd had a talk with his sister while I was at Rose's. We kept our voices low, with occasional glances toward the stairs to the bedrooms.

I was glad I had errands and a hair appointment, and would be leaving the house before Jean was awake. *Or maybe she'll hide in her room till she hears my car pull away,* I thought.

"Jean promised to be more open to this change. You know, she had a hard time adjusting to her husband's death. She has Chet's photos all over the house, and still doesn't even date after ten years."

I was glad Matt hadn't kept such a strict mourning regime. "Having two small children would make a difference," I said, by way of excusing her.

He shook his head. "It's not the kids at this point. They'd love it if she had a social life of her own. I told her she had made her choice, and it was fine, but I'd made a different one. It wasn't going to do anyone any good, us mourning together for the rest of our lives." He put his hand on mine. "I know you're doing your best. It will all work out."

"I thought she liked me the first time I met her," I told him. "But then she got colder and colder. Am I doing something in particular that offends her?"

"No, I'm sure it's because you kept showing up, and now that you've moved in, it looks like you're here to stay." He smiled at me. "You are, aren't you?"

I nodded, touched at his care of me.

I considered telling Matt the round of pregnant jokes Rose and I had engaged in, but thought it might fall flat. Or sound disrespectful to the mothers of the world. Sometimes with these funny stories you had to be there.

I PARKED AROUND THE CORNER from the high school for my late-afternoon, after-classes appearance at the Science Club meeting.

I'd prepared an outline of my talk, taking the students from the basic facts on carbon to the latest in carbon research—carbon nanotubes. *Buckytubes,* I said to myself, rehearsing my opening, *one of the versatile new materials of nanotechnology.* I'd talked MC into joining the Science Club program, thinking it would be a nice introduction to what a career in high school teaching might be like. For this topic, I'd give the first lecture, laying the groundwork and providing some physical applications; MC would do a follow-up talk emphasizing the chemical and biological applications she was more familiar with.

I'd laid out a timeline with the highlights that preceded the nanotech revolution: the development of the electron microscope and new coating techniques; the discovery of buckyballs by two experimental chemists; and the discovery of the carbon nanotube, which opened the door to advances in all fields from medicine to computing to building materials.

Daniel Endicott, young, tall, and fit, met me at the front door of the school and relieved me of some of my props. His haircut would have been an embarrassment for any boy in my high school class, looking as though his mother had put a soup bowl on his head and shaved around it, leaving the effect of a blond weeping willow at the top.

I'd met Daniel only once before, at the orientation session at the beginning of the school year. He impressed me as one of those dedicated teachers we hope are the norm, not the exception. He'd set up partnerships with Boston colleges, which allowed his students to get involved in real-life science activities. I was thrilled that Revere High students were being exposed to equipment and techniques used by professional scientists such as the field biologists working on the Rumney Marsh project.

"I like to give my students opportunities to *be* scientists, as opposed to being told what scientists do," Daniel told me at our first meeting. I wanted to adopt him.

Besides a binder filled with transparencies, I'd brought materials to build models of a soccer-ball-shaped buckyball molecule and a long, slim "nanotube." I carried tote bags of Styrofoam balls, drinking straws, wire mesh, a sturdy metal T-square, scissors. Arts and crafts gear.

"I hope this won't be too juvenile for them," I said to Daniel.

He shook his head. "Nah, all students love crafts. Hands-on, visuals, field trips, demos, anything but listening to a lecture." A blush started at his neck and spread to his face. Poor guy, I thought, a blusher, like most fair-skinned people. "I didn't mean—"

I laughed. "Don't worry, Daniel, I know what you meant. I thought I'd start the session with an overview of Buckminster Fuller's life. How's this? An amazing journey from a desperately poor man with a young family, on the brink of suicide, to a life of invention in service to humanity. And now a whole series of molecules named after him. What do you think?"

"Wow, I think it's great. I told you, I'm a huge fan of Bucky's. Are you going to talk about how his ideas were so efficient, no one wanted them because it would upset the economy? I mean, if you can build homes that are cheap, strong, and safe, for everybody in society, who would want to spend a third of their income on some square box with endless decorations, right? And renewable energy sources." He shook his blond locks. "Let's not even go there."

I cleared my throat. "Hmm, is this a political science class?" I smiled to show I wasn't some good old boy who was afraid to second-guess the American capitalistic system. Even if I was. "And how about that Dymaxion map of his—the first to show the continents on a flat surface, appearing as a one-world island in a one-world ocean."

"Right," Daniel said, shaking his head. "One world. As if."

I knew I'd lose any debate on the basis of language alone, and knew also that Daniel's dream, like Fuller's, of "more with less" technology was basically a good one. Back to hard science, I decided.

"You know, carbon itself has an exciting story. We thought we knew everything about it, until 1985, when this new, third pure form, after graphite and diamond, was discovered."

Daniel laughed, and stroked his hairless chin. "Just remember, to these kids 1985 was a long time ago. You might as well be talking about Abraham Lincoln."

"Good point."

I showed him a transparency for buckyballs, a graphic with a caption that explained its shape:

C-60, NAMED BUCKMINSTERFULLERENE, BE-CAUSE THE SIXTY CARBON ATOMS FORM THE SHAPE OF AN ICOSAHEDRON, OR GEODESIC DOME, LIKE THE KIND INVENTED BY BUCKMIN-STER FULLER. LARGER FULLERENES CONTAIN AS MANY AS FIVE HUNDRED CARBON ATOMS.

Buzzzzzzz!

The buzzer for the start of class startled me, a loud Klaxon sound as if to call inmates in from the yard.

Daniel laughed. "I think there was a sale on those bells last year."

In came about fifteen students. And one very tall, bald gentleman with thick glasses. Dr. Timothy Schofield, I presumed. In expensive-looking navy slacks and a beige cardigan, he was by far the best-dressed person in the room. Maybe even the oldest, I thought. He wore a pleasant expression as he extended his hand.

"I've heard so much about you, Dr. Lamerino," he said. I doubted it, since I barely knew Daniel, but it was a nice way to start off. "I hope you don't mind my dropping in on your talk. I thought this might be a good way to get to know the students and hear what kinds of questions they ask."

"I'm glad you could join us. Daniel's told me about your coyote project," I said. I'd never met a veterinarian and wondered what kinds of question *he* might ask.

Once the class was settled, I launched into a tribute to carbon, the sixth element of the periodic table, and its all-pervasiveness, in our food, clothing, cosmetics, and gasoline.

"And they're a girl's best friend," said June-Anne, a tiny Asian student.

I was happy June-Anne could relate carbon to diamond, one of its three pure forms, but Lynda with a y, as she called herself, poked June-Anne. "Better not say that. Dr. Lamerino doesn't like sexist remarks. I've been in her class before."

"How is that sexist?" June-Anne wanted to know.

"Well, girls should be thinking of more than bracelets and rings, for one thing, like school and all, and then the whole, like, cliché involves a guy giving a girl expensive jewelry, when why doesn't she just get, like, a great career and make a lot of money and buy her own diamonds? Right, Dr. Lamerino?"

I nodded. Lynda soared to the top of my Smartest Teen list; if I were giving grades, she'd have gone up a point at that moment, her quirky grammar and my lack of interest in diamond jewelry notwithstanding.

"I'm so not into all that," June-Anne said.

One to one. I decided not to take a further vote, unwilling to risk another cause for depression. I stole a glance at Dr. Schofield. He seemed amused, but didn't give away his philosophical position on girls and diamonds.

After we constructed our nanotube—a hexagonal network of carbon atoms rolled up to make a seamless cylinder, capped at each end with half of a fullerene molecule—I showed slides of real-world nanotubes being prepared in a furnace operating at more than one thousand degrees centigrade. I was happy with the respectable numbers of *wows* and *cools*.

Daniel remained quiet through my presentation, until near the end, when Nathan, a young man with several earrings in places other than his ears, made a comment.

"There's one of those domes in Atlantic City. And there's this totally cool video game called 'Spaceship Earth,'" Nathan said. "Maybe that's where this guy Fuller got the idea."

Daniel jumped up. I thought he might attack Nathan, but he attacked the whiteboard instead.

RIP OFF, he wrote in red dry-erase letters.

"They have completely ripped off Fuller's ideas and themes. And they give him no credit, not even a plaque." Daniel wrote CREDIT on the board, then drew a circle around it, and a line through it. The international, intergenerational symbol for no. "The term 'Spaceship Earth' was coined by Fuller, not by some action hero."

I'd stepped back when Daniel came to the front of the room, unsure whether to interrupt. It was his club, after all, and not having children, I'd never been to a theme park and was unaware of this controversy. Daniel went on for a few more minutes; then I raised my hand and asked permission to give an example of a physical application of nanotubes.

Daniel smiled. "Okay, the student with the great pin can have the floor," he said. It was the first I knew that he'd noticed the replica of a carbon atom that I wore on my lapel.

"Thanks, Mr. Endicott, and I appreciate the way you give your students a well-rounded perspective. Science is part of society, and at the same time it impacts our culture as if it were an external force. Maybe sometime we can do a whole class on that subject."

Daniel seemed pleased with the resolution. Dr. Schofield nodded agreement, but said nothing. In fact, he'd said nothing beyond his initial greeting, and I began to wonder if he'd been sent by the administration to evaluate me.

I described briefly the excitement for physicists, the remarkable electronic and mechanical properties of carbon nanotubes. I thought Daniel and the budding environmentalists in front of me would appreciate the application to new hydrogen storage methods that were important if we were ever to have an alternative to fossil fuels. I flipped to my transparency showing a sleek, environmentally friendly, fuel-efficient vehicle, and ended with a list of URLs for those interested in pursuing dome-related topics in more depth.

Once the students left, I started packing up my materials.

"Very nicely done," Dr. Schofield said. "I've always admired people who understood physics."

"And I can't imagine knowing the details required of a medical person." I thought of asking him why he didn't become a human doctor, the kind who could help Matt. But he might ask the same of me.

"I hope you'll feel free to come to my talk next week," he said.

"Thanks," I said, noncommittal. I didn't think I had the time or the interest in learning how microchips were implanted in coyotes. Besides, what if he brought a real coyote to class? I didn't trust anything faster than I was that couldn't talk.

Daniel offered to help carry the tote bags to my car, but I declined, citing a need to use the rest room and make a couple of calls. The truth was that I'd had enough interaction for the day. I loved being in the classroom, but found it draining in a way that hours of research were not. I wasn't used to being around so many high-energy people at once, from Daniel to the fifteen or so well-fed, lively teenagers.

I looked forward to the solo ride home and then to the espresso maker only a few feet from my couch.

EIGHTEEN

IT WAS NEARLY FIVE and dark as I headed to my car. The street was full of vehicles, but empty of people. I had my remote ready and pressed it to open the door of my Caddie. The interior light did not come on, meaning the door locks hadn't snapped up, either. I pressed a few more times, as if I didn't know a thing about dead batteries and how they didn't resuscitate spontaneously. Clearly I'd need my backup system. I dug out my keys, flipped around the ring until I fingered the long, thin key that opened the driver's door the old-fashioned way.

Matt would have laughed, I thought. He never used the remote that came with his Camry. "There's not enough return for the extra space the square thing takes up on my key ring," he'd said.

There was no streetlight close to my car, and I knew I'd have a hard time seeing the lock. I put my bags down on the sidewalk, fumbling in my purse for the small flashlight I always carried.

Clank!

I turned to see one of my tote bags knocked over, my metal T-square hitting the pavement. Small white atoms rolled out of the bag and into the gutter. I worried momentarily about the storm drain, but figured the tiny balls wouldn't be the worst of the contaminants headed that way on an average day.

"Let me help you with that." A deep, unfamiliar voice. I started at the sound, seeming to come from nowhere, yet so close that I bumped into him—a man I didn't know—when I turned around. I gasped, a wave of fear coursing through my body. I looked around at the street, not exactly deserted, but no one within range of my voice, either. He leaned into me. An unwashed smell attacked my nostrils. Perspiration, cigarette smoke, foul breath. A homeless person? No. In the next moment I knew who he was, though I'd never met him.

Wayne Gallen

He'd used surprise to his advantage and taken my keys from me, knocking over more of my bags in the process. He pressed himself against me, so that my back was arched against the hood of the Cadillac, my knees unnaturally bent. Pain shot through my lower body.

"Nice wheels, Aunt G," He said. My eyes widened. "Oh, yes, MC and I used to talk a lot, back in Houston. She sure is crazy about you."

I'd always thought a Southern drawl would sound soothing, even sweet. Not this one, however. His voice was strident, threatening, on the edge of malice. I tried to breathe, to sound normal. Not easy with my hips and knees at the wrong angle to each other. But even through the pain, I thought, *Just what he did with MC— this man has no imagination.*

"Mr.…Gallen, is it?"

He eased his upper torso away, pinning me, knees to knees, and tipped his filthy cap. "Yes, ma'am. Wayne Gallen himself. Listen, I need to talk to you, but let's get inside where it's private."

What is this? I wondered. *A new kind of stalker? The Unwanted Passenger Stalker?* I also wondered why a certain inappropriate flipness always accompanied the moments of crisis in my life.

"My husband is a policeman," I said, "and he's expecting—"

Wayne smiled, a crooked grin, but not at a pleasant angle as Matt's skewed smile was. Wayne's was more like a sneer. He shook his finger at me in mock reprimand. "You are not married, Aunt G. Don't go lying now, or neither me nor MC will be able to trust you."

Well, we're practically married, I thought. Maybe we should tie the knot, just for situations like this.

A few cars passed us, but I was parked on the left side of a one-way street, with the driver's side next to the sidewalk, unable to signal anyone. Besides, our relative positions against the car probably led people to think they were witnessing a romantic interlude. No help needed.

Wayne held me with one hand, inserted the key in the door with the other. I made no attempt to get away, knowing he was stronger and faster than I. Most people were. He must have realized I wasn't about to bolt, because he relaxed his hold a bit. He ushered me into the back seat of my car, not pushing hard, almost as if he were my chauffeur having a bad night.

"I need you to talk to MC," he said, settling himself into the back seat beside me. "I know she trusts you. You need to explain, A, that she's in a lot of danger here, and B, that she needs to come away with me. It's the only solution."

Half of me was scared to death, trying to plot a getaway. The other half was happy to have located Wayne Gallen, or vice versa. I wished I had a copy of the PFA the police couldn't seem to issue in the last forty-eight hours. It was small consolation that the order was in effect whether the respondent, in legalese, knew it or not.

He didn't really hurt MC, I reminded myself. *Maybe I can get some information out of him.*

"What kind of danger is MC in?" I asked him, just an interested Aunt G.

Wayne lit a cigarette from a new package. Evidently the surgeon general's message hadn't reached Texas. He carefully removed the red cellophane strip from around the top and tucked it into his jacket pocket. A neat, environmentally conscious captor, despite his lack of grooming. I thought about bolting while he focused on keeping his thin, handlebar mustache from going up in flames from his lighter. "My boss won't like it if I tell you, believe me."

Some magic links connected in my brain, and I thought of my session with MC and her e-mails. I tried to remember the sender. Sampson? No, that was Carol Sampson, an editor I knew at BUL in Berkeley. Stinson? No, that was the beach in Northern California. Swanson? Early TV dinners. Then it came.

"You mean Dr. Simpson?" I asked. Wayne squinted and thrust his chin forward. I knew I'd hit it right.

"Maybe," Wayne said, drawing on his cigarette. I coughed, unused to being so close to a smoker.

"What is it that Dr. Simpson thinks MC knows, Wayne? May I call you Wayne?" Get cozy, something I learned from the few times I'd watched crime dramas on television. Matt outlawed them in his presence, however, and I hadn't really missed them.

I'd calmed myself considerably now that Wayne had distanced himself from me physically and mentally. I couldn't help thinking of how MC had been in this same situation not long ago. Wayne was no longer touching me, and his concentration seemed to be on his cigarette, and on how or whether to answer me. He breathed heavily. More secondhand smoke for me and my Cadillac, a first in its lifetime.

"She got an e-mail with some information that no one except me was supposed to get. See, there's stuff going on with the money and all. Some creative diverting of funds, you might say."

Never mind escaping; I couldn't miss this. "Diverting of research funds? So Lorna Frederick's annual reports don't tell the whole story?"

Wayne checked me out again, with the same squint and chin thrust. I'd hit it again, apparently, by guessing that Lorna was involved, and that some clues might be in the reports Andrea had dug out for me. I wished I'd gotten to read them, but they were still in my briefcase, my retirement being a lot busier than my regular full-time working life had been. I wondered if Lorna could be reinterviewed based on Wayne's weird expression.

Wayne opened his mouth to say something, then stopped, his eyes widening as he looked over my right shoulder toward the street. I turned to see what caught his attention. A car had pulled up next to mine. The young male driver casually glanced our way. In fact, his sedan was the last of a whole line of cars piled up for a red light. My captor and I were suddenly in the middle of a traffic jam. I'd heard bells chime five o'clock a few minutes before, possibly from the nearby Immaculate Conception Church, and guessed that we were seeing a brief local tie-up from retail businesses or offices closing for the day.

This new opportunity for me to summon help dawned on both of us at the same time. Wayne's response was to grab the door handle and move his feet to leave the car. Mine, strangely, was to reach out, as if to hold him back, my need for information dwarfing my initial fears for my safety.

"Let's talk this out, Wayne," I said. "If I know more about what MC should be worried about, I might be able to—"

He shook his head and spoke around his cigarette. "I don't think so. Just talk some sense into her," he said. He slammed the door and ran in the direction of the bushes that lined the sidewalk.

I scrambled across the seat and opened the door again, annoyed that he'd rushed off without giving me any satisfying information. *What's wrong with me?* I wondered. I should have been happy to be alive, needing only a painkiller for my backache and air freshener for my car. Maybe I was a victim of the Stockholm Syndrome, bonding with my hostage-taker.

I got out of my car, switched on my flashlight, and started toward the bushes Wayne had ducked into. On the other side was a small, dirt parking lot with a clear view to a building on the next street, but Wayne was nowhere in sight. I let out a heavy sigh and returned to my car to gather up the spilled contents of my totes. I felt I'd been close to something important, something that would have shed light on MC's predicament.

Diversion of research funds. Something missing from the annual reports. That was the phrase Wayne had responded to. I needed to commit it to memory, to keep in mind for when I was safe at home examining the reports Andrea had given me.

With the next traffic signal cycle, the street became nearly deserted again. I thought I should leave in case Wayne came back, but I continued to pick up my faux atoms, as if three dollar's worth of Styrofoam were important enough to risk being manhandled again.

Between two pretend carbon atoms I saw something wrinkled and shiny enough to catch the headlights of a passing car. I picked it up, gingerly, the way Jean had fingered the soap in the guest room. An empty cigarette package, most likely Wayne's, since he'd opened a new one after he entered my car. I spread open the crumpled package. Camels. Who smoked Camels these days?

While I was bent over, I played the light around the area. Maybe Wayne left a trail of butts and I could find out where he's staying. Fairy-tale reasoning. I thought of Hansel and Gretel, though I'd never liked such stories as a child. Like the Bible stories Sister Pauline told us, they all failed my logic test. "Why didn't the glass slipper disappear at midnight, too, like her beautiful new clothes?" I'd asked the lady in the library at the Saturday morning reading session.

I went back to the edge of the bushes, this time looking at the ground. A few steps in I found a cigarette butt, a Camel, next to tire tracks that were too narrow for a motorcycle and too wide for the kind of bike I had as a kid. Some in-between off-road bike, I figured. The on-and-off rainy weather made the perfect mold for the tracks and I could make out the design in some detail.

I followed the bike tracks to the back of the lot, which ended at the asphalt driveway of an office building. Along the way, wherever the indentation seemed deeper, there were one or two Camel butts alongside it, as if Wayne had made his way across the lot riding, lighting up, waiting, then repeating the cycle. I shuddered at the image of Wayne Gallen sitting on his bike, enjoying a smoke while lying in wait for me. I shuddered again thinking of MC as the object of his stakeout. I realized the whole episode in my car had lasted fewer than ten minutes, but that's long enough when you know you've lost control of your life.

I made my way back to my car, beaming my flashlight back and forth in front of me, collecting cigarette butts. Overkill, probably, but why not? I gathered three butts into a tissue and put them in my pocket. I foresaw more midnight activity at our washer/dryer.

At least now I knew how Wayne was getting around. No rental car or local taxis, all of which had been checked by the police. Wayne was riding a bike. Now the police could carry Wayne's photo to bike shops and possibly get an address or phone number. The idea that I'd come away from my frightening ambush with some information excited me. This time I didn't rule out the possibility that Matt had come up with it already, as with the Lorna Frederick connection. As long as we got that man off the street.

I felt a drop. Rain would be nice, I thought, to wash away the presence of Wayne Gallen around my car. Then I looked at the bike track at my feet and got it in my head that the tire treads might also be helpful, though I didn't have time to figure out why. I realized they would soon be washed away if I didn't preserve them. Not that I carry plaster of Paris around in my trunk. But I did have some supplies. *Think,* I told myself as the raindrops came faster.

I went back to my totes and pulled out some extra clear transparencies that I'd brought to class, to use in real time with the overhead projector. I peeled one off the stack, grabbed a marker, and went to the nearest track with good definition. I made a little pile of rocks and propped my flashlight on it. By now my knit suit was wet and dirty, my shoes caked with mud. Police work could ruin a good wardrobe, I thought, and it was a good thing I didn't have one to begin with.

It was pouring now, water filling the grooves of the track as well as the space between my collar and my neck. I rushed to make a trace of the pattern on the clear, stiff plastic, using a blue marker to follow the design. Straight line, zigzag, reverse zigzag, straight, curvy, reverse curvy, straight, and back to the zigzags. I lifted the transparency from the ground and held it near my flashlight. Nothing that would stand up in court, but I had the dimensions correct, and a good representation of the angles of the zigzags and the wavelengths of the curves.

I held the transparency between my shirt and my jacket, both soaking wet, but some protection from the now-pelting rain as I walked back to my car. I found my keys on the floor of the back seat where Wayne had thrown them. I held them out the window to wash him off.

If the remote got scrambled from the rain, I'd resort to Matt's old-fashioned method of unlocking doors.

NINETEEN

MC FISHED A COUPLE of clean mugs and silverware out of the dishwasher. The smells of fresh coffee and the peppery Tex-Mex frittata brought back old memories, the good ones. She carried the mugs and forks to the small dining table between the kitchen and the living room, pleased she'd been able to find her favorite pale blue and white mats in her still mostly unpacked boxes of household goods.

"Smells terrific," Jake said, pouring coffee for them. He ran his finger down the side of a small ceramic vase holding the purple and white icicle pansies MC had picked from her mother's yard yesterday. "I miss all your nice little touches."

MC smiled and sat across from him. He'd come by last evening, low-key and attentive, showing her his new, reformed self. He'd looked so great in a light denim shirt and the leather jacket she'd bought him last year—a cross between brown and red, a rusty, cowboy color, she thought. They'd laughed over the style, how it had no "Texas fringes."

"I haven't even had a beer since Sunday," he'd told her last night.

He'd learned his lesson, he'd said. He'd go to therapy with her as she'd asked him to do in Houston. He'd do whatever it took to have her back in his life. Looking into his brown eyes, she really believed him.

But this morning Jake seemed different, jumpy and preoccupied. He'd gone to the window and peeked out several times while he prepared the frittata. At one point he'd carried the mixing bowl with chilies, red peppers, and cheese to the window, stirring as he walked.

She looked at him across the table, breathed the smell of warm tortillas. His face was tense. He'd drawn in his lower lip, ready to break some news. But what? After all this, was he dumping her? Not after last night, she thought. Maybe his talk at the expo didn't go well. She decided not to ask, in case it was a sore spot.

"Is something wrong?" she asked him instead.

He flexed his fingers, a tension-relieving gesture she'd seen often. "Nah, I'm just rehashing that Liverpool jump I didn't make a couple of weeks ago."

The stadium jump over a small pool of water, she remembered. MC knew Jake was evading the truth, but she wasn't going to push him. "You got a second-place ribbon though, right?"

"Yeah. That has to do."

MC knew how important winning was to Jake Powers, the only son of L. Edward Powers of big oil fame. The limos in MC's childhood carried grieving families to and from Holy Family Cemetery; the limos in Jake's young life were his regular transportation to school and riding lessons, to the airport for trips to Paris and London. He'd told MC how hard it was for his father to accept Jake's decision to be "just a scientist." He was still on Jake's case, nagging him to use his science simply as a stepping stone to taking over the company one day.

"Want to hear a horse story?" Jake asked.

"Sure," MC said. She loved watching Jake and Spartan Q perform, and had often videotaped the shows, but she'd made a personal vow never to get up on a horse. Too scary.

"Remember that old guy you met—Andy Hunter?"

"The one who owns all those European horses?"

"Right. He owns, maybe, ten Hannoverians. Well, he killed one of them for the insurance money. The horse was not performing to expectations, and these guys are ruthless. He gave the horse an electric shock, which looks like a heart attack." Jack used his butter knife to mime a stab in the heart. "Awful. The guy's in jail, which is where people who hurt animals belong."

"How did they find out about it?"

"Some kid who works for him was rolling around in the hay with his girlfriend and saw the whole thing."

Jake's eyes darted to the window all during the story, and he'd hardly touched his frittata.

"Jake, these horse stories are fascinating, but tell me what's making you nervous."

He breathed heavily. "I'm not sure. But something's up, MC, something illegal or immoral or…something. I have to do a little more investigating before I start pointing fingers."

MC put down her fork, which was filled with what would have been her first bite of potato and sour cream. "You must know more than that, Jake. And why do you keep looking out the window?"

MC hadn't told Jake about either of the Wayne Gallen incidents, not the knocking on her basement window and certainly not the near-attack in the parking lot. She figured Wayne had been served the restraining order by now, and it was likely that he'd have headed back to Texas rather than be embarrassed by police action again.

Now she wondered if Jake's nervousness had anything to do with whatever Wayne had warned her about. She thought about showing Jake the e-mail from Alex Simpson.

"I've had this creepy feeling that someone's following me ever since I started looking into this," Jake said.

Now MC's eyes darted toward the window. Was this all part of Wayne's campaign of fear? Was he now harassing her boyfriend? "Have you by any chance seen Wayne Gallen around?" she asked.

Jake started, frowned. "Don't tell me Gallen followed you to Revere?" He banged the table with his fist, startling MC. "He implied as much to me a week or so ago, you know. Said he'd heard a certain Massachusetts girl was now single again." He pounded the table again, setting the plates rattling, and MC worried that the old Jake Powers was making a comeback.

MC played with her fork, twirling the stringy melted cheese around the tines. "Jake, don't worry about Wayne. It's not as if I'm the slightest bit attracted to him. Except for his mustache, of course."

Jake smiled, gave her that intense look she couldn't resist. He leaned toward her and they used their fingers to trace two long handlebar mustaches, curved at the ends, in the air between them. This was the Jake she loved, teasing, giving her adoring looks, abandoning entire meals to be with her.

LATER, AT THE DOORWAY, she kissed him. "Don't go," she whispered.

"I have to get this settled. When I come back, shall I bring my suitcase?" He gave her a sheepish look, as if to ask if he'd behaved well enough for her to take him back.

She smiled and shrugged her shoulders. "Let's go slow, Jake." He kissed her and she knew he could tell she didn't mean it.

MC leaned against the open door, watching Jake skip down the stairs. All the old feelings had come back and this time she felt it could really work. No one was more a turn-on than Jake Powers at his peak of charm. Not that she had any intention of rushing back to Houston with Jake, at least not until he proved he could last more than four days without a beer.

TWENTY

"YOU DID GOOD," Matt told me, using our traditional complimentary phrase from our first case together. "Berger says they were able to trace the tire tread to a low-end motorcycle made by Melrose Company and sold in only one shop in Revere. The owner ID'd Gallen based on the photo we took of him the night MC called in the nine-twenty-one."

I was excited that I had at last contributed to an investigation, if only the one relating to the whereabouts of Wayne Gallen, which, now that I thought of it, wasn't really an investigation in the eyes of the police. Matt had taken the report of my late-afternoon encounter with Wayne better than I thought he would, probably because I downplayed the fright I'd felt when he first entered my car.

"And the bike shop had an address for him?" I asked, with great hope.

He shook his head. "Not that lucky. But now we know how he's traveling and the uniforms are checking local biker hangouts; it could be he's trying to blend in that way."

"If he really wanted to blend in, he'd wash up and shave off that mustache."

I brushed out a jacket Matt would wear the next morning to his "modeling appointment," as we were calling it. I was uneasy about their using Styrofoam in a serious medical diagnostic, and felt better reading the new paperwork we'd been given, which called it a thermoplastic mold.

"What about Alex Simpson?" I asked. I'd decided Simpson must be in Revere, too, since all the other Texans involved with MC were.

"Negative. It's possible that Gallen is with Simpson in a motel, but if so Simpson's using a different name."

"I don't think Gallen's in a motel room. Why wouldn't he clean himself up if he were? Gallen smells as though he's been on the street half his life."

"You were that close?"

"I...uh...heard MC say that."

"Uh-huh. Because you made it sound no more intimidating than a guy just stopping to ask directions, and if he'd gotten close or threatened you, you'd have told me. Right?"

"Of course."

MATT'S SIMULATION was scheduled for Friday morning. This would take about an hour and would help pinpoint the tumor, according to Dr. Abeles. Matt's pelvic area would be scanned, and a three-dimensional image would be generated. A technician would make marks on Matt's skin to indicate the area to be radiated, a large area compared to what would be required with the new small-molecule medicine I'd been reading about.

"I'm supposed to leave the marks there, and not wash them off for the whole treatment cycle, just pat with water and then a dry towel," Matt said. "That ought to look cute. A nice decoration, like a tattoo. Maybe I'll get a navel ring to match."

I laughed. "You're doing a great job putting me at ease about this. How are *you* doing?"

"I'm nervous, but I'm feeling no pain," he said. "I even have some pre-pre-premedication to help prevent nausea and diarrhea once the treatments start."

He read through the booklet one last time, mumbling reminders to himself not to use moisturizers or powders, as if that were his habit.

Jean had been in and out the day before, visiting other friends and clients in Revere, and was now back so she could join Matt and me for the trip to the clinic. Once Jean saw that her brother was fine, she'd head south to the Cape.

That was the arrangement, until Berger showed up at our door. The rain was in full swing again, and he stomped the water off his rubbers—the kind I hadn't seen since I was a kid, requiring untold strength to overcome the friction as you pulled them on or off your regular shoes. "I'll keep these on if you don't mind," he said, and we waved our approval.

"Sorry to bother you so early," Berger said, accepting a cup of coffee. He leaned his elbows on our tile tabletop and held the mug with two hands as he drank, as if he were a very old man who'd slept outside in a storm. The image caused me to wonder whether Wayne Gallen had any protection from the nasty weather. Ugly as he was in all ways, I didn't want him out of commission before I had some answers.

Matt introduced Jean, who'd entered the kitchen when she heard the doorbell. She'd gone for a run already, and had changed from one expensive-looking sweatsuit to another. They were the kind Rose might wear, I noted, and wondered why I didn't resent the same look on Rose.

Jean shook Berger's hand, her head half-turned to me. "Matt's *real* partner? So glad to meet you, Detective Berger."

Then I remembered why the fancy sweatsuits appeared pretentious on Jean, but classy on Rose.

Berger gave no indication that he caught her hostility to me, possibly recalling a period when he might have felt the same way. "Ah, this coffee's good," he said, reaching for a bagel to go with it. "I'm beat. I feel like I've been working two jobs."

Matt sighed heavily, and Berger, flustered by his own remark, rushed in. "I don't mean it that way, Matt. You take all the time you need. Cynthia and Rebecca both have bad colds, and I was up all night listening to them coughing. And—"

Matt held up his hand. "It's okay. I know I'm slacking off here. What do you have?"

Berger put his mug down and flipped open his notebook, from the same supply closet Matt used, apparently, and put it on the table in front of him. "Lorna Frederick called yesterday afternoon, late. She wants to talk to someone at the department, preferably you and Gloria." He swung his mug at me. "Ms. Frederick…I guess it's Dr. Frederick, said she may have been abrupt at the interview you had the other day, and she does not in any way want us to think she is not cooperative, blah blah blah." Berger twirled his bagel in the air to indicate that the rest of Lorna's words were not worth repeating exactly. He closed his notebook, which, as far as I could tell, he hadn't glanced at while he talked.

My excitement that we didn't have to wheedle Lorna into a second interview took a back seat to Matt's needs. "Matt has a medical appointment this morning," I said.

"He needs to have his simulation done." From Jean, not to be outdone in mothering.

"I know," Berger said. "So, I thought you might come with me, Gloria. We should move on this while she's willing, and I could use a little, you know, technical assistance."

Matt, who'd been a good sport about being talked about in the third person, now raised his eyebrows and gave me a quick wink. We both knew what a breakthrough this represented. Berger had gone from not wanting me around the department when I first signed on, to now wanting me as a partner on an interview. Very flattering, but bad timing, however. I wasn't about to leave Matt's side.

"Can't this wait until later today, or tomorrow?"

"I don't mind at all taking care of my brother," Jean said, her delicate chin in the air. Matt gave her a look that I assumed was supposed to remind her of her recent promise to work on accepting me. I did my best not to look in her direction. It was hard, and even harder not to come back with the fourteen retorts on my lips, like "How sweet of you," or "Maybe you could leave your Cape Cod estate and move in with us."

"Gloria, I'd feel much better if you'd go with Berger," Matt said. "This simulating thing is nothing anyway. It's just pretend, right? And this way, I'd feel like my job was being taken care of."

I sighed. "If you put it that way..." I turned to Berger. "I'd love to come with you, though I'm sure you could handle it yourself." One more shot at being let off the hook, without alienating my new partner.

"Well, it's always nice to have someone else around, and since this lady is a scientist..."

I looked at Matt. He nodded. "What time?" I asked.

"Matt's office, eleven o'clock." He smiled at Matt. "Your office is bigger."

I checked my watch. I had two hours to go over the reports Andrea had given me. Two hours to pull something useful out of my next interview with the scientist-cum-horsewoman Lorna Frederick. After Berger left, I kissed Matt, ignored Jean, and went to work.

I LIKED my newly arranged office, in the second-floor guest room, facing the busy Fernwood Avenue. I worked better with worldly noises like traffic and neighborhood sounds around me, probably a holdover from having to share lab space all my professional life. Old Mr. Dorlando next door often obliged, using his power mower on his front lawn at all hours. This morning delivery trucks made a clamor on their way to and from a supermarket at the end of the street, their alternate route when there was construction work or repairs on Broadway, which seemed to occur frequently.

Too late I'd realized this was the room Jean had always used when she visited, and she was now relegated to the smaller downstairs bedroom at the back of the house. Another reason for her to resent me, I figured. Matt had shrugged and said, "It's your house," when I asked why he hadn't advised me against the choice. My house—I wondered why that hadn't immediately leapt to my mind.

I set a mug of fresh coffee on the little table next to a high-back wooden rocker and piled the stack of papers on my lap. I'd started in the same way several times since Andrea had given me the reports, and each time I'd been distracted by one of Matt's many brochures on his cancer. I slid easily from science to medicine lately. Last night he'd placed a new leaflet on my desk since I was the keeper of the files, and I glanced through a tri-fold on male sex hormones and a new agent, ketoconazole, that blocks their production. I tried to adjust my mind to the idea that blockage was a desirable outcome in this case—we did not want cells in a cancer patient to grow, but to be inhibited. It was a technology pharmaceutical companies were working on, but not quickly enough to suit me.

I filed the pamphlet, and focused on the nanotechnology group reports and grant proposals. I'd written my share of funding documents, and recognized the forms and summary charts. Project name, principal investigator, action items, delivery schedule, contacts. The government usually awarded researchers money based on a record of research and development activity and tangible signs of progress in a certain direction.

Trying to make sense of Wayne Gallen's comment about a diversion of funds got me nowhere. I was hopeless at financial auditing; reports of income and spending were meaningless to me.

The Charger Street scientists were promoting their ongoing work in nanoropes, bundles of nanotubes that would be valuable in HIV studies. Nanoropes could be used as probes to explore the core structure of the HIV virus.

I enjoyed reviewing an image gallery of beautiful graphics that made up an appendix of one report. A small, bright green rope of buckytubes. Vials of buckytubes in colorful solutions, three shades of red. A green buckytube with four red peptide rings wrapped around it like a Christmas garland. Who needed a museum?

A half hour of my allotted two hours had passed and I had nothing that would be useful in the upcoming interview with Lorna Frederick. I realized the reason for my failure was that I had no clear idea what I was looking for; I knew only my primary mission—determine why MC was being stalked, warned, and cajoled into leaving Revere.

I abandoned my star method of a few days before and went into a linear organizing mode, writing down what I had, what was missing.

Q.: Why was private investigator Nina Martin murdered in Revere?

A.:1. She was on a job in Revere and her death was related to that job.

2.: She happened to be in Revere when she was murdered, but the killing was random, or related to another assignment.

I wrote *NO* next to number two. No coincidences allowed at this point.

So, given that her murder was related to an assignment that took her to Revere, the surrounding facts must all be connected. I wrote them down.

The job Nina Martin was working on had something to do with:

1. her enrollment in MC's chemistry class.

2. the Houston Poly buckyball team (since she used the class to instigate contact with them through a pretend term paper).

3. the Charger Street lab buckyball team (since she was in Revere with Lorna Frederick's card in her pocket).

4. the FDA (since she had their card in her pocket also).

5. (possibly) the e-mail matter Wayne Gallen was keeping to himself, but which should force MC to run away with him, like some Romeo and Juliet escaping their feuding families.

Brilliant, I thought. I still had no clue what tied all these together.

From Matt, I knew that the Texas agencies had shared very little information. I assumed that was because Nina Martin's murder was essentially solved and they might see no further need to investigate. Rusty shoots Nina; Nina shoots Rusty; both die.

I made a note to ask Matt if there were any chance Houston police would question Alex Simpson, based only on Wayne's ravings and an admittedly innocuous, possibly misdelivered e-mail. I doubted it.

Dejected, I straightened the papers and shoved them into my briefcase, catching them on the yellow-lined pad I kept in it. I pulled out the pad and scanned the notes I'd made while Andrea and I talked about the reports. I'd generated a checklist, and forgotten to follow through. Reading down the items, I saw that I'd done everything except check the contacts, to see if I recognized the names of any of the researchers on the payroll. I still had another ten minutes before I had to leave, so I pulled out the contact list and read down.

The consultants for Lorna's team represented a wide variety of research, government, and educational institutions, with an impressive array of credentials. I ran my finger along the column. MD, MS, PhD, MChem.

I scanned down.

Alex Simpson, PhD, Houston Polytechnical Institute. An *aha* went through my body, though I already knew the two labs were connected through common research. I searched for Wayne Gallen's name, but couldn't find it. I did find more MDs, an MBio., and a DVM.

A DVM? I looked again. Dr. Timothy Schofield, DVM, of Revere, Massachusetts. Daniel Endicott's vet. Why was there a veterinarian on the contact list?

Finally, I had a couple of questions for Lorna Frederick.

I looked out the window to see Matt and Jean pull away in Jean's new black BMW. Matt had come up to say goodbye and wish me luck at the interview; Jean had not.

TWENTY-ONE

Lorna Frederick did not disappoint me with her second outfit. Green enough for a St. Patrick's Day parade, swirly enough for belly dancing, enough layers for a silicon chip on a wafer. I hadn't forewarned Berger about her flamboyant appearance—a good partner would have, I thought, too late—and I saw him swallow his surprise as Lorna swept into Matt's office.

"I'm so sorry to hear that Detective Gennaro is not feeling well," she said. I wondered who had told her what, about why Matt was missing this meeting.

"Nice of you to come in," Berger said. He pulled out a chair for her on the opposite side of Matt's desk.

I sat to the side, and had a view of the photo of Matt and me that he kept on his desk next to the Massachusetts penal code.

Lorna folded herself and her fabric into the gray chair, an unworthy background for her costume, and smiled. "I certainly didn't mean to be uncooperative when Detective Gennaro came out to the lab," she said. "I was taken by surprise, I guess, and felt uncomfortable, but of course I'd be glad to answer any questions about our work, or anything else that might be helpful to you."

"You've met Dr. Lamerino, our science consultant," Berger said, nodding my way.

Lorna smiled at me. "Indeed I have. It seems I'm the last to know of your sterling reputation around the lab."

"Sterling" sounded like a horse word, or maybe that was "gelding." In any case, I couldn't gauge her level of sincerity.

Lorna had the shortest distance I'd ever seen between an adult's forehead and chin, as if her features had been squeezed together in an accident with a vise. A remarkable contrast between her tiny face, topped by tight blondish curls, on the one hand, and her dramatic costumes and gesticulations on the other.

For about a half hour the three of us talked, Lorna establishing that she still hadn't been able to come up with a single reason why a murdered private detective would be carrying around her phone number. She'd done a little research, however, and come up with several numbers close to hers, she said—a dry cleaning establishment, a fast-food restaurant, and assorted citizens of Revere and Winthrop. Berger wrote down the information and promised to follow up.

Lorna brought out a folder with current publications from her group, most of which I had already received from Andrea.

"I'm most proud of our work in materials enhancement," she said. "We're taking the lead nationally in producing tougher ceramics and even sunblocks for UV and IR." Lorna used a well-manicured finger to march down the explanatory bullets, holding the page in front of her flat, green chest. I was tempted to offer her the use of the laser pointer I kept in my briefcase, but saved my intimidation for something more important.

I pulled the grant proposal contact list from my stack and placed it on top of the pile of reports on my lap. "I have a couple of questions, Dr. Frederick."

She extended her arm full length, as I knew she would, her hand in a *halt* position. "Call me Lorna, please."

I smiled a thank-you. "Lorna, I notice Dr. Alex Simpson's name here, from Houston Poly. Do you work closely with him?"

Lorna cleared her throat and fidgeted, catching one of the slits in her cloak in the arm of the chair. Her tiny, dark eyes darted around the room, as if she were looking for a TelePrompTer. I tried to remember what her behavior meant in terms of how credible her next words would be. In what amounted to a training session for me, Matt had showed me a video of an RPD detective interviewing a woman caught robbing a bank. She claimed the man she was with had held her hostage and forced her to assist him. Matt point out one clue that indicated she was most likely lying. Several times the woman referred to "we," as in "we drove down the street," instead of "he drove me down the street."

When was I going to stop piecing together a degree in police work? If I'd approached my career in physics this way, I thought, I'd have been thrown out of the American Institute of Physics long ago.

Lorna stopped squirming abruptly, switched to a thoughtful pose, during which I supposed we were to assume she was searching her memory banks. She moved her head up and down slowly. A reflective nod. "Yes, I do remember the name. You understand, I don't personally interact with everyone on the list. It's a composite of all the contacts of all my groups."

"But you're the group's leader, aren't you? The head of the whole nanotechnology program?" I asked.

"Yes, but—well, let me ask you this. Do all of you law enforcement people work closely together? For example, do you immediately share whatever I tell you here with other agencies?"

Berger gave her a questioning look, but I knew where Lorna was going. And I finally understood the real reason she'd offered to come in and "cooperate." She'd been visited by FDA agents, who probably told her less than they told us, and she was fishing for information. She'd come to get information, not to give it. Very nice trick, I told her, but not out loud.

I struck a pensive pose myself. "I guess the FDA agents asked you for an alibi?" I asked her in a light tone, almost sympathetic.

Lorna sighed heavily. "They did, and I just wondered…" She threw up her hands.

"If the Revere police consider you a suspect in Nina Martin's death?" I finished for her, compassionate. *How could they?* my tone said.

Lorna relaxed a bit and Berger took the opportunity to jump in. "What *were* you doing that night, by the way, Dr. Frederick?" He tapped his pen on the desk pad, his slightly pudgy face expressionless. Warm cop, cold cop. *Maybe Matt and I should adopt this interview strategy,* I thought.

"I rode my horse, as I often do after work, then went home. I already told this to Detective Gennaro."

Berger nodded, wrote in his notebook, and studied the page for several seconds.

"And you don't know Dr. Simpson?" he asked, tapping again, suspicious.

"I know him, but not really well."

Lorna stood, her habit when she lost control of a meeting, it seemed. But I had one more question.

"I see you've listed a veterinarian on your contact page. Dr. Timothy Schofield. I happen to know Dr. Schofield from our volunteer work with Revere High students."

A friendly comment about a mutual acquaintance, casually made, but Lorna's swallow was audible. "Oh?" The reaction I'd hoped for. She didn't have to know I could barely describe the man. I remembered little other than his exceptionally shiny bald head.

"How are veterinarians connected to the buckyball program?"

Another flustered movement as she caught part of her bright green fringe on a deep scratch in the metal chair. She bit her lip, then said, "Probably as consultants on animal testing."

"So, some of your programs require testing on animals?"

"Not exactly." She picked up her briefcase and gave it an annoyed tug, as if it were at fault for a meeting gone wrong. "Well, thank you for seeing me. I won't take any more of your time."

Lorna Frederick's exit had less flair than her entrance.

"NICE JOB," BERGER SAID, after Lorna left. It seemed strange coming from him, and not my real partner, now encased in a Styrofoam cradle. "What was that about a vet?"

"Someone I found at the last minute, on her consultant list. It so happens I know this vet, and I plan to ask him about his connection to her." I paused. This was not Matt. I couldn't appear to investigate on my own. "If that's okay with you," I said, trying to sound meek,

Berger smiled. "Go for it."

I could only hope my relationship with Jean would develop as well.

HALFWAY DOWN Fernwood Avenue, I could see that Jean's BMW was gone. A flood of relief came over me, not just because I'd had enough of her, but it meant Matt was fine; otherwise, I was sure, she'd have stayed.

"Good news,' Matt said, as soon as he heard me come through the door.

I stopped in my tracks.

"Oh?"

No cancer, I thought. *No tumor, no treatments. A miracle, like the Virgin Birth or the resurrection of Lazarus.*

"They found Wayne Gallen and issued his PFA. The bike shop owner gave them the lead."

This information paled next to the wonders I'd come up with, but I was relieved nonetheless.

"Terrific, now let's hope it doesn't make him even angrier at MC." *Or me.* "How are you?"

"The tire tracks did it, you know." Not answering my question, but I smiled, accepting the compliment, a new skill I was learning, thanks to Matt especially. "Gallen got himself involved with a bike group, like a poor man's motorcycle club. Not your Harleys or Yamahas. They meet every night at a truck stop on One-A, near Saugus, past the marsh. They're into a lot of noise and bar fights, near as anyone can tell, but nothing violent."

"Maybe they've upgraded to murder in the marsh?" I asked.

Matt rocked his hand back and forth. A favorite gesture of my father's. *Mezza mezza.* Maybe yes, maybe no.

I briefed Matt on my meeting with Berger and Lorna Frederick, including a description of her costume.

He laughed. "Well, it's almost Halloween."

"She knows something," I said, taking the easy chair opposite him.

"Can you be more specific?"

"No, but I'm closing in on it." I told Matt about Dr. Schofield and Berger's go-ahead for me to talk to him.

"You two are getting to be good buddies. I'm glad."

"Me, too."

The coffee table between us was littered with yet more brochures and flyers from the clinic. A huge orange warning against wearing perfumed lotions within two hours of treatment.

A list of possible side effects of external beam radiation therapy. Unpleasant words stood out. Irritation. Inflammation. Dysfunction.

"Now are you going to tell me about your appointment?" I asked him.

He waved his hand. "It was nothing. First they made the mold, then I got in it, and they X-rayed the area. They say the hormone medication worked, which is good, so that means the radiation treatments can start right away."

"When?"

"Monday morning."

"So soon?"

I should have been happy to get started, and therefore, be finished. Instead, I choked up, something I hadn't done until now. I considered the irrationality of crying over the treatment rather than the diagnosis.

Matt came over and pulled me off the chair.

"I'm not saying I'm not worried or scared, Gloria. But if we don't have faith and hope for the best, well…"

"I know."

"Come on, I'll show you the marks the technician made on my skin."

I recovered quickly and followed him upstairs.

TWENTY-TWO

ON FRIDAY EVENING, things looked brighter. Matt had talked to me for a long time about the great confidence he had in Dr. Abeles. He recited the names of several men he knew who had recovered completely from prostate cancer. Plus, Wayne Gallen was being PFA'd away from MC, and Matt and I were invited to dinner with the Galiganis.

"And there's a surprise," Rose told me when she called to confirm our presence at seven for drinks—a French wine for them, I was sure, and mineral water for Matt and me. "Guess who's coming to dinner?"

"Spencer Tracy."

Rose laughed. "No, and anyway it would be Sidney Poitier. He was the guest in that film."

"You should be surprised I even know the movie."

"I am. And it's Jake Powers." I paused to process the information, and Rose filled the space. "MC is bringing Jake Powers to dinner."

I sensed Rose's mixed feelings, like my own. "Well, it's good that we'll get to meet him."

"I hope this doesn't mean anything," Rose said.

"It might mean she wants your opinion of him."

Rose blew out her breath, a scoffing sound rippling across her lips. "I'm only the mother. Well, we'll see—let's be nice to him."

"I wouldn't dream of anything else."

"I would," she said, and hung up.

JAKE POWERS WAS a delightful guest. Physically he was a lot like Frank Galigani, small, dark, impeccably groomed. Maybe we all choose our fathers, I thought, realizing how much Matt was like my own father, minus the tiny mustache Marco Lamerino had always kept carefully trimmed. I hadn't seen MC so relaxed since she arrived in Revere. We'd told her that the PFA had been issued, and that probably accounted for a lot of her equanimity. But most of it, I suspected, had to do with things going well with Jake.

For once it was not Frank's stories that held the dinner table captive. Jake was out to charm MC's parents, and by extension, Matt and me. Rose and I had sneaked glances now and then, sending messages that couldn't be spoken aloud. *Who does he think he's fooling?* was one of them. *We'll talk later,* was another.

"Tell them about the guy raising the pole, Jake," MC said, nudging him.

Jake managed to affect a bow, even though he was sitting, as if to say MC's wish was his command. He picked up his knife and balanced it across the top of a set of salt and pepper shakers. "Okay, say this is the pole the horse has to clear in the competition. Okay?"

We all nodded our okays. "I see that on TV sometimes," Rose said. Not surprising, she'd been the perfect hostess, even trying her version of Texas cuisine. "This is called ranch chicken," she said, placing the main course between the guacamole and the jalapeño corn bread.

Jake breathed in the aroma and gave an enthusiastic thumbs-up. "What you don't see on TV is what happens before the competition. Owners, or sometimes stable boys, ride the horse around a warm-up arena, with one or two fences. During warm-up there are two people, one on each end of the jump. Maybe they're coaches, maybe grooms, with a final chance to tell you 'get your shoulders back,' or something, you know." Jake pointed to the salt and pepper ends of the steak knife. "What they do is, when the horse is just about over the jump, they raise the top pole ever so slightly, so it scrapes the horse's ankle."

"Ouch," Rose said, taking her seat and starting the serving bowls in a counterclockwise direction.

"Ouch, exactly. Because during the next few jumps—which

would be in the competition—the horse will go higher over the pole so as not to get hurt again." Jake sat back, his story finished.

We sat in silence, except for a *hmm,* from Rose.

"I'll bite," Frank aid. "What's wrong with that?"

"It's illegal," MC said. "Tell them why, Jake. I know it's called poling, but I'm not sure I get it myself, why it's illegal."

"Essentially, you've enhanced the horse's performance. You're not supposed to do *anything* to affect the performance, you know, except practice, practice, practice. Same with horse racing, dog racing. You can't even give the animal bute."

Crumbs of jalapeño corn bread caught in my throat, and I coughed embarrassingly loud and long. I glanced at MC to see if she'd noticed it—the word Alex Simpson had used in his e-mail. She seemed to give a start, and I guessed she had, but thanks to her habit of taking nanoparticle-size bites of food, she did not end up choking.

"What's bute?" MC asked Jake, casually, long before I physically could have. She looked at him intently. Foolishly, I wished I were sitting next to her so we could pass notes.

"Phenylbutazone, an oral painkiller-slash-anti-inflammatory, which is perfectly okay to give a horse outside of competition, for normal aches and pains."

I was amazed there were people who could tell if a horse had sciatica or a crick in its knee. How did the horse signify it had a headache when it couldn't put a hoof up to its forehead? Or maybe it could, if it was lying down?

My own headache was developing as I fought the urge to leave the table and go to MC's apartment and check her e-mail from Alex Simpson again. I tried to recall the sentence or phrase he'd written about bute, and at the same time pay attention to Jake in case there was more to learn.

"Bute is one of the best meds you can give to improve a horse's ability to perform. It's entirely against the rules for competition, however, as governed by USA Equestrian and by the FEI in the international arena. FEI is the *Federation Equestre Internationale,*" he said, with a French flair.

"Jake's been to Olympic equestrian shows all over the world,"

MC said. Her tone was informational and automatic and I could tell by her concentrated frown that she was also trying to remember the exact words of her e-mail.

"How do you give a horse a pill?" Frank asked. The anatomist, interested in bodies, human or animal, dead or alive.

Jake laughed, thinking *city folk,* I supposed. "You crush the tablets and mix them into grain, or you make a paste with molasses or honey and you put it on the horse's tongue."

"Does it take a veterinarian to give the medicine?" I asked Jake. I thought I'd zeroed in on Dr. Schofield's part in this…this what? Just because his name showed up as a grant consultant didn't make him part of anything but normal, legal research.

Jake shook his head. "No, no, the vet distributes it, but anyone can give it to the horse." Not anyone. I cringed at the thought of my fingers being in a horse's mouth.

"There must be a way to test whether the horse has been given something illegal, the way they do with athletes," Frank said. I wondered if Frank knew as much about horse anatomy as he did about humans. Were horses embalmed? And where would you bury a dead horse? These were questions that also came to my mind.

Jake nodded. "Sure, it would come out in a urine test, but those are random. So either you'd take a chance that your horse wouldn't be singled out, or there's always—" Jake rubbed his thumb and fingers together in the international gesture for money "—paying off the testers."

"Fascinating," Frank said. A compliment, I thought, from one who had so many captivating stories of his own. I thought of asking him to tell one of my favorites—about the deceased prostitute whose friends came and re-did her makeup before the public viewing, or the family who propped up their embalmed grandpa for one last reunion photograph. But for once I didn't want to stay very long at the Galiganis'. I kept trying to remember the exact text of MC's bute e-mail.

Matt had been very quiet during Jake's stories. I'd looked over a couple of times and thought I saw closed eyelids. Another of his naps, but the first time at a dinner table.

Now I thought maybe I could use his fatigue as an excuse to get us home early. I wanted to share the new insight about bute with him, and then to make a trip to the Galigani Mortuary and MC's computer. I hadn't worked out how to help her get away early, too.

I looked back and saw Matt sway, a small circular motion from the waist up. Fortunately Rose's dining set was an old, sturdy kind with arms on the chairs, or Matt would have fallen to the floor.

As it was, he was unconscious.

TWENTY-THREE

THE SIGHT OF MATT in a narrow hospital bed, looking pale and weak, frightened me as nothing before in my life. It was more terrifying than being run off the road in the Berkeley, California, hills, or being trapped with a double murderer in the Galigani Mortuary prep room. Certainly worse than being cooped up in my car for ten minutes with Wayne Gallen.

The time between seeing Matt slumped onto the arm of Rose's mahogany dining room chair and now, in his thin white gown with tiny polka dots, was a blur. I knew that Frank had taken over, calling a number probably only morticians had, and an ambulance arrived in an instant. I remembered getting into Rose's car, and then waiting outside Matt's hospital door, refusing coffee from MC and Jake. I thought I'd never be able to drink from a Styrofoam cup again without thinking of Matt's disease.

Matt looked at me now, the tiny smile on his lips forced, like a stretched spring that would snap back as soon as it was released. He was attached to the bed by tubes of three different sizes; a green display followed the pulses of his heart. I realized I was angry at someone or something. I'd dutifully gone through all the literature Matt had brought home, plus my own on-line research, and could not recall a side effect that occurred *before* the treatment started. This did not make sense; therefore it had no place in my life.

Matt pulled at the neck of his gown. "Silly, huh?" he said.

"You look fine, really. How do you feel?"

What I meant was—*What happened to you? Are you going to live? Please do not leave me.* I felt as though my entire Texas dinner was at the edge of my throat, the taste of chili powder and bell peppers overwhelming my senses.

"I'm not ready to run the Boston Marathon. But when was I ever?"

"What did the doctor say?"

"A confluence of medications. Nice term, isn't it? Apparently the two medicines I've been taking are incompatible, and I had a reaction."

A reaction. Good. Not an attack or a stroke, both of which had a finality to them. Reactions were temporary, fixable, like a harmless rash or an upset stomach. Or at least I hoped so. I held that thought as the door opened and a young woman with a dark ponytail and a clipboard entered—a candy striper?

"I'm Dr. Rosen," she said. "How are we doing here?" She looked and sounded too much like a cheerleader to suit me, but I realized that professionals seemed younger and younger to me as my sixth decade was coming to an end. MC was a skilled chemist, I reminded myself, and probably no older than this woman.

"We're doing fine," Matt said.

Young Dr. Rosen looked at me. "Are you his wife?"

"This is Gloria Lamerino," Matt said quickly, introducing me politely even as he seemed to struggle for breath. "She's my fiancée."

This night was full of surprises. It had begun with bute—I hardly remembered why the word mattered—and now I was pseudo-betrothed to a man in a hospital johnny.

"Well, if it's all the same to you, and even if it isn't…" Dr. Rosen laughed. Perhaps lightheartedness was a new technique taught in medical school these days. "We're going to keep you at least overnight. You can stay another five minutes, Ms. Marino, then lights out."

Marino, close enough for someone with a name as simple as Rosen. Ordinarily, I'd be tempted to call her Dr. Rose, but not tonight. I followed her to the door and asked if I could talk to her privately in the hallway. She looked at her watch and nodded.

I went back to Matt's bed and took his hand, ready to utter a soothing good night.

He was asleep.

ALL I WAS ABLE TO LEARN in my sixty-second consultation with the very busy Dr. Rosen was that Matt's hormone treatment and the antinausea medicine he'd been given were incompatible, or that he'd had an allergic reaction to one of them.

Dr. Rosen flipped through Matt's folder, the way I'd seen Matt manipulate the pages of a felon's record, dozens of times. "Hmm, it's pretty big, isn't it?" she said, clicking her tongue against her teeth.

Not what I wanted to hear, tongue-clicking from a doctor. "What's pretty big?"

"Oh, I'm sorry, the, uh, tumor. It's a good size."

"Isn't *small* a good size for a tumor?" Here I was, alienating one of Matt's doctors with my smart mouth. "I'm nervous," I told her.

She put her hand on mine, gave me her bedside smile. "I'm sure his doctor has everything under control. Now, you go home and get some rest. I assure you, he's not going to wake up very soon." She turned from me and walked away briskly, her pony-tail waving like a horse's tail. *So that's where the name comes from,* I thought.

The Galiganis had stood discreetly back while I'd been with Dr. Rosen. My friends seemed very far away, down a long green cor-ridor with side hallways shooting off, and color-coded footprints to take Hansel and Gretel to X-ray, to admissions, to surgery.

Rose came up to me and gave me her best hug. "Is everything okay? What are they saying?"

I told her about the "pretty big, isn't it" remark. "Why didn't Matt tell me the tumor was big?" I asked her, as if she'd have an idea that would put my mind at ease.

"Probably it's just big to her," Rose said, tilting her head in the direction Dr. Rosen had gone.

"What if something else is going on and it's worse than we thought?"

Rose shook her head, hooked her arm in mine as we walked to her car. "How old is she? Is she even twenty? This may be her first tumor. Like Frank with his first client. Shall I tell you about that?"

I smiled and squeezed Rose's arm. She was just what I needed but I shook my head *no* on the client story. Rose either didn't notice, or decided I should hear it then and there.

"Well, you know, when a client's brought into the prep room from the hospital or wherever, it's usually on a stretcher. You position the stretcher next to the embalming table and slide the body over." Rose removed her arm from mine to demonstrate a sliding motion. "Many times the body will give out a gasp, like it's moaning."

I gave out a gasp myself. "Rose…" I wanted to tell her Frank had told this story many times, but my voice has always been weaker than hers, and she was already into the sound-effects part.

"It sounds like *mooooooooan.* This is only air being expelled out of the lungs because of the movement, but when Frank heard it the first time, it was night and he was alone in the Sasso Brothers prep room where he worked as an intern, and he thought the person was still alive. He nearly dropped the client. Of course now he loves to be with a rookie when it happens, to see the reaction."

"Thanks, Rose. I feel so much better now."

AT MIDNIGHT I HAD Fernwood Avenue all to myself. The street was slick from a brief shower while I'd been in the hospital; the streetlights picked up the fine mist still in the air. I'd declined all of Rose's offers—to drive me straight home and leave my car in their driveway, to come and stay with me, to have me sleep overnight at their house.

"I need to be near the phone," I'd said. "Remember that was my condition for agreeing to leave the hospital." I'd assured her I'd be fine and promised to let her know if I heard anything.

Now as I drove down the deserted street, I wished I'd said yes to one of the Galiganis' suggestions. The dark brown, shingle house seemed enormous as I approached, too big for one person. Darkness surrounded it, though I could have sworn we'd left the porch light on. In fact, I knew I'd flicked the switch just before leaving for dinner. A burned-out bulb, I thought. One more household chore.

I slowed down in front of the house, preparing to make the turn into the driveway, which was on the left side. A movement caught my eye, a shadowy form that seemed to hurl itself over the porch railing and into the bushes. A rush of fear came over me and I shivered in spite of the warm interior of the Caddie.

I tried to talk myself into a rational state. It was probably Mr. Dorlando's cat, a frequent visitor to our property. There was no need to feel uneasy, just because I'd be alone all night—I'd lived without a roommate of any kind nearly all my adult life. But I had quickly accustomed myself to cohabitation. I realized I'd never entered the Fernwood Avenue house this late without Matt's being there. No wonder I'd imagined an eerie visitor at our front door.

I pulled in and pressed the button to close the garage door immediately behind me, glad that an automatic system had been among our recent upgrades. From the driver's seat, doors still locked, I peered into every garage corner I could see and listened for sounds. Finally, I got out of my car and entered the house through the kitchen door. Unlike my mortuary apartment, my new home did not have an alarm system. I was on my own.

I switched on the light and blinked until my pupils adjusted. The espresso maker came into focus, the toaster, the small ceramic kettle Elaine had sent from a pottery shop in Berkeley. Everything looked normal, the way we'd left it only six or seven hours ago. I stood in place, scanning the room, my keys at the ready for a quick getaway. Two mugs on the drain board, pot holders on the counter, a clean saucepan on the back burner. Nothing out of place. I could move to the next room.

RRRRRRRing!

I dropped my keys. *It's only the phone.* I was utterly annoyed with myself for reacting like a scared child. In the time it took to put the receiver to my ear, I was able to imagine a too-solemn voice on the other end, a doctor summoning me back to Matt's bedside.

"Aunt G? Oh, good. I knew you couldn't be sleeping already." MC's voice. I took a breath.

"No, no, I just got in." *This is about bute,* I thought. MC and I can finally talk about the emerging scoop on bute. I could get her to read Alex Simpson's e-mail to me over the phone, or better yet, forward it to me.

"It's awful, Aunt G. I got home and there was a note on my door." I waited, unable for a moment to remember the name of the person who'd harassed both of us. "From Wayne Gallen."

"I thought he'd be halfway to Houston by now."

"No such luck."

MC read the note she'd found on her door: NO POLICE ORDERS WILL PROTECT YOU. IF IT WEREN'T FOR ME YOU'D ALREADY BE DEAD.

I shivered, silently, I hoped, so that MC wouldn't be even more upset. "How did he get far enough to put something on your front door?"

"Martha, Mom's assistant—well, of course, you'd know her." MC uttered a frustrated sound, like a breath that lost its way from her throat. "Martha stayed late today, and he probably sweet-talked her into letting him go up for a minute. The note was in a regular, long, business-size envelope, so she wouldn't have thought anything of it. Or he might have gotten her to put it there. I don't know. I just know he's freaking me out."

"Did you call the police?"

"No. I'm not sure what good it would do, unless I could talk to Matt. Wayne didn't even sign it, so how could I prove he violated the order?"

"Well, Martha will remember a red handlebar mustache."

"True. But now I'm afraid to leave the house. First, he might be out there, and second, maybe he's right that I'm in danger. Jake said something, too, about something funny going on."

"Tell me about that."

"Jake has a hunch something illegal is going on and he's doing a little 'investigating,' he called it. Also, he's had the feeling someone's been following him. Sound familiar?"

"It does. MC, I think we need to tackle *bute*." I told her about the Dr. Schofield link. I now had two equestrians, an animal medication, and a veterinarian. Out of my field, with buckyballs far behind, but still I felt a rush that always accompanied making a connection, however tenuous. "Bute might be the key. Can you forward the e-mail to me?"

"Done. I sent it as soon as I got in."

"I'll read it, and call you right back."

Except I had one more thing to do before going to my computer.

I left the kitchen light on, but turned on no others as I made my way to the front door. I crossed the carpeted dining room where I took my shoes off, then walked barefoot on the hardwood and tiled entryway. I wished I'd turned on music or news to act as white noise over the normal creaks and groans of an old building. I felt my every step generated a seismic wave inside and outside the house.

As I thought, the porch light switch, an old-fashioned up and down single-throw variety, was in the up position, indicating that I had indeed turned it on before leaving for dinner.

Two tiny decorative strips of etched glass were embedded vertically in the oak door, so I should have been able to see the edge at least of a note tacked anywhere on it. I stood close to the glass and ran my eyes up and down both strips. Nothing. Unless the note was less than five inches wide, the width of the opaque part of the door. But MC's note was in a size-ten envelope and there was no reason to think mine would be different.

I moved through various angles, looking past the decorative trim, catching the bushes, the tree near the curb, the edge of Mr. Dorlando's lawn. Nothing threatening or even interesting.

I was about to turn away when a patch of moonlight seeped through a gap in the rain clouds and reflected off a piece of glass on the floor of the porch. Many pieces of glass. The lightbulb, in shreds on the porch.

Next to the largest piece was a rock.

TWENTY-FOUR

I JUMPED BACK FROM THE DOOR, as if the frosty surface of the light-bulb might defy entropy, gather itself together, and attack me. I told myself it wasn't out of the question that an unruly adolescent had decided to terrorize Fernwood Avenue by throwing rocks at selected porch lights. I wasn't about to test the theory, however; or do anything else that required leaving the house.

My second, more likely theory was that Wayne Gallen, upset by the PFA, had decided to intimidate Matt and me, perhaps to lurk in the darkness he'd created by smashing our porch light. It was possible that composing one note to MC had taken all the creative energy he had for the evening. This juvenile, mental scoffing at Wayne Gallen seemed to help make him less fearful to me, and got my pulse rate back to normal.

I stayed at the door a few minutes longer, uncomfortable with my stocking feet on the cold tile. I gave the already tight dead bolt an extra twist and listened for out-of-the-ordinary movement; I heard none and eventually put my shoes back on and went up to my office.

At my computer, I clicked on the Alex Simpson e-mail MC had forwarded to me, and read carefully.

There's good news and bad news. Our contact sees no problem delivering the package, but one unfortunate outcome—the bute that's not bute—might bring trouble.

Was it as simple as Alex Simpson giving show horses a dose of bute before a competition? Illegal, according to Jake Powers, but was it an FDA matter? I made a note to ask Matt about the mission and jurisdiction of the FDA. Matt, who seemed very far away at the moment, but would soon be home and we'd work cases together as usual, for a long time. Wasn't there a philosophy that said positive thinking brings about the reality?

I got out my case folder, now labeled MARTIN/FORMAN, for the two murdered Texans. I doodled around the star I'd drawn, the one that had led me to Lorna Frederick. Suppose the FDA, or whichever regulating body cared, got wind of a bute coalition, with Alex and Lorna working together, drugging show horses before competitions? They'd need a vet, at least to obtain the bute, if not to administer it, and Dr. Schofield was the one. What part they played in the research project, I didn't know—a loose end I'd have to work on.

Nina would have taken MC's class to get close to Alex, then might have come to Revere to track down Lorna. But was this scam worth the risk Alex and Lorna would be taking?

Maybe MC had a better idea.

"Not really," she said when I got her on the phone. "That's all I came up with, too."

"Is Alex Simpson also an equestrian?"

"Not as far as I know, and I think I would. The guy doesn't miss an opportunity to brag, if you know what I mean."

"So his bute reference might be something entirely different."

"It could be some shorthand for a completely unrelated compound."

"Lorna gave us the impression that there isn't a lot of money in equestrian sport, nothing worth killing people over. Is that your understanding?"

"Uh-huh. Jumpers—that's what show jumping horses are called—can be very expensive, and some of the bigger competitions have pretty hefty prize money, but not in the league of racing horses, for example. I can ask Jake."

"Is he there?"

MC laughed. "Smooth move, Aunt G. No, he's not here. And if you want to know if we're getting back together, I don't know. We're taking it slow."

"If you ever want to talk…"

"I know. And maybe I will. Soon. Right now though, sleep is sounding really good. I'm glad I have a burglar alarm."

I didn't need the reminder of my vulnerable state. When Matt returned, I told myself, we would revisit the need for increased security in our house. Whether or not it had anything to do with Alfred Hitchcock, I knew I could not take a shower. I felt defenseless enough fully clothed. I pulled my white flannel robe over my knit pantsuit, already wrinkled from sitting around the hospital waiting room, and settled on the overstuffed chair in our bedroom.

The last time I looked at the clock it was three in the morning.

I WOKE AT SIX, stiff from the chair/footstool combination that had served as a bed. *Psycho* or not, my need for a shower and a change of clothes won out. I carried my cell phone into the bathroom and got ready for the day.

I knew I should have called Jean last night, but it was very late when I got home. And now it was very early. But Jean was a morning person, and I couldn't put it off any longer. *If I'm lucky,* I thought, *she'll be jogging and I can leave a message on her answering machine.*

I wasn't lucky,

"What's wrong?" Jean asked as soon as she heard my voice. A normal reaction, I told myself, when a call comes before seven on a Saturday morning.

"Matt had a slight reaction to his medication. They kept him at the hospital overnight for observation. Nothing serious, I just thought you'd want to know." I had no idea why I downplayed Matt's condition. Certainly not because I was at ease with it.

"I'll be there by noon," she said, and hung up.

I glared at the receiver, as if it had rudely broken its electromagnetic connection to Cape Cod on its own. "You're welcome," I said.

MATT LOOKED MUCH BETTER. I'd stopped at the nurses' station first, and learned that he'd had a good night. If he promised to rest for a couple of days I'd be able to take him home after the doctor checked in.

I took a seat next to his bed, happy to see the diagnostics had been turned off.

"I miss our tutorials," Matt said. "Tell me something technical."

"This is because we can't leave here until Dr. Rosen comes by, isn't it?"

He gave me a sheepish smile and looked up at the clock, next to the tiny television set hanging from the ceiling. "We have at least a half hour."

"Okay, then," I said, rubbing my hands together and assuming a professional voice. "Today we'll discuss tachyons." For relief from all the chemistry and pharmacology I'd had to study lately, I brought up a pure physics factoid. "They're small particles that have a strange property—when they lose energy, they gain speed. And, the slowest a tachyon can go is the speed of light. Also, I think 'tachy' means 'fast' in some ancient language. How am I doing?"

"Tachyon." Matt stretched out the syllables, seeming to like the sound of the word. Then he snapped his fingers. "That's what I had. Tachycardia. Rapid heartbeat. That's what caused the fainting."

Of all the particles of physics, I'd picked the one that matched Matt's *reaction*. "Maybe there is something to the idea of being on the same wavelength," I said.

Matt smiled. "And I almost know what a wavelength is. Is this tachyon one of those particles no one has actually seen yet, but there are a million papers written that predict it and how much it weighs, and everything about it, so when it shows up, we're ready?"

I gave him an approving look. "I didn't know you'd been listening."

"I hear everything," he said.

"I know. It's what you do." I reached over and tucked the thin cotton blanket around him, taking the opportunity for a long, if awkward, embrace.

"Remember when I first met you—you'd come up with all those facts, like Einstein's birthday, or some atomic number?"

"March fourteenth, and the number is six for carbon," I said.

He laughed. "Aren't you going to draw me some pictures?"

I took a pen and small notebook from my purse and sketched the standard graphic of a carbon atom, or any atom—the familiar solar system model with negatively charged electrons orbiting a positively charged nucleus. It always bothered me to perpetuate a model that had been superceded in the 1920s, but the old representation was easier to picture than the "clouds of charge" of the new physics. I consoled myself with the fact that for some phenomena, the solar system paradigm still worked.

"Aren't you going to tell me how no one model accounts for all behavior, and you're using the simple model to make a point?"

"Like human behavior," I said. "Your field."

Matt knew my deep-seated belief that we would always have better physical models than human models. I thought of Wayne Gallen, and how psychology couldn't possibly describe his behavior using the same model as the one for Matt Gennaro's behavior.

"Tell me about Buckminster Fuller. A good quote, maybe."

"Fuller was only five two," I said.

He laughed, and raised his arm in the air. "Let's hear it for short men," said the five-foot-seven detective.

"Here's a quote, as near as I can remember it: 'When people discard the notion that ownership is important, they will not be burdened with possessions. The less we own, the greater our mobility.'"

"Didn't Jesus say that?"

"And Chairman Mao, I think."

Matt pointed to the clock. Dr. Rosen was late. "My doctor is probably making a prom date," he said.

I smiled. "She is young, isn't she? But that doesn't mean you don't have to follow her orders and go to bed when you get home."

"I'm ready to promise anything as long as they let me out of here," he said.

"Isn't the food scrumptious?"

Matt frowned. "Even your cousin's fruitcake is better."

"I'll be sure to tell her."

Enough, I thought. This was the kind of hospital small talk people made when someone was dying. "Are you up for some real work?" I asked him.

"You bet. What do you have?"

I reviewed Jake Powers's remarks, the ones Matt had missed when he inconveniently lost consciousness. I used the notepad to emphasize key words and possible links.

"So you think this bute is the key? Maybe an illegal drug? And the vet you met at the high school is involved?"

I nodded. "The trouble is, there doesn't seem to be enough at stake to kill someone over it. You remember what Lorna Frederick said about prize money and—"

"What is this?" A loud, reprimanding voice. Jean Mottolo, nee Gennaro, entered the room. She was in nicely tailored casual pants and a thick Irish sweater, comfortable for driving, but not inappropriate if a prospective client came her way. She stood at the foot of Matt's bed, arms folded, and glowered at me. "I can't believe you're making him work. Don't you care at all about him?"

I was dumbstruck. First, I'd forgotten she'd said she'd be coming to the hospital, and second, I hadn't been scolded in a long time.

Matt recovered from the outburst quickly. He pointed to an orange chair stuffed under the television set. "Jean, pull up that seat please, and sit down."

Jean obeyed, breathing heavily. *She's nervous and worried about her brother,* I told myself.

"I'm sure you didn't drive all this way to upset us." He took her hand. "You know I wouldn't be 'working,' as you call it, unless I wanted to. What's going on with you, Jeannie?"

I'd never heard Matt call his sister "Jeannie" and suspected it was meant to recall happier days of their childhood. I could see her body respond to the endearment. She took a deep breath.

"I'm sorry, Gloria," she said, using the correct words, but in a tone that sounded like a homework assignment from her brother. She swiveled her head to face first me, then Matt, and back to me. "What's going on is, I feel very left out of all this. Is there something you want to tell me?"

Matt and I looked at each other. "I told you everything I know, on the phone, Jean," I said, proud of my adult behavior so far.

"How nice of you to call my sister, Gloria," Matt said, with a teasing smile to both of us.

I went on, needing to finish my defense. "The doctor will be by in a few minutes and then Matt should be able to leave, but I didn't know that until I got here."

"That's not what I mean."

"Then what do you mean, Jeannie?"

She looked at Matt, tilted her head toward the door and reception area beyond. "The nurse told me your fiancée was in here."

Matt and I looked at each other and burst into a reasonably decorous laugh; the rattle of the food carts passing by provided the perfect background music.

Matt held up his hand in a *let me explain* gesture. "We told them that because hospitals have a hard time with people who are unrelated. You can't get information, can't come and go—"

"So it's not true?" Jean sat back, apparently immensely relieved.

"I haven't gotten down on one knee yet, but…did you think we were just temporarily playing house?"

Jean gave a loud sigh. "So are you getting married or not?"

I stood and picked up my purse, headed toward the door. "Anyone want a cup of coffee?" I asked.

TWENTY-FIVE

IT FELT SO GOOD TO HAVE Matt back from the hospital. He sat in the living room wrapped in a new flannel blanket I'd ordered online, but his color was returning, and his appetite was excellent. Even I had a hard time eating two whole cannoli in one sitting, but he managed, within an hour of being home.

"Don't want to insult Rose," he said, as if she were present to witness any restraint.

Jean had left his hospital room by the time I got back from the vending machine with a coffee-colored beverage. She had a client to see in Medford, she'd told Matt, and would be back to Fernwood Avenue in the afternoon. I didn't ask how the marriage conversation turned out. It seemed ironic that the subject had been instigated by a nurse who happened to be on duty when Matt was wheeled in.

When the doorbell rang, Matt flicked his blanket off and went to answer. The simple movement lifted my spirits, and I felt great hope that his previous listless behavior was due to the medication that had put him in the hospital. The doctors had yet to tell us what would replace those drugs, but a moment of respite was welcome.

"Looking good, buddy," I heard George Berger say, as the two men walked toward the living room.

Berger reached down to the plate on the coffee table and scooped up the last cannoli, the one both Matt and I had avoided because of the chocolate chips mixed into the cream. Not authentic, but Berger wouldn't know that.

He offered a treat of his own, wrapped in a blue RPD folder. "We got a transcript from the Houston PD. They had a joint interview with the party who hired Nina Martin and an FDA inspector. They've released the text to us."

I made a grabbing motion, and Berger pulled the file back, teasing. "Martin was hired by a woman named Penny Trumble. That's going to be PT in the margin. And the interviewers are just listed as HPD for Houston PD, and FDA, for…"

The last words, fortunately unnecessary, were buried under chewing sounds.

"Thanks for dropping this by," Matt said.

"Okay, have fun. And be prepared. Nina Martin was in Revere about a horse."

"A horse," Matt and I said, almost at the same time, with different tones. Mine was questioning; his was more like *I thought so*.

Berger had eaten his entire cannoli standing at the table. He brushed his hands together, sending powdered sugar into the air, and gave us a wave. "I got to take my nephews to soccer."

"If you need me to explain icosahedrons…"

Berger smiled. "Thanks, Gloria. I'll let you know."

I turned immediately to Matt. "You sounded as though you expected a horse."

He shrugged. "Not exactly, but I have been asking myself what are the possibilities why Nina would have Lorna's phone number. One would be the connection to Lorna as a scientist, and the other would be to Lorna as a horsewoman. Trouble with you is, you always think science is the only thing someone does."

I cleared my throat. "Is that a criticism?"

"Does it matter?"

"No. Let's get to the transcript."

A transcript. Something official, *how different*, I thought, *from what we had so far*—a wayward e-mail, babbling from under Wayne's handlebar mustache, Jake's casual remarks at dinner. I rubbed my hands together the way Elaine would do when she saw a new hardback by one of her favorite writers. Berger, who was turning into my best friend, was smart enough to bring a copy each for Matt and me. We retreated to our reading corner and turned pages almost simultaneously, skipping the boilerplate such as time and place, and getting to the heart of the matter.

HPD: So you hired Ms. Martin when your horse died.

PT: Yes, Lucian Five. He was an Andalusian.

HPD: That's a breed?

HPD: You have to say it out loud for the tape.

PT: Yes, Andalusian is a breed. He had the most beautiful mane.

HPD: And the animal lived on the ranch with you and your niece?

PT: Yes. My brother's girl. She stays with me and works on the ranch full-time. The Trumble X Ranch.

HPD: Okay. So you thought something was funny about how the horse died?

PT: Yes, it was horrible. He...beat himself to death, flailing around inside his stall. He tore the stall apart. We heard the noise, but thought it was just the wind since it had been stormy all evening; then in the morning, there he was. There was so much blood, and his face was disfigured...

I imagined PT was upset at reliving such a horrible scene. Nothing the transcript would pick up, however. We needed video, I thought, for a true representation of an interview.

FDA: Ms. Trumble, you said that just before this, you'd had a veterinarian install a microchip in the animal's body?

PT: Lucian Five.

FDA: In Lucian Five's body.

PT: Yes, on the side of his neck under the mane, so if he had a bad initial reaction, like a rash or anything, it would be hidden by the hair.

FDA: Because if the rash showed, there might be points taken off at the show. Is that correct?

PT: Yes, dressage judges can be influenced by how well

your horse appears to be taken care of, the grooming, how intricately his mane is braided, even the rider's outfit.

FDA: And you took very good care of Lucian Five? Had regular checkups, that kind of thing?

PT: Of course. I know what you're getting at. Lucian Five had the best in medical care. I'm telling you it was that chip.

FDA: Can you tell us why you had that chip implanted?

PT: One of the vendors at a show I was at was offering a very good deal. And I'd read about how it was important for identification in case Lucian Five was lost or stolen. We'd be able to prove it was really Lucian Five.

FDA: What makes you think the microchip was responsible for your horse's death?

PT: Lucian Five was fine before the implant. He's an older horse, and he's allergic to a lot of things he could take when he was younger. Some common sedatives act as a stimulant for him. He can't even take bute, except in very small doses. He didn't react right away, so maybe the chip was like those time-release cold capsules. I'm not a vet, but I've been around horses and vets all my life, and I know there was something strange about that chip.

Bute. It might as well have been written in red. I highlighted it on my copy of the transcript, so it was at least in pink. I looked over at Matt, who seemed engrossed, and not sleepy. And anyway, Trumble had mentioned bute only peripherally. Nothing to stop for right away.

FDA: So you hired a private detective. Why not report the incident to whoever takes care of medical regulations for shows?

PT: They just care whether some competition rule was violated. I wanted to know what happened to my horse. I wanted some proof that the chips were responsible, so I hired Ms. Martin to find out what they were made of, or something—without alerting the vet who put it there. She specializes in crimes against animals, and she said she would take care of reporting her findings to the proper authorities, once she figured out what happened.

I put the transcript on my lap and stared up at the ceiling, as if the textured white paint swirls were the repository of all my knowledge.

Matt stopped, too. "Here's one big loop closed," he said.

I nodded. "From a dead horse in Houston to Nina Martin in Revere with horsewoman Lorna Frederick's phone number in her pocket."

"So it's possible her murder and all the other side problems have nothing to do with the Charger Street lab. It could be just Lorna the equestrian who's involved," Matt said.

I was only too eager to dismiss Lorna the scientist from wrongdoing. I hated having members of my profession caught at being less than perfect. Much more acceptable if Lorna the horsewoman committed the crimes.

"The FDA link is strange," I said.

Matt nodded. "I see your thinking. According to Jake Powers, the regulating body for drugs in show horses is USA Equestrian. So why did Nina have an FDA card in her pocket?"

"Presumably, USA Equestrian monitors drugs that are already approved by the FDA, and they would only care about certain dosages that would affect a horse's performance."

"I'm thinking Nina Martin must have stumbled upon something bigger than a horse show," Matt said.

"A drug that's regulated not only by horse show rules, but by the U.S. government."

"Then how do Wayne Gallen and his warnings and pranks fit in? Was he just blowing smoke to get close to MC?" Matt asked.

I blew out my own smoke, in the form of a loud, confused sigh, and shook my head. "And the Alex Simpson e-mail? And the reference to bute in the transcript?"

"But according to what Jake said, bute is almost like aspirin, so who knows?"

"Has Houston been able to connect Rusty Forman to anyone?"

"Negative. It's like he walked out of prison and flew to Revere to kill Martin."

We both shrugged and returned to the transcript.

FDA: You said the vet who did the implant was a Dr. Owen Evans?

PT: Right. He's new, but my old doctor retired and recommended him.

FDA: And Ms. Martin told you she was going to investigate Dr. Evans.

PT: Yes, when she made her initial report to me. She said she planned to look into other deaths of Dr. Evans's patients, and also the people who made the microchip. Next thing I knew she was off to Houston Poly. She was such a nice lady, born right here in Houston, a real Southern lady, if you know what I mean, even though she was in a kind of unladylike line of work. Do you really think she was murdered because of this investigation?

HPD: Is there anything else you can tell us about the circumstances? Anything else you think we should know about?

PT: I don't think so.

"Well, there it is," I said.

Matt looked up. "Yes?"

"Nina was looking into a vet, and that took her to Houston Poly where we know she signed up for MC's class. So her vet investigation must have led her to the Houston Poly buckyball people. Remember she asked MC to put her in contact with someone who could help her with her fullerene paper."

Matt nodded in a way that said he was with me, and maybe ahead of me. "And there's a vet on the payroll at the Charger Street lab."

"Vet plus scientists in Houston and vet plus scientists in Revere."

"Lorna the scientist *and* Lorna the horsewoman."

"I love it when we're both right," I said.

When the phone rang, neither of us wanted to stop the momentum.

"I'm weak," Matt said, flipping back through the transcript.

I let him get away with the ploy and took the call. The message made *me* the weak one in the house, sending a disturbing wave through my body, turning my muscles to plasma. Except for my mind, which whipped across the city to MC on Tuttle Street and then back across town to Revere High's young Science Club students.

Jake Powers was dead. His body had been found in Rumney Marsh by one of Daniel Endicott's students.

Another eruption in a case—a life—that was full of priority interrupts.

TWENTY-SIX

MC HUNG UP THE PHONE and stumbled back to bed.

She tossed around for hours, it seemed, throwing off her blankets, tucking them back under her chin when she felt chilled, throwing them off again when a cold sweat came over her. She rolled onto her back, then to her left side, then to her right side. She got up several times to straighten her oversized T-shirt, a souvenir from one of Jake's shows, and her holey black tights. She went to the window and peeked out, for a reason she couldn't remember, then finally cried herself to sleep.

MC HEARS THE BELLS from St. Anthony's Church. Since when do they chime all night long? The digital clock on her nightstand flashes on and off, running backward. Three A.M. Blink. Two A.M. Blink. One A.M. Blink.

She hears a thumping noise at the door of her bedroom. Why had she closed it tonight? She never closes it. And there's a peephole in the door. How did that get there, an enormous peephole on an inside door? She stumbles out of bed and looks through the peephole. She can see all of Houston through that peephole. All of Revere Beach. She sees Jake and the spotted gray Spartan Q sail over the brush jump. Then a trot half-pass right. Then a fan oxer. *Good Spartan Q.* But why are dressage movements and jumps all in the same show? No matter. Spartan Q will get treats tonight.

She squints as Jake and Spartan Q do the final halt and salute, then ride away. She looks again. There's Rumney Marsh right outside her bedroom. Jake and Spartan Q ride into Rumney Marsh. She strains to see them.

Buzzzzzzzz!

MC jumps back as her buzzer rings. Why is there a doorbell at the threshold of her bedroom? It must be Aunt G's bell. She lives in Aunt G's apartment now, she remembers. She hears a low moan, and then soft scratching on the lower part of the door. A puppy? She's always wanted a dog but Jake won't let her have one.

The scratching continues; the moan grows louder.

"Who's there?" she yells. It's *Jake,* she thinks. She'll ask him again for a puppy.

"MC."

She can just make out her name, and now she's sure it's Jake. He sounds drunk. Or hurt. That's it; Jake is hurt.

MC opens the door, ready to rail at him for getting into some bar fight again.

Jake falls onto the threshold; his bleeding head touches her soft brown carpet.

MC gets on her knees, cradles his head in her hands. Blood is pouring out of his head; his rusty leather jacket is sticky with blood and dirt. She wants to ask him what happened, but when she opens her mouth, no sounds come out.

MC sees a trocar sticking out of Jake's stomach. When she was a little girl, she begged her father to let her watch while he showed Robert how to use it. The trocar is sticking out from the right side of Jake's stomach. MC knows this is the last step, after Jake has been embalmed. He doesn't look embalmed. She sees her father injecting a fluid and hears him tell Robert, "We need to pay special attention to the bowels and the liver. We don't want any problems upstairs in the parlor."

She hears Jake whisper her name. He's alive; he can't be embalmed. She bends low to hear, but she can't tell what he's saying. She knows he's telling her who did this to him, who put him on the embalming table, but she can't hear. She is useless. Jake is dying and she is useless.

She brushes her hair back; it's sticky where it has fallen over Jake's wound. She swallows and tastes frittata with chilies. She pulls the phone off the table near Jake's body and pushes 911, but the buttons don't move. She presses hard; they won't budge.

When she turns back to Jake, he seems to have fallen asleep. He's curled up, his breathing faint. She stuffs a pillow from the couch under his head and goes to her bathroom. She finds a box of gauze, scissors, and alcohol, and carries them back to the living room.

MC kneels down by Jake. He's rolled partway onto his back. His face is pasty, but he looks strangely relaxed. Her heart clutches as she reaches for his wrist.

She lays her head on his shoulder and goes to sleep with him.

MC WOKE UP CRYING and shivering, all the covers on the floor. Her clock had stopped.

TWENTY-SEVEN

Coyotes? In Revere?" Rose asked me, for once giving me the upper hand in local lore.

I decided to give her a taste of being on the receiving end of an avalanche of information.

"Absolutely. The Revere High Science Club is doing a project called 'The Urban Coyote Field Study.' I have the full report if you need it, with appendices on the current poor state of science education in the United States, how students seldom actually experience real-life science. Daniel Endicott's students are also contributing to correcting the misperception of coyotes as dangerous predators that should be eliminated. They have a trap at a North Revere site, and they've captured a twenty-seven-pound female, which they named Cinnamon, for her color and spiciness. Her age can be determined from the wear on her teeth. They're working with Tufts and BC and with local veterinarians." I stopped for a breath, and started again. "Several students have been able to observe coyote pups raised in captivity—"

I took a deep breath, and a drink of water.

Rose laughed heartily and held up her hand. "You need water? You're not as good as I am at holding your breath for an entire story. But, okay. I get it. Sometimes I go on too long." She paused, her face reconfiguring into a serious expression. "I guess we shouldn't be joking this way. MC is very, very upset, and I don't want anyone to think that I'm glad in any way—"

"Rose, no one would think that. Not MC, not me. We'll just have to give her a little time to adjust to this. It's awful for everyone."

"Thanks, Gloria. And you'll find out who did it, you and Matt, I know."

I hoped she was right. I'd never had such a case, barely able to follow one lead when another crisis turned up. Matt and I had been so excited about what the Houston transcript revealed. Berger had missed some connections, mostly because neither he nor anyone in the department was seriously working on the Nina Martin case. With Matt out a good part of the time, everyone's load had increased, and for all they knew, they'd found the only killer—Rusty Forman might even have been Nina's jealous boyfriend, coincidentally an ex-con.

I hated to admit, too, that Jean had a point—I knew that if MC were not involved, I would also have abandoned the case long ago, and focused completely on taking care of Matt.

We expected that Jake's murder would reopen the entire investigation, however, and I felt optimistic that all the threads would come together soon.

As far as Matt knew, Rose had casually stopped by to see him. It was pure coincidence that she might hang around with him while his partner and I went to interview fifteen-year-old Jacqueline Peters, the RHS freshman who'd stumbled onto Jake Powers's body. Matt, asleep at the moment, was doing well, but I still didn't like the idea of his being left alone. What if he had a relapse and fainted again, this time without a dining room chair to support him? And what if Jean dropped in, found him unattended, and sued for custody? This was my next uncharitable thought.

"Why did they leave him alive, I wonder?" Rose asked, her ad hoc remarks often leaving me speechless for a moment. *She means Jake, not Matt,* I instructed my brain.

"Whoever shot him probably didn't dream anyone would be crawling around the marsh late at night. But as I learned from Daniel, coyotes are nocturnal and—"

Rose rolled her eyes here. "No, no."

I laughed. "I'm not going on with this, just to tell you that the class did the tracking during hours of darkness."

"Interesting. That poor child."

"Jacqueline Peters. Aren't you going to tell me about her family?"

"Only because you ask. Her mother used to be married to Timmy Peters, who did some handiwork for us on Tuttle, but then ran off not long after Jacqueline's little brother was born. Then the mother remarried." She leaned in close. "To tell you the truth, I think the little one was the new husband's, before the fact, if you know what I mean. Don't you love these information sessions?"

I did.

"How is MC doing? This must be very hard for her."

"She finally picked up the phone this morning. She sounds awful. I'm giving her another day, and then I'm going to force her to go shopping."

She gave me a weak smile, one that said she knew this was not something a trip to Boston's Copley Place, one of Rose's favorite shopping venues, could fix.

"Is Frank going to take care of Jake's body?"

Rose nodded. "Frank will prepare it for delivery to Texas. MC knows to keep away from the prep room."

I heard Berger climb the steps to the porch and headed him off, opening the door before he could ring the bell and wake Matt up. I wasn't really ready for an interview with a teenager. My brain felt crowded with information I hadn't had time to process. It seemed every time I was ready to put two and two together, I was jerked away by another crisis. Stalkers, one murder after another, Matt's illness, Jean's hostility.

I knew that there were still more clues to be followed in MC's e-mail, in Lorna's records, in Jake Powers's bute reference, in the HPD transcript, maybe even in Wayne Gallen's ramblings. Suddenly I felt as tired as Matt and wanted to sleep more than anything.

"Are you ready?" Berger asked.

"You bet," I said.

JACQUELINE PETERS lived on the left side of a duplex with its unkempt front on Hutchins Street. The pale blue paint was chipped, the garden tools rusted, the chain-link fence lopsided and full of holes. George Berger and I climbed shaky steps to a tiny porch and rang the tiny metal doorbell, what I would have called "original equipment" in lab talk, meaning it had come with the house, probably built in the 1940s. I smiled as Berger pointed silently to dropping strings of Christmas lights around the edge of the Peters side of the porch—either two months early, or ten months overdue for dismantling.

"Mrs. Peters?" Berger asked, holding his badge against a dirty storm door, in the face of a wiry young woman.

"I'm Jacqueline's mother. Mrs. Ramos," she said in a voice so constricted I wondered if she had something to hide. Then I remembered how intimidating a police officer could be to someone who didn't live with one.

Mrs. Ramos, in stocking feet and tight, black Capri pants, formerly known as pedal pushers, led us through an uncarpeted living room and dining room to a large kitchen area that smelled of unhealthy breakfast meat. We passed two small children and two television sets on the way. I had the feeling Mrs. Ramos had been watching at least one of the shows, neither of which was Sunday morning political commentary.

"Someone go get Jacqueline," Mrs. Ramos yelled. Her loud voice caught me off guard, and I jumped. "Sorry, didn't mean to scare you. They never hear me over the TVs. Jacqueline's upstairs. Don't keep her too long, okay? This thing's got her upset."

Berger and I gave reassuring nods. "We have just a few questions," he said. "This is Dr. Gloria Lamerino, our consultant. She's very good with young people—she's had a lot of experience with this kind of thing."

Making me sound like a child psychologist, something Matt would never do. Berger had prepared me to take the lead, however, pleading incompetence with teenagers. "Besides there's the woman thing, you know," he'd said, making curly motions with his index finger in the air next to his head.

I sighed. *This partnership is temporary,* I told myself, and Berger's doing his best.

Jacqueline Peters, chubby enough to remind me of myself in high school, came down the stairs. She was a large-framed girl and I figured Timmy Peters, wherever he was, had contributed the body-shape gene, since the now-Mrs. Ramos was filament-wire thin. Jacqueline joined Berger and me at the Formica kitchen table while her mother, arms crossed in front of her, leaned against a stove piled high with sticky saucepans and a skillet.

"Am I supposed to leave?" Mrs. Ramos asked, tapping her foot on the linoleum.

Berger shrugged. "Sometimes when parents are around, kids tend to—"

"It would probably go much quicker if you were to wait in the other room," I said with a smile.

"Right," Berger said.

Mrs. Ramos pushed herself off the stove, went into the living room, and pulled an accordion door many shades of brown behind her, closing us in with Jacqueline and the heavy, greasy odor, but letting through the sounds of daytime television.

"Do you remember when I came to your classroom?" I asked Jacqueline. A blank look. "I brought some materials and we made a geodesic dome." I pushed aside the reminder of the little Styrofoam balls rolling into the watery gutter, of Wayne Gallen in my car.

Jacqueline shrugged. "I guess." Not flattering to a would-be teacher, or someone as good with children as Berger claimed I was, but then I didn't especially remember her being there that day, either. Maybe she was absent, I thought, consoling myself.

"What you saw in the marsh—it must have been awful for you, Jacqueline." I leaned across the shiny red table, trying to land my elbows between drips of milk and syrup.

Jacqueline nodded, lifting her eyebrows, widening her eyes, as if she were being surprised all over again by a dead body in the marsh. The cheers of a game show audience rose up behind the accordion door.

"Is there anything I can do to make it easier for you to talk about what happened? Would you like to get yourself a glass of milk or some water?"

She shook her head, causing large amounts of dark, curly hair to swing back and forth. Jacqueline was the best-groomed person in the Peters-Ramos household, her black T-shirt looking clean and smoothed out, if not pressed. No food stains were visible on its rubbery neon cartoon picture of a music group I've never heard of. I wondered if she'd dressed for this interview.

'Okay. What happened was, Cinnamon had some pups and we were trying to find them, 'cause they got separated from their mother, and we wanted to feed them. We had meat and stuff. And it was dark. We always go in the dark. Coyotes are nocturnal animals." Jacqueline sounded like a bright student. I hoped her home environment was supportive of good study habits. "I went off on my own 'cause I saw a huge bird, maybe a vulture, although I'm not sure what they look like except for our science book, or even if there are any in Revere. Mr. Endicott gives us extra points for spotting something unusual, so I went to check."

Jacqueline sniffed and rubbed her eyes. I stole a look at Berger. He sat back far enough from the table that he could keep his notebook hidden on his lap. I dug out a packet of tissues and put it in front of Jacqueline. The televisions blared on.

"Take your time. You're doing really fine."

Another loud sniff. "Okay. I was sneaking up on this bird that was maybe a vulture, but I made a noise on a loose rock or something and the bird flew away. Then I saw something right under where it was. This, like, bright blue jacket—I thought it was empty, I mean, you know, just the jacket. And when I got close it started moving, and I went over and it was—this man, really bleeding and moaning. I was going to do some CPR but we just learned it last week, and I was afraid I'd hurt him even more. And…and…"

Jacqueline broke into tears, quite out of proportion to the situation. It's not as if she'd known Jake, I thought. Then I guessed the problem. I patted her head.

"I'll bet you were nervous about putting your mouth on his, too?"

She raised her shoulders and shivered. "Uh-huh. So I probably killed him."

I glanced at the accordion door, expecting her mother to come and rescue her, but realized the television sounds would mask Jacqueline's breakdown. I felt so sorry for the child, imagining the burden of guilt she'd been carrying, that I came up with a lie. Berger's influence, I thought.

"Jacqueline, the doctors said the man had been so badly hurt, nothing you could have done would have helped."

Sniff. "Really?"

"Really. This might be a lesson for you, though, to get some more training, in case you need it again." Jacqueline gave me an *I don't think so* look. "But not for a long, long time," I said.

A smile, finally. "We're almost through, Jacqueline. Just one or two more questions."

"Okay."

"Did you see anyone in the marsh? Anyone besides Mr. Endicott and your classmates?"

She shook her head.

"Did the man say anything before—did you hear anything from the man before you called for Mr. Endicott?"

"He was moaning a lot and he said something like 'Sarta's dead' or 'Satan's dead,' maybe, I don't know. It was hard to tell."

"Could it have been 'Spartan's dead'?" I asked.

Jacqueline shrugged. "I guess. Yeah, it could have been Spartan."

Spartan Q. Jake's horse.

Another dead horse?

TWENTY-EIGHT

MATT AND I FOLLOWED the hospital's faded blue dots to the waiting room for radiation therapy. This would be our route five days a week for six weeks. We'd re-read all the literature, which predicted no ill effects until well into the treatment, if at all. We'd stocked up on bouillon and cranberry juice. No citrus or food with small seeds. Matt had circled in red an item on controlling fatigue: *Let others cook for you and eat six or seven small meals a day.*

"Do you really think two cannoli are what they mean by a meal?" I'd asked.

We'd both finally finished the transcript from Houston, the RPD was investigating Jake Powers's murder, and the problem of locating his horse, dead or alive, was also theirs, I decided. I could focus on Matt. And MC, in her grief over Jake Powers's death. And the microchip problem that had brought Nina Martin to Revere. Not too bad a workload.

I thought how different our conversation probably sounded, compared to that of other couples—normal couples, I meant—on their way to X-ray.

"It's just like a regular microchip, with an integrated circuit coil," I explained, as we turned corner after corner, avoiding the yellow triangles and green squares that would have sent us off to obstetrics or orthopedics. "The only difference is that the IC—the integrated circuit—for an identification implant would be in a container that's biofriendly."

"Is that a real word, 'biofriendly'?"

"I don't think so. I made it up just for you."

"I'm flattered. I thought I'd been reading about this for years, though. Don't they monitor railroad cars with the same kind of device in the track?"

"You're right. Remote sensing of passive identification isn't new."

"Is that what I said? I'm smarter than I think."

I loved Matt's jovial mood, his normal self. I loved thinking the time he'd spend under an X-ray machine would be a tiny blip in his day, not affecting his positive outlook and his sense of humor.

I smiled and nodded. "What's different is the miniaturization that's possible with new materials, and also the fact that we now have sealants like biocompatible glass to encase the device. I'll know more after I talk to Dr. Schofield."

I'd managed to convince Berger that I was the best one to talk to Dr. Schofield since he wasn't officially a suspect in anything—his name had come up only in the parallel constructions Matt and I had made from the horse/vet/buckyball equation we derived from the Houston transcript. I also shaded the truth a bit by letting Berger think "Scho"—the nickname Daniel Endicott used for him—and I were buddies.

When a nurse appeared and called Matt's name, she seemed to be out of context. Weren't we at home or in a car, at one of our usual tutorial sessions? Either from Matt to me about some new police protocol, or from me to him on one of the elements of the periodic table. I'd forgotten we were in a hospital waiting for Matt to climb into his custom-fit Styrofoam mold and be pummeled with high-energy electromagnetic radiation. Just as well.

Matt left me for what was billed as a fifteen-minute procedure, but was closer to forty minutes. I hoped the X-ray event itself took up only a small fraction of that time.

I'd left my own reading material in the car, so I flipped through out-of-date, sticky magazines. Fortunately, there was no story I cared about enough to miss the torn-out pages. I scanned a women's publication. Better than auto racing, fishing, professional sports. At least there were interesting recipes. I read the ten best fashion tips for the long-gone summer season, a reported coupling between celebrities that had probably been dissolved by now, a review of a movie that featured famous human voices coming out of animated animal bodies, and the progress of sextuplets that arrived courtesy of a fertility drug. I wondered who subscribed to this kind of periodical at home, when there was *Scientific American, Technology Review, Discover.*

"Done," Matt said, re-entering the waiting room.

"Good. We're on our way," I said, meaning many things.

DR. SCHOFIELD was most accommodating, agreeing to meet me on short notice on Monday afternoon. His office had fewer animal pictures than Lorna's, I noticed. During the few minutes I had to wait, I availed myself of yet another stack of "foreign" waiting-room magazines. *Veterinary Forum, Veterinary Industry, DVM News,* and *Compendium—Continuing Education for the Practicing Veterinarian.*

I glanced at an article on a new technique for removing a horse's ovaries and an ad for an analyzer of what were euphemistically termed "canine, feline, and equine veterinary samples."

I'm going to have to start carrying around Physics Today, I thought.

Dr. Schofield ushered me into his office. In his white lab coat, he could have been a spectroscopist, like me—not that he would be flattered by the comparison. What Dr. Schofield did not look like was a murderer, especially standing in front of a coffee grinder in his office, the mark of a gentleman. But I'd learned that even murderers might dress well, have nice smiles, and be fussy about their coffee.

We started on a friendly note, commending each other for our work with Revere High students, discussing how important it was to get young people interested in science. We'd both read an article about resources teachers could use to bring the science classroom to life.

"I'm interested in knowing more about your project with Daniel Endicott's students," I told him once we were settled with excellent espressos. "I'd like to see the microchips you use to track the coyotes."

"I doubt it," he said, with a satisfied grin.

"I, uh…" Caught. Clearly, Scho—he'd asked me to use his

nickname—wasn't one to waffle. I felt my face flush, and tried not to squirm to add to the pitiful sight.

He smiled, but not offensively, even though he'd exposed me as a poor excuse for a detective. "Lorna Frederick phoned me over the weekend and told me to expect you. It seems we're both suspects in a murder."

Two murders, maybe three, I noted. Dr. Schofield's—I abandoned the notion of calling this imposing gentleman "Scho"— pleasant tone and demeanor said he wasn't worried a bit. I wondered if Lorna was.

I stared past his bald head to an anatomy chart of a horse, noting with interest where the various organs lay. I wondered if I could stall by asking the resting pulse of, say, a thoroughbred.

I cleared my throat. "Well, you know what the police say— everyone's a suspect until the killer is found."

"Nicely put. Are you the police?"

I laughed. "Not quite, but I am a consultant, and since you brought up the most unfortunate subject of murder—did you know Nina Martin or Jake Powers?"

I watched for signs of guilt, as if I had an infallible list of symptoms. In any case, Dr. Schofield was calm, sure of himself.

"Not Nina Martin, I'm afraid, and Jake Powers was just a passing acquaintance. I met him once or twice through Lorna."

"And Lorna knew him through equestrian activities."

"That's my understanding."

"Did you by any chance implant a microchip into Jake Powers's horse?"

"Hmm." Dr. Schofield went into a modified *Thinker* posture, elbow in hand, and seemed genuinely pondering the question. "If I did it would be in my records. I must admit often my technician does the actual insertion."

"Can you check your files, if they're handy?"

"Not a problem." Dr. Schofield's records were as well-kept on the inside as the outside, and he quickly pulled a printout from a folder in his desk drawer.

Listed were the horse's name, the owner, an ID number for the chip, the location, the breed, and a column for comments.

We read down the list and stopped at a line near the bottom. "Here it is," Dr. Schofield said.

SPARTAN Q POWERS 87&541*27 MA APPALOOSA NONE

If he knew that Spartan Q was dead, he gave no indication. I didn't know why I didn't tell him my suspicions about the dead horse at that moment, except that I felt I'd get more information if I withheld that fact.

I wondered about the state of health of the other horses on the list, and whether one of them might be the horse whose death PI Nina Martin was investigating.

"May I have a copy of this list?" I asked, aiming my tone halfway between casual and authoritative. *If you don't give it to me*, I tried to imply, *someone more official will be by later with a court order.*

Dr. Schofield's confident, almost fatherly presence intimidated me, and strictly speaking I had no authorization to ask for an alibi or question him further about the murders. I'd told Berger I'd restrict myself to learning about microchip ID technology so we could understand better if Ms. Trumble in Houston had a case.

"I'll bet Houston PD doesn't have a consultant like you," Berger had told me.

I bet they did, especially since nanotechnology was commonly thought to have been born in that city, but I'd accepted the compliment graciously.

Dr. Schofield weighed my request only a few seconds, then buzzed his secretary and asked her to have a copy for me before I left.

Too easy, I thought. It was time for a technology lesson from Dr. Schofield.

I gave him an open, honest smile. "I really do want to know about microchip ID technology. Unless Lorna has advised you not to talk about it?"

He laughed. "Or my attorney? No, I'd be happy to talk to you about the new chips. I'm afraid it might be boring, given your background."

I shook my head and ran the fingers of my left hand over the back of my right hand. "My expertise ends at skin level. I'm out of my league with biological sciences."

"Well, I'm sure you're a quick study." Dr. Schofield pulled a binder from a row of them lined up across the top of his fine oak bookcase. The dark blue binders were different sizes, but matched in color, with neatly typed labels, all in the same font. Not the eclectic mix of office supplies in my former labs. I figured it might be more necessary to give attention to décor when the public was paying directly for your expertise. My old lab, with constantly recycled, relabeled folders, wouldn't have inspired confidence from outside visitors.

Dr. Schofield opened the binder to a page with a circuit diagram. A thing of beauty, compared to an anatomy chart. No messy blood flow, for one thing. No possibility of cancer, for another.

"We can skip the schematic, I'm sure," he said, moving on to a specifications sheet for an EID, an electronic identification device. He followed the items down the page with his finger, summarizing the structure. "A tiny passive transponder, small enough to fit inside a hypodermic needle, is encapsulated in biocompatible glass. Each transponder is preprogrammed with a unique multi-digit, unalterable alphanumeric code. Depending on the brand, there are billions or even trillions of possible combinations of strings, without duplication."

Nothing new so far. Unlike a tracking circuit, which gave out a signal of its own, a passive circuit like the EID was closer to a bar code on a supermarket item, requiring a reader to scan it for the information.

"It's like a bar code, only using radio frequency," I said.

"Good analogy. When a reader is passed over the implantation site, a radio signal activates the transponder and the detector receives the ID, which the user sees as an LCD. With one phone call, the number can be traced back to the owner."

"Very nice. Why doesn't every horse owner do this? Is it very expensive?"

"No, not really. A lot of horse owners think their animals are in a secure location and don't need one, or perhaps that their horses aren't very valuable."

"A little like the rationale for home security systems, isn't it?" I said, thinking of the lack of an alarm in my Fernwood Avenue home.

He nodded. "Indeed. Also, there's no standardization. Company A's chips cannot be read by Company B's equipment, so that's a nuisance. What else is new, huh?"

I nodded and we chatted amiably about the drawbacks of the great American capitalist system with its lack of industry standardization—automobiles, computers, and even commercial nuclear power reactors.

I eased us back into the microchip industry.

"How do you implant the device?"

"With a simple hypodermic. The chips have a special coating so they don't migrate through the animal's body. We inject under the skin and very soon a layer of connective tissue forms around the chip and it stays there forever. It's quick and painless. And of course we keep a record of which chip went into which horse, so it's easy to track the horse's medical history."

I was ready for the big questions. The first one surprised even me. "Do you know Dr. Owen Evans in Houston?" The doctor who installed the chip into the Houston horse—it occurred to me that if there was some kind of scam going on, they'd all know each other. Scam Theory, by police consultant Gloria Lamerino. I was amazed I remembered the Texas doctor's name.

Dr. Schofield leaned back and folded his arms. *Uh-oh.* "I've never met him, but I've seen his name."

"Here's another question I have, Scho." *Now that you're squirming.* "What exactly are you doing for the buckyball program at the Charger Street lab?"

Dr. Schofield rotated his expensive-looking pen around an axis perpendicular to its length. First one end hit his desk, then the other.

"Let's say we're an investment in the future."

I didn't budge. *Try the Matt Gennaro technique,* I told myself, *and wait him out.* Dr. Schofield came through.

"As you know, Lorna's nanotechnology program is geared to

smart medicines, and eventually will develop a small molecule drug that will need to be tested."

I nodded but said nothing, maintaining an interested if noncommittal look.

"On animals," Dr. Schofield said. "Now, they're not ready for that quite yet—even that phase has to have FDA approval, of course. But eventually—"

Now I was starting to feel sorry for Scho and thought I'd help him out.

"Let me see if I have this right—you and Dr. Evans are on the nanotechnology payroll now, just for putting in EID chips, so you'll be on board when the animal testing starts at some unspecified time in the future? Even though the chips really have nothing to do with any of the nanotechnology projects in Lorna's program?"

He nodded—a flushed, embarrassed nod.

I sat back. Could this be it? Did Lorna kill Nina Martin in order not to expose this? I'd already ruled out Scho as the killer. I believed he didn't know that Spartan Q was dead. In fact, even I didn't know for sure that Jake's horse was dead; we had assumed it from Jacqueline Peters's statement. As far as I knew Spartan Q's body hadn't been found.

I wondered where and how horses died. Did they all turn violent like Ms. Trumble's horse at the end? And how did you bury an animal that probably weighed more than half a ton?

I blinked my eyes, returning to Dr. Schofield's office. I noticed increasing perspiration on his wide brow, a film that extended over his bald head to the back of his neck.

"You may think this is out of the ordinary, Gloria." *Fraud* is what I was thinking. "But what we're doing is not uncommon. It's not as if we're—"

"One more question, Scho." I interrupted, not about to let a scientist, medical or otherwise, off the hook for even the slightest misconduct. If indeed that's all this was. "Are you familiar with bute?"

Dr. Schofield relaxed considerably, as if this were his physics doctoral oral examination and he'd finally been asked an easy question, like "What are Newton's Laws?" after a round of quizzing on Einstein's Unified Field Theory.

"Bute—our shorthand for phenylbutazone. A nonsteroidal anti-inflammatory drug and cyclooxygenase inhibitor. We give it typically for lameness, which might be the result of soft tissue injury, or muscle soreness, or bone and joint problems. Bute can be administered intravenously or orally and—"

"Thank you, Scho. That will be all for now."

I stood and gathered my purse and briefcase. I picked up a copy of the microchip printout on my way out.

I didn't even care what cyclooxygenase was.

TWENTY-NINE

I HATED IMPURE SCIENTISTS. But was Dr. Schofield a killer? Over a few dollars garnered to establish a relationship between himself and a laboratory? It didn't fit.

The streets between Dr. Schofield's office on Squire Road and the mortuary on Tuttle Street hadn't changed much since I'd lived in Revere during the first years of my life. Squire Road was dominated by a large outdoor strip mall and the unimposing entrance to the Charger Street lab. As I passed the road to the research facility, I thought of the scientists, engineers, and other staff I'd met since I returned to my hometown. Of all of them, Andrea Cabrini was the only one I'd maintained contact with. Of course, some of them were now in prison. Others were dead.

I passed Tomasso's Restaurant and Coffee Annex and hoped our Tuesday Girls' Night Out would be resurrected soon.

I tried to concentrate on what I'd learned from this interview. Dr. Schofield's attitude and confession confused me. His connection to Lorna Frederick hadn't posed any problems initially—he'd even joked about Lorna's phone call and about being a murder suspect. He must have learned from her that I'd found his name on her payroll. My guess was that they'd discussed me extensively and decided what to let me in on, that he'd confess to getting paid for implanting chips for which his clients also paid him.

I got no insight into the murder of either Nina Martin or Jake Powers. Either those were entirely separate issues, or Dr. Schofield was holding back, perhaps under Lorna Frederick's orders. *Or I'm grasping at straws,* I thought.

I reached for the notebook and pen I kept in my front seat console and scribbled at red lights. No law against that, I hoped, con-

sidering the growing number of states legislating against cell
phone use while driving. With the pad balanced on the cup
holder, I wrote in my personal shorthand.

> EIDs con'ction to bucky?
> Scho and Owens—Vet scam?
> Bute?

My lists were starting to replicate each other. The same questions, and no answers.

I KNOCKED ON THE DOOR of my old apartment. I knew MC was
home. Martha, Rose's very observant assistant, had told me she'd
seen MC looking out her bedroom window as Martha pulled into
the driveway.

"I wanted to tell her how sorry I am about her friend's death,
but she's not answering her door or her phone," Martha had said,
waving the can of air freshener that was as much a part of her
look as her trendy jewelry. Martha typically wore a necklace,
bracelets, and earrings—a matched set, as if they'd come as
prizes in successive cereal boxes.

"She needs a little time, I guess," I'd said.

"Oh, for sure. And, oh, I'm real sorry about Detective Gennaro's—" Martha leaned closer to me "—illness." *A non-cancer-
speaker,* I thought. "But he's lucky to have you to cover for him
on these terrible Rumney Marsh cases."

I smiled a thank-you, having long ago stopped correcting
Martha's notion that I was a "real policewoman," as she'd introduced me to her second-grader twin boys.

"I'm on it," I'd said, and climbed the last flight to MC's door,
barely ducking a spray of cedar-smelling freshener. I wondered
if Martha would be so obsessive about odors if she worked in a
bank or a bookstore instead of a funeral home. Yes, I decided.

I stood on the maroon-carpeted landing, my eyes passing
fondly over the familiar setting—the polished mahogany railing
and baseboard, the subtle swirling pattern in the wallpaper, the
pair of shell-shaped sconces that gave out a pinkish light. I

knocked again, and called MC's name. I chose not to use the ir-
ritating door buzzer, in case she was asleep. But if she was awake
anywhere in the apartment, she'd hear me and she'd know I'd
keep at it.

I put my eye to the peephole—I remembered the unhappy circumstances that had precipitated its installation—and made a
silly face.

I heard the dead bolt click. It worked.

MC fell against me and sobbed. I patted her back and made
soothing sounds. Nothing articulate seemed appropriate until
MC was ready. Her own words were scattered, but I understood
that she felt guilty.

"I should have told Jake about how crazy Wayne's been lately.
What if I could have prevented Wayne from killing him?"

"We don't know for sure that Wayne killed him, MC, and we
can't be sure it would have made a difference anyway, whether
you'd said something or not."

MC was in dark blue sweats that looked like she'd slept—or
not slept—in them. We sat on a small couch Rose had bought
for the apartment, in purples and blues that were of a different
color family than my blue rockers. I suspected the old rockers
would become a charitable donation the next time MC took a
close look at her décor.

MC brought her breathing under control. "You probably
haven't heard this. The police have witnesses that say they saw
Jake and Wayne fighting outside that bar by the marsh. They were
threatening each other."

I'd gone from Dr. Schofield's office to the mortuary, with only
one quick stop at the grocery store to pick up a treat for MC. It
had been about two hours since I'd checked my phone messages. It didn't take long for me to fall behind in this case, I noted.

"Is Wayne MIA again?"

She nodded. "He seems to just disappear." She snapped her
fingers. "Like that. You'd think he'd stand out in Revere with
those filthy cowboy clothes and that mustache."

"Missing or not, it doesn't make Wayne guilty."

"I suppose."

"Do you know anyone else Jake might have had a run-in with? Anyone from his work, or from his horse interests?"

She shook her head. "Not really. He managed hydrocarbon conversion technology—so we'd all have enough fuel for our SUVs, you might say. He rode horses." She shrugged her shoulders. "It's not like he was connected, or anything."

"'Connected'? You sound like your mother." I meant it as endearment, but my comment did nothing to help MC relax.

Time to bring out the treat. "Why don't I fix you our special comfort drink?"

MC smiled. She knew what I meant. "I don't have any—"

"I do."

I dug into my oversized purse, and made a dramatic showing of a can of Ghirardelli chocolate, a San Francisco staple that had happily made its way to East Coast groceries.

MC clapped, as if acknowledging the performance. "Remember going to that factory every year? Having humungous ice cream sundaes and planning how we'd wait until no one was looking and then vault ourselves into that big vat of melted chocolate?"

"I certainly do. And there's more." I pulled out a quart of milk. "The real thing. I figured you'd have only low-fat."

She smiled and nodded. "I drink two percent. But not today. Let's go for the butterfat."

The hot drink did wonders to calm MC, making me question the myth that there was caffeine in chocolate. We sipped quietly for a few minutes, but the parade of expressions on MC's face told me we were far from finished with our conversation.

"Aunt G, do you ever think you just don't know how to live?"

"All the time."

"No, really. I mean like you don't even know the basics of living? Like maybe all these years you've been brushing your teeth the wrong way…and that every single choice you've ever made was the wrong one."

It wasn't a question, but I answered anyway. "We all feel that way sometimes, MC, especially when something as horrible as this happens."

"I have no idea right now how I'm supposed to feel, where I want to live, what I want to do with my life. No idea at all."

"Probably because you have an overabundance of choices. You can do anything. You're intelligent, healthy, nothing's closed to you, except you're perilously close to the cutoff age for military service." I welcomed MC's smile at that observation. "Too many choices can be as bad as none. No wonder you have a headache."

Her eyes were red and puffy and her hair not as fresh and bouncy as it should have been, but I thought I saw signs of recovery in her smooth breathing and relaxed shoulders.

"Have you always known what you want, Aunt G?"

I laughed. "You mean you haven't noticed my erratic migration patterns? Anyway, times are different now. When I got out of college, the options were few. Women became either teachers or nurses, until they got married. I didn't really want to do that—be a housewife—mostly because my own mother didn't make that life look very good. But I was ready to follow the rules, until…well, you know about Al."

MC nodded and gave me a wide-eyed look. "How could I have forgotten? How hard that must have been. Here I am whining about Jake, and you lost your fiancé right before your wedding."

I didn't believe in that kind of comparison, but I let MC think about it, hoping it would give her perspective.

"You probably don't want to handle the loss the way I did," I said. "Move away, hole up, in many ways avoid the problem."

"If Al hadn't died, you might have stayed in Revere all your life, had three kids, like my mother. I'm sure she's never looked back."

Poor MC, I thought, *if she's trying to reproduce her parents' relationship.* I couldn't contradict her notion that Rose and Frank Galigani had the perfect marriage and every intention of keeping it that way.

"And nothing would have been wrong with my remaining in Revere with a husband and three children, either. It's not what you do, it's whether you have the sense of contributing to life in some way…well, now I really am going off, aren't I?"

"I hear you though. It's just that I did so many things wrong with Jake. I let him get away with so much when we lived together. Then, just as we were finally starting to get it right…he's gone."

I didn't want to tell her what I'd learned from Matt about DVR—domestic violence recidivism. An abuser seldom gets converted, he'd told me. If he stops, it's usually because he's gotten beat up himself and is no longer strong enough to batter someone else.

I noticed for the first time a photo of Jake Powers in a frame on MC's end table. He was astride a spotted gray horse, the deceased Spartan Q, I presumed. Jake sat erect, a high white collar that could have been a scarf or a turtleneck jersey keeping his head straight and his neck rigid. I wondered if Jake had as many horse-related tchotchkes as Lorna, or if collecting symbols of your interest—like my large assortment of science-related pins— was a female thing. I fingered the pin I wore today, a square representation of an integrated circuit, bought from an on-line computer club.

MC had followed my gaze to Jake's photo. She put down her mug and picked up the photo, holding it in both hands. "I found this in a box I hadn't unpacked. Jake was so happy when he was riding. And competing—he loved winning. He loved Spartan Q, his jumper, and Werner, his dressage horse. He gave them only the best treats, home-baked cookies he bought from a friend who had a side business. No store-bought generics for Spartan Q or Werner."

MC talked more about Jake, and I let her show me a video of dressage. I had no interest in a competition with prancing horses, but at that moment I would even have watched slapstick comedy, which I hated, if MC wanted me to.

MC scanned through to a prize-winning performance by Jake and the dark brown Werner. She narrated the moves for me. Canter pirouette right, extended trot, zigzag half-pass, and a gentle tap dance called a piaffe. Or it might have been pilaf.

Knowing I'd never be tested on the information, I concentrated instead on the peripherals. The ring, or corral, or whatever the fenced-in area was called, was draped in the banners of advertising sponsors. I checked off the obvious ads for saddles, insurance, riding apparel. But a beef restaurant? Would these equestrians who treated their horses like crown princes really have dinner later at the expense of a cow?

I also tried to apply a bit of basic physics, calculating the tension in each very skinny leg of a horse weighing about fifteen hundred pounds.

MC's video camera lingered on the score chart, presumably to show Jake Powers and Werner in first place, with 76.525 percent.

MC laughed and held up her hand. "Don't say it, Aunt G. I know what you're thinking."

But I had to say it. "Three significant decimal places! It looks like a freshman lab report."

MC stopped the tape. "Okay, that's it. Thanks for being a good sport, Aunt G. I feel a lot better."

"I know it doesn't seem so now, MC, but you'll meet someone you won't have to work so hard with."

MC shook her head, drained her hot chocolate. "I don't think so. I feel like I've hit the wall here. I'm getting too old for the dating scene."

"I managed to skip that scene," I said. I spread my arms wide, as if to encompass an absent Matt Gennaro. "And look at me."

"I hope I do as well," MC said.

I did, too.

One other concern had been crowding my thoughts, and as much as I didn't want to worry MC, I decided I couldn't let it go.

"Have you thought about what Jake's murder means to you, MC? I mean in terms of your own safety?"

She nodded. "I sure have. When Nina Martin was murdered, I thought maybe she was the one they, whoever they are, were after all along. Now, Jake. Either it's over, or…"

I was torn—should I try to put her mind at ease or keep her alert? Should I protect her from any notions of danger? MC was an adult, I reminded myself, not the little girl I waited for at a gate in San Francisco International Airport every summer.

"It's probably over," I said. "But please be careful until we have Jake's murderer."

"You're still working on it, right?"

"I certainly am. Just be careful, okay?"

MC gave me a hug. "You already said that. I love you, Aunt G."

"And I love you." *And woe to him who hurts you,* I thought.

THIRTY

I TURNED ONTO Fernwood Avenue from Broadway, passing the former site of a favorite high schoolers' pizza parlor, now a professional building. I could almost hear the parade of Italian-American crooners that we all loved, coming from the small jukeboxes attached to the wall of each red booth. Frank Sinatra, Perry Como, Julius La Rosa, and Jerry Vale, nee Vitaliano.

We'd walk down School Street, picking up classmates along the way, singing "Don't Let the Stars Get in Your Eyes," "There's No Tomorrow," "Love and Marriage," "Pretend You Don't See Her," as if we understood the words. As if any of our hearts had been broken, or our dreams crushed, as they would be later in life—when Connie would lose a twelve-year-old daughter in a diving accident and Olga's husband would be fired from his job and commit suicide.

I wondered what songs Alysse and Petey, Jean's children, listened to and what their dreams were.

Not that anyone has a choice, but I was content with my age, with not being part of the dating scene that MC loathed to re-enter, not needing to worry about career advancement or any other issues of the young.

I know Matt agreed. One time his nephew Petey, the philosophical one in the Mottolo family, asked Matt if he wished he were still a kid.

"Not if I'd have to see the Ice Capades again," Matt had replied.

As if to confirm my feelings of domestic satisfaction, I opened the door to the aroma of steaming New England clam chowder.

"I thought I was supposed to cook for *you?*" I said, ninety-nine percent sure all he'd done was heat up a pot that Rose had brought over.

He smiled and wiped his brow. "The hardest part was traipsing the beach in my hip boots digging for the clams."

The same Matt. No ill effects from the radiation treatment he'd had that morning. So far, so good.

"Seems I missed a lot," I said. "Witnesses saw Wayne Gallen and Jake Powers in a bar fight, threatening each other?"

Matt nodded. "I don't suppose you'd want to look at the report?"

I smiled, shed my jacket, and walked to the coffee table where Matt's papers were spread out. I picked out the ones headed POLICE REPORT—STATEMENT. I'd seen a number of these reports in my consultant work, but I'd never before paid attention to the check-off squares at the upper left where there were options for the type of report: CRIM., INCID., COMPL., INSUR., DOMES. VIOL.

I wondered if MC would feel better or worse if she knew that domestic violence was so common that it had its own line on police forms. It made me feel worse.

Statements taken at the scene weren't as easy to read as formally typed transcripts, but I made my way through the handwriting of Officer Benjamin R. Di Palma.

The narrative told the story of two white males, later identified as Jake Powers and Wayne Gallen, both similar build, one dark coloring, the other redhead with a "barbershop mustache," the witness had called it. They'd started to argue in the One A Bar, I read, then had taken it outside to the parking lot, where many patrons formed a ring around them and watched. Two witnesses claimed there were more verbal hits than physical; a third said the opposite.

I sighed. "Do men still really do this? It's not just in old western movies?"

"You should pay more attention to the police blotter," Matt said. "Di Palma did a good job on this. He located three different witnesses who'd talk to him. Very unusual in these circumstances. Guys don't want to be known as spectators for this kind of thing. In fact, most of them don't even want to be known as ever having been in the One A."

Had I ever been in a place I wouldn't want to be seen in? I asked myself. Maybe an ice cream shop alone, feeding my habit with a hot fudge sundae.

I looked at accounts of the words flung about along with the fists of the two men.

All three witnesses reported either, "I'll kill you," from Wayne, and "Not if I kill you first," from Jake, or vice versa.

I read a few of the alleged quotes from the brawl aloud, though Matt had already seen the narrative.

"'You're breaking the law.'"

"'I'll break your jaw.'"

"Do you think that was deliberate poetry?" I asked him, not waiting for an answer.

"'I can't believe you thought you'd get away with it.'"

"'You'll keep your trap shut if you know what's good for you.'"

"'Not in a million years. You are going down, friend, you are going down.'"

"'I don't know what you're so upset over.'"

"'She was mine.'"

"'She was mine'?" I repeated, incredulous. "As if he owned MC? Whichever one said this—"

"Keep reading," Matt said.

"'Damn your Suzy Q.'"

"'You'll pay for what you did to her.'"

"'Suzy Q. Suzy Q.'" [Witnesses' interpretation: taunting.]

"Doesn't sound like jealous guys fighting over a girl, does it?" Matt said.

"No, it doesn't. And Suzy Q. Do you suppose that could be—" I asked.

"Spartan Q is my thought. They're fighting over a horse."

"A dead horse."

"So this brings Gallen back into the case."

"And therefore maybe Alex Simpson."

Matt sat down, and I served the chowder and sourdough bread, another San Francisco treat that had also made it to Revere's grocers.

"This gets weirder and weirder," he said.

I thought of the elements of the case. Three dead people and two dead horses. Buckyball scientists, vets, and equestrians. Houston, Texas, and Revere, Massachusetts.

"I agree. The case is weird," I said. "And I haven't even told you yet about *my* day."

MATT HAD THE SAME REACTION I did to Dr. Schofield's confession.

"Not enough to worry about," he said.

"Unless you're the funding sponsor. Not that I'm going to report him." I waved my hand. "It's his conscience."

Matt gave me a sympathetic look. "I know it's tough on you when a scientist doesn't live up to…what would this be, the Hippocratic oath, maybe?"

I shrugged my shoulders. Were veterinarians also regular MDs who took an oath? At the moment I didn't care at all.

Well, maybe I cared a little. Once Matt and I finished dinner, I reached for my briefcase and retrieved the printout with the list I'd gotten from Dr. Schofield's secretary—horses with microchip implants. I might have been influenced to remain in the western/horse-related mood by the words to Perry Como's "Tumbling Tumbleweeds," coming from an "old crooners" CD in the background, my choice for the evening.

I scanned the list.

SALLY'S RIDE	BILLINGS	012#11994	MA	HUNTER PONY
NIGHTWALK	THOMAS	7421710^3	TX	ARABIAN
BIG MAX	HAMILTON	05#43&98	MA	CLEVELAND BAY

Clever names, I thought, wondering if astronaut Dr. Sally Ride or the owner of McDonald's restaurants had given permission for use of their names. Or if they owned the horses. Inventive, either way.

SPANISH LADY	GOMEZ	049*106^6	MA	LIPIZZAN
LUCIAN FIVE	TRUMBLE	7545753^0	TX	ANDALUSIAN

There it was. Lucian Five. The names of horses didn't have a long shelf-life in my brain, but I recognized Penny Trumble's deceased horse.

"What if all these horses are dead?" I asked Matt. I tapped my pencil the way Dr. Schofield had, end on end.

Matt lowered his *Revere Journal*. "I doubt it. That would raise a flag." He came to my chair and peered at the list. "There's one I know," he said.

I gave him a strange look, as if he'd just admitted to having fathered a child now living on a ranch in Texas with its mother. "What else are you keeping from me?"

He laughed and pointed to a line on the chart.

UNCLE SAM MERCATI 012#68488 MA SADDLEBRED

"Mike Mercati used to be on the job. He went into private practice a couple of years ago and opened an agency in Saugus. This is probably his middle daughter, I remember she was into horses as a teenager." Matt sounded like Rose. It seemed I was the only one who had forfeited my knowledge of Revere history.

We looked up simultaneously, our heads making a nearly identical angle, its sides being parallel lines from my chair to the old analog clock on the mantel. I had the fleeting thought that we should implant an identification microchip in the clock, a valuable antique.

At the same time that I said, "It's only ten o'clock," Matt said, "It's ten o'clock already."

"I said it first." I kissed his cheek and handed him the phone. The crooning had stopped, but neither of us bothered to reload the player. The evening had turned into a work session where the words to "Catch a Falling Star" would only be distracting.

I waited through a catch-up session between Matt and his old friend, hearing Matt's easy comments, as if he had all the time in the world. How nice that Sheila was teacher of the year at Saugus High. Did Uncle Bill ever buy that cottage by the ocean? And yes, Matt was still on Fernwood Avenue and things were fine. I noticed he left out both me and his cancer. I heard a few more pleasantries, then finally, the reason for the call.

"Okay, yeah. And I'm glad to hear Uncle Sam is doing so well." A pause. "No, no, I'm just following up with some statistics for a case. Thanks a lot, Mike."

"Alive?" I asked. I was glad Mr. Mercati couldn't hear my disappointment.

Matt nodded. "Uncle Sam won a second in a show yesterday."

"So the chips don't kill all the horses."

"Or any of them, as far as we know."

"Right. Coffee break?" I asked, already at the espresso maker.

IT HAD BEEN A LONG TIME since I'd responded to a dream by waking up with an idea. I got out of bed as quietly as I could and went down to the living room.

In my dream I kept forgetting to put cash or credit cards or my checkbook into my purse, so I couldn't pay for what I was buying. I had no idea what I was trying to buy, but the dream crisis reminded me that I hadn't looked at the financial details of the Charger Street reports. Sometime later I might delve into what the dream really meant. As far as I knew, I was solvent.

I pulled the stack of material onto my lap—I'd read the same annual summaries of the projects over and over and thought I knew them by heart, but had just skimmed the financial reports. Not the most interesting to me. I riffled through and found the money sections, appearing as appendices to the reports.

Since most of Lorna Frederick's program money was from government sources, the financial aspects were a matter of public record, just as my salary at mostly DOE-funded BUL had been. I checked the Revere payroll for Dr. Timothy Schofield, and the Houston payroll for Dr. Owen Evans. Both were listed at an hourly rate that was reasonable—for doctors or lawyers, though high for consultants in general. And certainly high for people who weren't working for the program yet.

I found the input/output sheets for the microchips.

QTY.	SUPPLIER	REC'D	COST/EA.	COST/DVM
10	ADVANCECHIP	7/13	$50`	$35

| 10 | SYCHIP | 8/1 | $48 | $34 |
| 10 | CHIPBASE | 8/8 | $65 | $46 |

If I was reading the sheet correctly, Lorna was buying chips from different manufacturers—probably to satisfy a government regulation to avoid sole sourcing—and then selling them to the veterinarians. But Lorna was giving a 30 percent discount to the doctors. I was amazed the sponsors wouldn't notice and question this. I had the feeling that somewhere in an executive summary meant for bureaucrats there was twisted jargon that made this seem reasonable. What else was being sanitized, I wondered.

Another perk for the doctors—I was willing to bet they were not passing the savings on to their clients.

I went back over the fiscal reports, looking for…something else. I didn't know what. Until, there it was. I knew I'd recognize it when I saw it. Another chart for microchips, with different parameters tabulated.

ID	SUPPLIER	REC'D	PROCESSING	TODVM
012#11994	ADVANCECHIP	7/13	GROUP A	8/12
74&1710^3	SYCHIP	8/1	GROUP B	9/2
7545**390	CHIPBASE	8/8	GROUP A	8/15

Lorna kept a record of each chip, with its history. The page wasn't numbered and I wondered if it had been submitted by mistake. Most intriguing was the column labeled PROCESSING.

The good doctors were installing "processed" chips? What kind of processing would take a month or more? I wondered why the chips couldn't go straight from the manufacturer to the veterinarians. Surely if the veterinarians bought the chips themselves they wouldn't "process" them. But, of course, why would they buy their own when they could get a huge discount from Lorna's program?

I looked through the technical reports one more time, to see if I could find anything on "processing." Nothing. Did Dr. Schofield and Dr. Evans know the chips were being processed before they received them for implantation? I wished I'd looked at the financial statements before interviewing Dr. Schofield. This case, plus all the time I'd been spending in hospital waiting rooms and in emotional stress over Matt's illness, had made me sloppy.

I got off the couch, pulled my navy corduroy bathrobe tighter, and walked around the living room and dining room to warm up and to reorganize my thoughts. I needed to talk to someone. Andrea Cabrini could help, but not at two o'clock in the morning. It was only eleven o'clock in California, but I hadn't given Elaine Cody running commentary on this case as I had on others. I had, however, poured all my stress over the phone lines to her.

I went upstairs to my office and found my notes from the first interview Matt and I had had with Lorna. I made noises, shuffled past the bedroom door, but not too loudly, just enough to wake Matt gently, I hoped. He slept on. I went back down with only my notes.

I'd recorded the dialogue as best as I could remember it, once we'd left Lorna's office. I read the section where I'd questioned her about having veterinarians on her payroll:

Q./me: Do some of your programs require testing on animals?
A./LF: Not exactly. (Annoyed. Ends meeting abruptly.)

The question of chips never came up. I started to blame Houston PD for not sharing the transcript sooner. If we'd known from the beginning Nina Martin was investigating the death of a horse, things might have moved more smoothly. Matt had defended them when I'd brought it up, however.

"It hasn't even been two weeks," he'd said. "And the HPD couldn't just walk into Nina's office and take her files. Not only that, once they had them, they had to sift through to find the case that might have sent her here."

"And it's not as if she had had an equestrian card in her pocket," I'd said, deciding to join his side.

After another fruitless half hour, I wanted to shake Matt awake and brainstorm, but I'd never keep him from the sleep he needed. It would be too rude, I concluded—unless he woke up from an odor, like the aroma of espresso.

Technically, I knew better—we can't smell in our sleep—but something worked, because Matt came downstairs a few minutes into my middle-of-the-night coffee break.

"I thought I was going to have to bake lemon cookies," I said. "Or try my new intense pesto sauce recipe."

"You mean if I'd held out a little longer, there'd be an extra treat?"

"Next time."

I summoned him to the coffee table and briefed him on my marked-up lists.

"What I don't understand—besides what processing they're doing—is why Lorna's giving us all this potentially incriminating evidence in nicely bound reports." I spread out the material on the coffee table, making a fan of the colorful plastic strips down the left-hand side of each report.

Matt shrugged. "You know what they say. If criminals didn't do dumb things…"

"None of them would get caught."

Matt pointed to other line items on the expense sheet. "Also, look at how expensive these other items are. Capital equipment, for one. Rare chemicals. CPU time, whatever that is. The chips are way down in the noise of the money they're spending. But Lorna certainly wants to be reimbursed for the full amount she's spending, so she sticks these little chip expenses in there. Why not, if she thinks no one will question her."

Good point. "So where are we on this?" I asked him, exhausted and frustrated. "Are we any closer to why Nina and Jake were murdered?"

"Maybe it will look better in the morning."

I was tired enough to wait.

Matt climbed the stairs extra slowly, holding on to the worn oak banister that was on our list to refinish some week. Along with repapering the hallway and buying new stairway lighting.

"Are you okay?"

"Yeah, but planning to sleep in."

"Me, too."

THIRTY-ONE

ON TUESDAY MORNING I was awakened by retching noises coming from the bathroom. I shot out of bed. Matt was doubled over, unable to tell me exactly what was wrong. He mumbled syllables I couldn't understand, then a few seconds later his eyes rolled to the back of his head, and he fell over, unconscious. I called 911, then Rose, and then George Berger, as if it would take all of them to save Matt.

How could I have been so selfish? I asked myself over and over as I sat in the hospital waiting room, dry-eyed, having used up my tears driving behind the ambulance. I'd kept Matt up late, luring him to work in the wee hours of the morning, helping him ignore his doctors' orders to rest. I'd even let him heat up the clam chowder himself, and forgotten to restock the cranberry juice.

Dr. Rosen had been assigned to Matt again. I hoped she would be a little less cheery now that she had at least more one week of experience, but her chestnut ponytail still bounced when she greeted me.

"Detective Gennaro's fiancée, right? I'll be back in a sec," she'd said, a half hour ago.

There was nothing I could do but wait. Wait for Rose, wait for Berger, wait for Dr. Rosen. I felt I'd read every old periodical in every waiting room in Suffolk County, though I'd have hated to be quizzed on the contents.

None of this had been predicted by the dozens of consultations, brochures, pamphlets, URLs, or wellness letters we'd drowned ourselves in. Side effects of external beam therapy for prostate cancer, if any, weren't due until well into the radiation program.

Matt had had only one treatment and had seemed fine the rest of that day. *Until I prodded him into working,* I told myself.

I'd dozed off in the stiff chair when I felt a sharp poke on my upper arm. I looked up to—none of the people I'd been waiting for—Jean Mottolo. I'd forgotten that I'd asked Rose to call Matt's sister. I wasn't ready for her criticism; I'd already given myself enough.

I was even less ready for her friendliness.

"Gloria, how are you? I can't believe this is happening. Did you talk to the doctor yet? You must be exhausted." Jean slung her burgundy shoulder bag onto the chair next to me and gave me a warm smile.

I waited for the zinger. *It's all your fault Matt's here and I had to drive all this way again,* my mind heard. But there was no zinger. Jean took off her coat, plunked down next to me with a big sigh, and put her hand on my arm. The way Rose would.

"I...uh...Dr. Rosen should be here any minute. I hope the traffic wasn't too bad."

Jean waved her hand and spoke rapidly, as if she wanted to close a deal quickly. "It took about an hour and a half. I was making good time until that Braintree split. Then things got bogged down. Thank God for easy-listening WQRC, and of course WBZ." She took a breath. "'Traffic on the threes,'" she said, mimicking the radio announcer's signature line. She looked at her watch, a fancy number with her children's birthstones along the band. I remembered the day she explained it to me—I'd tried to hide my imitation-leather-strapped drugstore watch under the sleeve of my jacket. "Anyway, I'm glad I'm here."

"So am I." I said this shakily, thinking Jean might be laying a trap. Trusting soul, that Gloria.

Jean patted my hand. "We'll get through this."

Rose arrived upon this scene, and gave me a look that was no more trusting than I felt. "Hi, Jean. You made great time." I heard the wariness in her voice.

"Rose, I'm so glad to see you." Jean stood up and hugged Rose. I saw Rose's arms stiffen, then make their way to patting Jean's back. She looked at me over Jean's shoulder—possible only because Jean had bent over to accommodate Rose's height. "How's your daughter? I heard the terrible news about her friend's death."

I wondered how Jean could have known about Jake's death. I didn't think the *Cape Cod Times* would carry stories or murder or mayhem in Revere. Most likely Matt had told her.

Dr. Rosen came through double doors that seemed to swing in tune with her hair. She beamed a big smile at us, and motioned me to come forward.

"You go ahead, Gloria. We'll be right here," Jean said, earning another strange look from Rose. I wondered briefly if Rose thought I'd decided to try one of the "I'm pregnant" stories on Jean.

"We just can't seem to get this right," Dr. Rosen told me. "Another bad reaction, this time to *no* medication. So, somewhere in the middle between too much and zero, that's where we're aiming."

I blinked my eyes at her glibness. This was my...fiancé, for all she knew, and her reporting came off as if she were trying to gauge the right distance to clear the highest pole in a competition. I took a breath before addressing her.

"So this reaction was to just one dose of the radiation?"

She nodded gaily, as if to commend me for getting the correct answer. "It doesn't happen often, but sometimes that's all it takes. He's presenting with exactly the symptoms we might expect in the fourth or fifth week. He's ahead of the class, you might say."

No, I might not say that.

"Can I see him?"

She shook her hair. "Not for a while. He's all doped up." Dr. Rosen checked her watch, more like mine than Jean's, with a plain brown strap. "I'd say come back at noon."

I gave her the best smile and thank-you I had available.

JEAN INSISTED she be allowed to treat Rose and me to an early lunch at a place of our choice, so at about eleven-thirty the three of us sat in Russo's, the elaborately decorated restaurant on Broadway where I'd met Matt for one of our first meals together. We called it our Half Meeting because it had been half work, half date, and, as Matt remembered, he'd half stood to greet me, not wanting to offend my sensibilities either way.

"I didn't know whether to expect a feminist or an old-fashioned girl," he'd told me once, reminiscing.

"Which was I?" I'd asked.

A crooked smile. "The best of both."

As I thought of him now, I turned my head away, having brought myself to the brink of tears. Rose and Jean kindly ignored me, but in a way that said, *We're here*. The best of both, I thought, mimicking Matt.

My friends—I was starting to include Jean in that group—ordered a bottle of wine and we clinked their wineglasses and my mineral water tumbler to Matt and his good health.

"I'm so glad to be with you both," Jean said. "I know you're not asking, but I have to tell you." She brushed back a faux fern that appeared to be growing out of an armless torso just over her left shoulder. Russo's seemed to add a little more of Old Rome every month or so, and Jean's eyes landed on each pink plaster cherub in turn. Any minute I expected criticism of my choice of restaurant, and the news that her hometown of Falmouth had rules against such cheesy artifacts.

"Tell us what?" Rose asked.

Jean looked at me. "Matt wrote me a letter."

Rose looked uncomfortable, as if she'd asked an embarrassing question and should excuse herself, but Jean apparently sensed it and held her arm. "This is for both of you. If I open my eyes, I can see how much Gloria cares for him, and I realized after reading Matt's letter how much both of you mean to my brother and well, you know, et cetera, et cetera."

"Well, you mean a lot to him, too, and we're all lucky, aren't we, because Matt is so wonderful. Thank you for sharing that, Jean."

That was Rose, the gracious lady of Revere, whose ability to rise to any social occasion often stunned me. I stared past Jean's shoulder at a fountain with water emanating from the mouth of an enormous winged creature, possibly Michael or Gabriel. Matt was not a letter writer. No notes, postcards, or Christmas cards. I had instituted the practice of sending birthday cards to Petey and Alysse. I couldn't imagine why Jean would make up such a story, however.

Way behind in the conversation, I said, "Matt wrote you a letter?"

Jean nodded. "He didn't say anything specific, but I know why he wrote it." She laughed. "He wanted me to stop being huffy—that's what he used to call me even when I was a little girl. Huffy." She cleared her throat. "I knew what he meant even then."

"We all get huffy now and then," Rose said, looking at me, not quite kicking me under the table, but nudging me with her eyes.

It was my turn to accept Jean's apology. I wanted to, but I was stuck on the image of Matt writing a letter. *Like a will,* I asked myself, *his last words?* I looked at Rose and she read the questions in my eyes. *Is Matt going to die? Is this the last scene, where the hero does after doing one last good deed for those he loves?*

"Gloria, this is a good thing," Rose said to me, locking her eyes on mine. "Matt is getting better as we speak."

Jean nodded.

The tears came again, filling my eyes. Jean moved her chair closer to me and hugged me. Rose gave us both a wide, beaming smile. I wondered if she was thinking of her dear departed mother-in-law.

THIRTY-TWO

By evening, Jean and I had seen Matt two or three times, separately, for a few minutes each time. Rose made trips back and forth, checking on us and bringing coffee. I knew she was dying to get me alone to discuss the new Jean Mottolo.

"It's Tuesday. Why don't you call MC, and maybe we can have a Girls' Night Out," I whispered during one of her appearances.

She brightened. "Even Girls' Night In would be great."

Dr. Rosen wanted to keep Matt overnight again, assuring me that they would "get it right" and this would be the last time Detective Gennaro would be spending a night away from his fiancée.

I went into Matt's room to say good-night. I'd decided he wasn't alert enough for a serious conversation, so I hadn't mentioned anything about microchips, buckyballs—or the bodies in the deadly Rumney Marsh—all day.

Jean hadn't held back, however, and he was up to date on my newly developed sisterhood with her.

"I guess it's okay, between you and Jean now?"

"Yes, it is, thanks to some missive you authored. Did you keep a copy?"

He smiled. "You mean on my computer?"

Matt and Rose were among the last holdouts—no computers, no e-mail, no Internet. They still wasted the cost of first-class stamps to pay their bills. Rose's assistant, Martha, had put the Galigani business files on a PC and it was Martha who accessed the data when needed.

"I have everything I need right up here," Rose would say, pointing to her lovely head, which got a more intense shade of auburn every year.

"Won't Thanksgiving be fine," Matt said. "One big, happy, Hallmark family."

I grinned. "Whatever you want."

"Well, good, now's my chance. I think we should get married."

I took a long breath. "Are you on something?" I asked.

"I was on two things. That apparently was the first problem. Now. I'm on nothing except some sleep medicine, I guess. But my head is clear. I just can't get down on my knees yet."

I thought of a conversation I'd heard in the last week or so between two young female clerks at Northgate's supermarket. I was next in line with my cart full of pastas and produce, unable to tune out the checker and the bagger, chatting about their love lives as they processed the items of the woman in front of me.

"Do you think Aaron's going to propose?" the dark-haired bagger asked, not losing her rhythm. Three large cans on the bottom, a head of lettuce on top. Bananas on the bottom, grapes on top, a baguette stuck down the side.

The blond checker, sporting inch-long fingernails with sparkly decals, shrugged her shoulders. "I wish I knew. I'd like to, you know, plan."

"Maybe he's waiting for Christmas, you know, to give you a ring?"

The checker shook her head. "Uh-uh. It'll be too late by then. I'm sure Billy will beat him to it. And I'll be all, Yes, yes, yes, Billy." They both laughed, seemingly at Aaron's misfortune.

I'd felt I'd been listening not only to a foreign language, but to another species, with different wiring from mine. I imagined the various brands of orange juice in Aisle 4 waiting on the shelf for a customer to choose one or the other, sighing with disappointment when Mrs. Kaplan passed them by, but acquiescing when selected by Mrs. Renaldo.

But I had no right to be disturbed by the scene, I thought— hadn't my engagement to Al Gravese been somewhat the same? He'd teased me about a special present coming up, and a certain question he wanted to ask me, and how I shouldn't have anything monogrammed for a while until he gave me this present. I shuddered at the silliness of it, dismayed that an important decision like the marriage of two people would be so controlled by one of them.

Matt tugged at my arm. "Are you with me here, Gloria? Jean's ready to pick out wedding favors. How about those little packages of Jordan almonds? I've always liked those."

I laughed. "We can have Jordan almonds anytime, and without the white netting and ribbon," I said. But I was surprisingly in tune with marrying Matt. *It doesn't have to be like the first time,* I told myself. Not all engagements end in the death of one party. Nor do all hospital stays have unhappy endings. Nor all cancers. "As long as we can have chocolate wedding cake, I'm there."

"Ahhh," Matt said. "Terrific. Think how nice it will be not to have to lie to the doctors and nurses."

I kissed him. "You're so romantic."

"You wouldn't stand for romance." He paused. "Gloria, will you do me the honor of becoming Mrs. Gennaro?" His voice was raised in pitch, a clue to his teasing.

Fortunately, Matt already knew how I felt about Mrs. Anybody. "Do you want my speech again about how women abandon their names and allow themselves to disappear into a man's family name, and then wonder why they don't get paid as much?"

Matt laughed, a weak laugh that caused me great pain. It seemed a long time since I'd seen him physically strong.

"See, I knew that's how you'd respond to romance. Listen, I'll probably be asleep again in a few minutes. But the next time I'm awake, have your calendar ready so we can pick a date, okay?"

"Matt…" I paused, partly because his eyes had already started to close, partly because I didn't know what to say. I love you? We'd said if often enough. Thank you? Not quite appropriate.

"Sorry, I'm all doped up. I feel like my tongue is coated with something thick." *Ith coded…*is what it sounded like. "See you tomorrow, Gloria?"

I stared at his body as he fell into a sleep, as if I were qualified to evaluate his health.

I kissed him, and left the hospital, engaged to be married.

I CALLED ROSE from my cell phone on my way home. "I've been in these clothes all day," I told her, involuntarily sniffing the sleeve of my merino wool jacket. "Do you think we can move Girls' Night Out to my house? I'd like to be in my bathrobe as soon as possible."

"No problem. MC can't make it anyway. She's started this new gym class." I heard a clicking sound. "Imagine paying to walk around a pool or exercise or whatever they do. I had enough of that in junior high."

"I don't think they call it gym class anymore. And I *know* they don't wear those awful blue outfits."

Rose laughed. "I forgot about those costumes. The itty-bitty dresses with the bloomers to match!"

"Mine wasn't so itty-bitty, remember?"

"Anyway, MC is doing so much better. I know you've been a great help to her, Gloria." I didn't want to mention that the person who killed her daughter's boyfriend was still at large. Rose had seemed more than willing to believe that the investigation was going well, and that it had nothing to do with her daughter. "I'll be over in a half hour and I'll bring some goodies."

"I'll have a goodie for you, too, when you get here. A bit of news."

What is this? I asked myself. *Have I been influenced by the checker/bagger duo, playing a silly guessing game about an engagement between two consenting adults?*

Rose gasped. "What fun. Is this about Jean?"

No going back now. Rose would be into this, and I owed it to her for all her trips to the hospital. For her big part in getting Matt and me together. For sticking with me when I'd tried to leave Revere behind forever.

I stopped at a light on Broadway just after the Chelsea overpass. Ahead of me to my left in the clear night was a building complex on the former site of the Revere Theater. The memory of Saturday matinees with newsreels, cartoons, and short subjects put me in the right frame to continue the little drama with Rose.

"Better than that," I said into my tiny cell phone speaker.

A pause. "You and Matt are engaged."

I moved with the green light. "Rose! How could you possibly...?"

"It's what I do."

BEFORE ROSE ARRIVED I had time for a shower and a phone call to Elaine Cody in Berkeley.

"I can't believe I'm not there to hug you, Gloria. I am so excited. You have to tell me immediately when you know the date. And I have dibs on providing the cake. There's this on-line wedding-cake site—I looked into it many times for my near-miss engagements. They do chocolate of course."

I laughed, remembering most of her near misses. Bruce, Paul, Jose, and others whose names escaped me. "Hold on," I said. "This is not going to be a big event."

I heard Elaine's sigh. "Never mind. I'll just deal with Rose."

I didn't have many friends, but I did know how to pick them, I told myself.

THIRTY-THREE

"HOW DO YOU FEEL, GLORIA?" Rose asked me from Matt's chair in the reading area.

She sipped white wine from a crystal glass that Matt owned from his marriage to Teresa. When I lived at the mortuary Rose kept a couple of her own wineglasses in my cupboard for emergencies like this. Elaine, whom Rose had met several times, had given her the idea.

"No need to use Gloria's recycled jelly jars," Elaine had teased.

I hoped my engagement wouldn't result in an influx of crystal and china and silverware. Managing household goods was boring, unlike inventorying and caring for lab equipment.

"I'm much better after my shower," I told Rose.

She waved one hand at me and with the other filled my wineglass with sparkling cider. "You know what I mean. Listen, we're going to have an engagement party, like it or not. I'll have to see if Elaine will come out. As soon as Matt is up to it."

"I'll never be up to a party." I sighed. "You know, maybe I should be all excited, but now that we've made the decision, in some ways I feel I've been engaged to Matt almost from the beginning."

"I've felt that way, too. You know, MC really likes that cute blond teacher—Daniel." A smooth segue to her daughter's love life. I'd introduced MC and Daniel only a couple of days ago so they could talk about MC's appearance at the Science Club. I doubted MC had told her mother anything about her personal feelings so quickly. "Did you know the Endicotts used to live across the street from the mortuary? Isn't that a coincidence? Right across from where MC lives now. The father worked in

City Hall for years, in the clerk's office, and the mother used to help out at a florist we dealt with back then."

I was sure the only engagement that Rose would have been happier about than mine was MC's. Preferably to a young man from Revere whose family Rose knew.

"Daniel's a nice guy," I said. I wasn't ready to vouch for him as anything but an excellent teacher.

Rose sighed and left me for a while, mentally. I watched her eyes roam the room without focusing. Her thin legs were crossed at the ankles, but the perfect creases in her beige wool slacks did not touch each other. Like Elaine, Rose would never dream of stepping outside her house without dressing well. The two of them joked about having nothing in their closets with elastic around the waist.

"I wish the guys were here tonight," Rose said when she came back from her trip—down the aisle with MC, I guessed. "We are definitely due for a celebration of good news. Too bad Frank is out of town, and Matt is doped up!"

Doped. A strange word. Until Matt's current intimacy with medicines, my first free-association matching word would have been *semiconductors*. Doping a semiconductor material meant adding "foreign" atoms to it, to increase the electron content, and therefore, the current flow. My mind shot off in the direction of semiconductor physics. Germanium could be doped. Also silicon. The stuff of microchips.

But the doping material would be trapped in the chip, of no use to the host. The horse in this case. What was the other word Matt had used? His tongue was…coated. He felt as though his tongue had been coated.

What if the microchips had been coated with something?

I sprang to life and off the chair. "A coating. That's it. The EID microchips are coated. That's what the processing step is all about. That's why Lorna gives the chips to the doctors at practically no cost. The vets think they're on the payroll for future animal testing. As far as they know, all they're doing is chip implantation and receiving money slightly illegally. They're making a big profit on the product, but that's it. As if that weren't enough. Or maybe the vets know about this scam. Maybe Dr. Schofield was confessing to the lesser crime to hide the bigger one. Hmm. I don't think so."

Rose knew better than to interrupt—it wasn't the first time she'd been present at one of my solo brainstorming sessions. By the time I finished talking I'd gathered all the material and spread it on the coffee table between us.

"This is great, Gloria. It's about the case, I know. Jake's murder. I haven't wanted to ask you about it, with Matt being sick and then the engagement." Rose shook her head and breathed out loudly. "Too much on our plates."

I gave Rose a briefing on what I'd learned from the horse ID charts. I pointed to the mysterious column in the appendix. "The only question I've had was, what's this step?" I tapped my pen on the heading. PROCESSING. "And now I think I know."

"Wow." Rose paused. "What?"

I laughed at her straight-woman caricature. "Coating. They— who, I'm not sure. Lorna and Alex and maybe both of their teams. But they must be sneaking in some drug, putting it onto the chips that are used for identification. It's like putting a rider on government legislation. Everyone's focused on the main text, but you've added a little clause at the bottom that has nothing to do with it, but that is your real purpose all along."

"Like the city council did last year, adding a nice little bonus for themselves to the school lunch bill." I nodded. That would do. "Why would they do that?" Rose asked.

"To get around FDA regulations and the interminably long time it takes to get a drug to market. And that would be why Nina Martin had an FDA business card in her pocket. She must have caught on to the scheme while she was investigating Lucian Five's death."

"Whose death?"

"He's a dead horse in Texas…never mind for now. And I imagine Jake Powers also caught on to them, probably when *his* horse died." I walked in front of the fireplace, which we had lit early in the evening. I removed the screen and added a log. Rose and I had a running disagreement about wood-burning fireplaces and the damage they did to the environment, but tonight I'd let her prevail. "I need to make some phone calls."

"Go right ahead. I'll put the coffee on. And then if you don't mind, I'll just sit here and watch a master at work."

I gave her a look that said I had no time for her snide remarks.

My first call was to George Berger, at home. I told him my coating theory so far.

"Can you get me Dr. Schofield's home phone number?" I asked him. "It's too late to reach him at the office, and he's not listed."

"Whatever the Revere Police Department can do to help you, Gloria, we are only too happy to assist."

Everyone was being snide, but I laughed at Berger's friendly tone. Matt's partner liked me, and now so did his sister. I had no enemies anymore.

With the possible exceptions of Lorna Frederick and Alex Simpson.

I DON'T KNOW WHAT I would have done if Dr. Schofield hadn't been at home. I was wired from my new theory and from the continuous coffee drinking Rose and I engaged in while we waited for Berger to call back with the telephone number.

The doctor sounded worried when he heard my voice. He must have guessed that I'd eventually uncover the microchip cost imbalance and jumped in quickly, before I could tell him my purpose in calling him at ten o'clock at night. Lately I'd been doing my best work after hours, like coyotes.

"Look, I've already decided to give all my customers a discount on the chips, starting now," he said, as if I were a traffic cop who'd pulled him over for speeding and then realized he didn't have his seat belt on, either.

"I'm pleased to hear that. But I have another reason for calling." I told him my theory of what the title PROCESSING meant in the Charger Street records. "What do you think of that?"

I heard a grunt of anger that I felt was genuine. "*We*—the veterinarians are being suckered into giving horses unapproved drugs? Without even a NADA?"

"Excuse me?"

"A New Animal Drug Application. There's a whole procedure set up through HHS. The Department of Health and Human Services. The FDA is under HHS." Dr. Schofield gave a low whistle. "If what you're saying is true, those guys at Charger Street and Houston Poly have it made. The ID chips make it possible for them to track the horses for as long as they want to. Geez."

"Track them?"

"Well, not exactly, not like we track the coyotes. But they can follow a particular horse's history through the ID chip."

"But the chip insertion is a one-time thing, so they wouldn't want to follow it for very long, right? Only as long as the drug, whatever it is, lasts from the one dose the horse gets."

"That's enough. Depending on the drug, they can get a lot of information from one injection. Let's say it's a time-release, and they're testing the effectiveness of it over time. And they can follow the horse's medical history, because…"

"Because they have their vets on their payroll."

I heard a weak, "Right."

"Lorna and Alex probably asked to be kept in the loop for all the horses that have their chips. You and Dr. Evans send them updated medical records for completeness, something like that?"

Another weak, "Right." I was getting too much enjoyment sensing Dr. Schofield's embarrassment and guilt.

"What's the packaging of the chips when you receive them?" I asked him. "Do they look different from the ones you might buy direct from the manufacturer?"

"Well, yeah, the ones I get are in a Charger Street lab wrapper. I figured they repackaged it for their inventory control."

"What would they be testing?" I asked, wanting to hear Dr. Schofield's theory before suggesting my own.

"It could be anything, I guess. Maybe they're just putting a different ceramic sealant around the chip, testing a new formula. That could be disastrous, of course, because then if the tissue didn't form correctly around it, there'd be problems. Foreign matter in the animal's body." I heard a long, low groan that might have been another "geez."

Dr. Schofield's voice rose and fell unevenly, not the relaxed tones I'd heard for most of my in-person interview with him.

Rose herself rose from and fell into the chair at intervals as she refilled my coffee and broke a biscotti into small enough pieces for me to nibble while I talked. She mimicked this behavior with her fingers to her mouth, but I shook my head *no*. I didn't need to add a choking hazard to my already overtaxed system.

"What about bute?" I asked Dr. Schofield, determined to tie up everything in the case together. "Could they be slipping bute into the chip to enhance the horses' performance? If they've strengthened the anti-inflammatory nature, for example, so the horse would be much more limber?"

"Bute. Is that why you were asking about bute this morning?"

"Yes."

"Well, that's $C_{19}H_{20}N_2O_2$ of course. I suppose they could be just adding that, but then they really would be getting short-term results. If they want to enhance a horse's performance, they'd have to be sure it was administered right before a competition. Unless they're adding a larger amount of bute than would usually be used. And they'd have to know that that particular horse was going to compete within a short time. And they'd be taking a chance on random testing. Of course, Lorna is so tied into the equestrian scene, she can follow the horses very closely, and maybe even has some of the medical people on her payroll."

"Maybe," I said, with a clearing of my throat that was meant to be another reminder that Dr. Schofield's own name was on Lorna's payroll.

"Yes, well, but still I don't see the point of it. My guess is that they're using horses to test a brand new drug and/or a new drug delivery system."

"Some experimental variation of bute, then?"

"I suppose. Why are you so bent on bute as opposed to a new drug?"

"It's hard to explain, but it has come up as another element of the scam. The alleged scam." A fine time for me to begin expressing myself as a careful police consultant.

"I can give it some thought, certainly. See if I can think how you'd change the composition of bute enough to result in a drug worth testing."

"Thanks. I'd appreciate that."

"Uh, Gloria, I just want to say…as bad as you think we've been to allow ourselves to be manipulated with the chip costs and so on, we…I think I can safely speak for Dr. Evans…we would never, never willingly participate in the kind of fraud you seem to have uncovered. For one thing, we would never do anything that could potentially harm an animal."

To say nothing of the human murders that may have resulted also.

"I believe you," I told him.

Rose had been patient through the call, satisfying herself with cleaning up the crumbs from the coffee table, stoking the fire, and gesturing meaningfully that I should sip my coffee, for instance, or take a bite of cookie. Now she burst forth with her questions.

"Are you going to tell Matt your theory?"

"Not until…he's well."

"Of course. Are they going to arrest the woman at the lab? Women these days, really."

"I'll have to call George Berger and see how he wants to proceed, based on what I have. I'm ninety-nine percent sure Alex Simpson is involved also. So they'll have to call the Houston PD."

"Do you think the drug companies are involved?"

"I doubt it, but that's something to investigate. Big sponsors like that don't usually take such chances in my experience. From what I've seen the biggest dollar amounts in Lorna's program are federal agencies of one kind or another."

"You mean it's easier to fool the government."

"Afraid so."

"I'll bet there's a lot of money at stake."

"Ultimately there might be a lot of money for pharmaceutical companies any time a successful drug is developed. But there's a lot of initial cost also, for the research. The Charge Street scientists don't work for the drug companies, however, and they would not be profiting financially in general."

"So you say."

"I know this sounds strange but scientists would rather have a unit named after them." *Or a molecule,* I thought. "Like Newton, Roentgen, Fermi, Volta."

"Volts is someone's name? Like a six-volt battery, that's someone's name?"

I nodded. "The volt is named after an Italian scientist, Alessandro Volta."

Rose shook her head. "The things you know."

"What's most important for a scientist like Lorna Frederick or Alex Simpson, who are on the cutting edge, is to keep their research going. Of course, they also want Nobel Prizes and recognition. They want to have breakthroughs and meet milestones before the people in Japan or Germany, but not for the money. More for the fact of doing it, getting into the science books of the future. They don't want yachts or mansions so much as the glory that comes with transforming the world."

"Better living through science," Rose said. "As long as it's *my* science."

"You've got it."

THIRTY-FOUR

AFTER ROSE LEFT, I went back through the reports. Often, I could hear Lorna's voice as I read the narrative in the research summaries she'd submitted to her sponsors.

A single nanotube can be ten to one hundred times stronger than steel. We've demonstrated that these tiny tubes can be opened, and filled with a variety of materials, including biological molecules, she'd written.

It was almost a clue, I thought—filling nanotubes with biological molecules—and I should have seen it sooner. But who would think that science as full of marvels as nanotechnology could be the vehicle for an elaborate fraud?

It bothered me deeply that a woman scientist would betray her profession. That she might also be a murderer left me unable to sleep.

I was so sorry Matt had to miss all the excitement, and hoped at least he was sleeping soundly and on the road to the relapse-free life Dr. Rosen predicted. I thought of the drugs he'd been given. He'd had a bad reaction to some of them, but ultimately it would be drugs and therapy that would help restore his health.

Did I care how the particular drug that saved him came to be developed? Through pure, honest research, or a scam that skirted long lead times and regulations? Through upstanding scientists, or men and women who cheated and even killed to further their work?

Thinking of Matt in the hospital, the long road of treatments ahead of him, our future together—I couldn't give the quick answer I might have given even a few months ago.

When the phone rang at one in the morning, I was awake and roaming the house. While my mind was picturing the structure of phenylbutazone and figuring how one might alter it, I'd changed the sheets, straightened pillows, hand-vacuumed crumbs here and there, and made a batch of brownies—more for the comforting aroma, I told myself.

"You sound chipper," Berger said. "I'm not."

"What's keeping you up?"

"Your theory, for one."

"Is that good news or bad?"

"It's very good, Gloria, especially with what else came up. I just had a chance to look at the report from the crime-scene people on the Jake Powers murder. He had a little something in his hand."

"Oh?"

"Yeah, a small piece of a mailing label from a horse magazine. We traced it back, because part of the subscription number was intact, and when they gave us the roll of possibles, you know, ending in that partial string, there was this name on the list...*ta da*..."

"Lorna Frederick."

"Yeah, and now that we have motive...another *ta da*, thanks to you and your chip story...we're good to go."

"And Simpson?"

"We'll give HPD what we have, and I think they'll be moving on him, too."

"So I can go to sleep now?"

"All the citizens of Revere, Massachusetts, and Houston, Texas, can sleep tonight. I'm going home. Say good night, Gloria."

"Good night, George."

When was the last time I'd thought of Burns and Allen? I wondered. Berger always brought out the 1950s in me. I smiled at the memory.

Until I remembered another citizen of Revere who might not be able to sleep safely.

Mary Catherine Galigani. MC, whose e-mails about bute had started my involvement in this case in the first place. I hadn't given MC a thought since I'd watched the horse-show video with her. It was as if I'd told her to be careful, and then dropped all attention to her. I should have tried to have surveillance ordered, at least. Did Lorna know where she lived? I wondered. I quickly realized she did. MC had filled out an application to work for her.

I picked up the phone and punched in Berger's cell phone number in case he'd already left the station.

Why hadn't Rose reminded me? I asked myself, as if to rationalize my neglect of her daughter.

"Hi, Gloria," Berger said, sounding pleased as most people with caller ID did, feeling ahead of the game.

I skipped opening remarks. "George, I'm worried about Mary Catherine Galigani. As long as Lorna is free, there's a chance she might go after MC. Remember the e-mail I told you about…"

"Right, right. Well, it's going to be a while before we can take Lorna in. I'm planning to organize the material in the morning. That's, uh, about six hours from now."

I laughed, a nervous chuckle that gave away my panicked state. "In other words, can't you get some sleep? I'm sorry, George, but isn't there a way you can put a car at either Lorna's or MC's place? Or both."

Berger sighed. "You know, nothing's changed as far as Lorna Frederick's concerned. It's not as if she was at your place when you figured this out."

"Well, she knows I've been talking to her vet. And…"

"And she knows you're smart."

"Thanks. And she knows you're smart, George, and that you move quickly."

"Okay, okay. Is this what you do to Matt?"

I laughed, a little more relaxed this time. "Sort of. Thanks, George."

THIRTY-FIVE

MC MOVED THE CURTAINS on her bedroom window and looked down on Tuttle Street. Just a check to see if the rain had stopped. Not looking for strange cars, no uneasiness. *Not.*

She considered a walk to the market near the circle. She'd heard that the rotary now had a formal name—the Albert J. Brown Circle. If she were a good daughter, MC thought, she'd give her mother a thrill and ask her who Albert J. Brown was, how he'd come to have a circle named after him.

MC was forcing herself to do normal things though she felt like she'd fallen under a stampede of wild horses. She'd been up early and gone for a run, lucky enough to miss both rain showers. Someday soon she'd set up an appointment with the Admissions Office at UMass to review her transcript and see about working toward a teaching credential. She could still keep her finger in research as a consultant. During the good five minutes that came about once an hour—progress, she thought—she envisioned using her contacts to develop a chemistry program as great as Daniel Endicott's environmental science program.

Aunt G had introduced MC to Daniel—to talk about MC's presentation to the Science Club, she'd said. Not too obvious: Daniel was single, MC's age, and loved science. Well, no way was she going to get involved again, no matter how cute he was.

She couldn't shake thoughts about what she could have had with Jake. She had fits of guilt when she wished she'd done more to make their relationship work. She could have started riding with him. Maybe if she'd given him support in the wholesome activities he'd embraced, he would have abandoned the other ones.

She felt proud of Jake, that he'd been willing to be sort of a whistle-blower, ready to confront people with their criminal behavior.

But basically she knew Aunt G was right—even though she didn't press the issue—the chances of people reforming from abusive behavior were very slim. Maybe if she held that thought, eventually she'd be able to move on.

MC was surprised to hear about the microchip scam and Lorna Frederick's connection to it. According to Mom, who'd called earlier, Aunt G had figured out the whole thing. MC shuddered. To think she'd almost taken a job with that woman. It was enough that she'd known Alex Simpson in Houston—Alex and Lorna were supposedly in it together, hiring that guy to kill Nina, too.

So everything that had been bothering her was over, all the mysteries cleared up. Alex and Lorna had been running a very clever scam that ended in the murder of two people she cared about. And Wayne—even weird Wayne was right about some things. That bute e-mail, for one thing. Not that MC ever would have known what it was about. If Alex had realized that, MC's life would have been a lot easier in the last few weeks.

RRRRRRRing!

MC jumped, stepped back, and folded her arms, involuntarily. Evidently she wasn't as relaxed as she thought. Even a phone call jarred her. She imagined it would be a long time before sudden noises would not scare her to death.

"MC? It's me, Wayne Gallen."

The connection was bad, but she heard the name. "Wayne? I hope you're calling from Houston."

He laughed, a strange sound. Probably he was on a cell phone. "It's…over, MC. I'm…you're happy."

"You're breaking up, Wayne, but anyway we don't have anything to talk about."

MC practically screamed into the phone, as if to make up for the bad connection. *I should just hang up,* she thought, *but Mom raised me better than that.*

"I saved…could have…chance with my own…ife," she heard.

If she understood correctly, Wayne was right in a way. He'd evidently crossed Alex Simpson and taken a chance with his own life in order to save hers. At least in his mind he'd saved hers. Also, she'd wrongly accused him, at least mentally, of murdering Jake.

"Okay, Wayne, maybe I owe you. I'm sorry I was rude to you, and I wish you the best."

"…like…meet you…last time, MC."

"What? Where are you, Wayne?"

"Beach Lodge."

That was clear. He was still in Revere. MC held the receiver away from her body and sighed loudly. No way was she going to that dump of a Beach Lodge, to meet Wayne or anyone else. "Wayne, it's not going to happen. We should just end on this note."

"No no,…worry. I'm all over…phase. I don't know what got into me. Let's just meet for a goodbye coffee. I'll be leaving for home soon."

MC was glad the line cleared up, but Wayne's voice still sounded strange. Should she trust him? What made her think he was any more stable just because he said so?

"Wayne—"

"MC, if we had a videophone I could show you my one-way ticket to Houston. Look, we can go to a coffee shop near your house. You pick it. Really quick, I promise. Heck, you can invite your Aunt G if you want."

MC pulled at the strings of her sweatshirt hood. *I'm going out, anyway,* she thought. *I could meet him someplace safe, quickly, and I'll never hear from him again. Otherwise he'll be bugging me from Texas. Why not get it over with? He certainly sounds a little more together, as opposed to being completely cracked up, asking me to go away with him.*

"Okay, Wayne. But I'm going to have Gloria with me, and maybe even Detective Gennaro." *The more the better,* MC thought, although she wasn't sure Matt was out of the hospital. But Wayne would behave himself even if just Aunt G were there.

"Let's meet at Tomasso's Coffee Annex on Squire Road. Do you know where that is?"

"You bet, MC. I…there."

Breaking up again. And that strangeness in Wayne's voice.

Too much twang, MC thought. Or maybe she was losing her tolerance of it.

"It'll take me about an hour," she said.

MC could be at Tomasso's in fifteen minutes, but she didn't feel like rushing—she'd had her run for the day—and also she wanted to stop at the florist near Oxford Park and have some flowers sent to Aunt G as a long overdue thank-you. It was way past the time when she should start showing adult behavior and not be everyone's little girl.

MC checked her watch, ambivalent about whether to call Aunt G about meeting Wayne. It was just before ten. She knew Aunt G was more likely to be up at two o'clock in the morning than ten, especially with Matt in the hospital and the crazy hours that must mean.

She picked up the phone, put it down, then picked it up and punched in Aunt G's number. Aunt G said to be careful, so that's what she'd be, even though Lorna was presumably wearing stripes by now. She waited through several rings and heard Matt's recorded voice.

She waited for the beep. "Hi, Aunt G and Matt if you're home. Wayne Gallen wants to meet me, one last time he promises, so I'm going. If you're around…hello…are you screening your calls? Guess not. Well, anyway, I'll be meeting him in about an hour, so, like eleven o'clock, and if you can meet me there it would be great, but if not, no prob, okay?"

MC was turning the corner from Tuttle Street onto Revere Street when she realized she hadn't told Aunt G *where* to meet her. Oh, well. It wasn't as though it was a dark and stormy night, she thought. And it would all be over soon anyway.

THIRTY-SIX

I WOKE UP ABOUT TWO MINUTES before ten o'clock, feeling rested for the first time in a while. At three—after a final call from Berger telling me they'd have Lorna brought in around ten-thirty in the morning—I'd unplugged the phone by my bed, knowing that anyone who needed me, like the hospital or George Berger, would use my cell phone. Nothing else would require immediate attention, I'd decided.

I was now running late, however, and rushed to get ready for a trip to the police station, happily only a short distance away. Within walking distance if I had time. I frowned at the thought of departmental coffee, but that's what sleeping in got me.

George Berger had suggested I be present when Lorna gave the technical details of the scam she was confessing to.

I called him cell phone to cell phone to say I was on my way.

"She's admitted to the illegal drug testing, but she still insists that she never killed anyone. She says she never even heard of Nina Martin and that whatever deaths resulted must have been orchestrated by Alex Simpson. She says she was suspicious as soon as a Houston PI showed up dead in Revere. The Houston PD can't find Simpson, by the way."

"Can't find him?"

"Nope. He was supposedly on vacation at a dude ranch in Montana. Did you know there really are dude ranches, not just in the movies? Simpson was due back yesterday, but never showed. Not home, either."

"Do they think he's running, or does he even know he's wanted for questioning?"

"Not clear. Oh, but guess who we did pick up, right her in Revere, Massachusetts, in the middle of the night?"

I was adjusting to George's game-show manner. I took it as a sign that he felt comfortable working with me. I wondered how Matt abided it on an ongoing basis.

"Who?" I asked brightly.

"Wayne got-a-mustache Gallen, on a D and D."

Drunk and disorderly. "Is that a big deal? I mean will he go to jail?"

"Briefly. I think the uniforms did it on general principles, you know. He's been such a nuisance. So when the call came in from the One A they went over and hauled him in. Just a little innocent revenge. They'll keep him twenty-four hours and let him go. No harm done."

I laughed, then caught myself. Uh-oh, not nice. Was I becoming a jaded policewoman who enjoyed cop pranks? I thought of Matt and wished he were around to keep me honest. Berger evidently thought of Matt at the same time.

"How's my other partner? Still in the hospital?"

"Yes, but coming home today. I'm going to pick him up as soon as I'm free this morning. By the way, we're…" I stopped. It suddenly didn't seem right that I'd be announcing our engagement without Matt at my side.

"Say what?"

"We're looking forward to having him home for good."

"I miss him."

"So do I."

FOR ONCE I WAS DRESSED better than Lorna Frederick. My fairly new charcoal gray sweater set outshone Lorna's faded blue sweats, which must have been what she was wearing when she was taken in for questioning. Lorna's hair was at least a day from being tended to, the formerly blond parts giving way to dull brown. Her lawyer, a sharp-nosed, well-dressed young man, was also on hand—to nudge her when there was a question she shouldn't answer, I presumed.

I listened to Berger's opening remarks to the tape recorder, picturing it later as a transcript.

Detective George Berger, Dr. Gloria Lamerino, Mr. Paul Di Marco, Dr. Lorna Frederick, on Wednesday...

"According to your statement, Dr. Frederick, you added illegal compounds to microchips intended for use as identification codes for horses. Is that correct?"

"I manipulated the ketone using a Grignard reagent. It involves adding a carbon anion. It's not illegal, just not approved for wide distribution."

"Not approved, thank you. And to your knowledge is it legal to use chemicals *not approved* by the Food and Drug Administration?"

Lorna sighed and leaned into her lawyer. Mr. Di Marco said something inaudible, covering the side of his face with long, slender fingers, one of which sported a large school ring.

"No, it is not," Lorna said.

"Not legal to use chemicals unapproved by the Food and Drug Administration?"

"No, it is not legal," Lorna said, with an exasperated sigh.

As if it's our fault that she's here, detained and unkempt, I thought. In her circumstances, I knew I'd be tense, not haughty. The gray interview room alone would have depressed me if I were on the wrong side of the questioning. Peeling paint; exposed pipes; dripping, clanging radiator; rust marks on the ceiling—all seemed to scream out that murder suspects weren't worth the price of decent space.

With a few more questions, Berger determined that Lorna had not enlisted pharmaceutical companies in her scheme, and had not involved her Charge Street research team.

"Alex masterminded this," she said. "He created the system that kept our bench people in Revere in the dark. They thought they were just repackaging. The Houston guys converted the compound and shipped us the chip, which we then put our label on."

An injectable form of bute was on the market, Lorna explained, but hers was a vastly improved version, and Charger Street had to take the opportunity to forge ahead, or they'd be left in the dust as far as research money. The derivative they'd used to coat the microchip—Alex Simpson's "bute that's not bute," I realized—was meant to be a longer lasting anti-inflammatory without the side effects that would accompany a larger dose of pure bute.

She followed all the competitions, so she knew when one of "her" horses had had a chip implanted within twenty-four hours. The derivative also had a different boiling point, and therefore would be missed by most of the systems used by competition officials to test for the presence of pure bute.

"This approach didn't give us an enormous number of samples, by the time you weeded out the non-show horses who had the chip implanted, plus the ones that didn't compete within a reasonable number of days of the implant. But we didn't need a lot, just enough to test whether we were going in the right direction."

"What did you and Dr. Simpson hope to gain by this scheme, Dr. Frederick?" Berger emphasized Alex's and Lorna's titles, as if to remind her of the incongruity between their behavior and the respect ordinarily due the profession.

"What did we hope to gain? *Please.*" Lorna contorted her face, sneering, her lips becoming nearly absorbed into the junction of her downward-curving nose and her upward-curving chin. "You're asking what did we hope to gain? How about progress? Cures for cancer. Relief from depression. Freedom from pain. How do you think all that comes about? The public doesn't want to know. The public just wants the results. They'd rather not know how these things are accomplished."

"We should thank you for murdering people and killing horses?" This was my first time witnessing Berger's interrogation style. Not much different from Matt, who wasn't above verbally taunting an arrestee.

"I've told you over and over, I did not murder anyone. See Dr. Simpson for that. And do you think I'm happy that two horses died from the error in dosage? I love horses. But I love people and my research even more. No one ever remembers the millions of successes."

It bothered me to admit that Lorna had a point. How many of us were aware of the animals that died even in legitimate drug testing? Not that I was going to join a protest group. Too many of my firmly held opinions were being challenged by this case. I'd have to rethink them all. But another time.

Maybe we'd all be saved from tough decisions by computer modeling, I thought. Weapons research was the most obvious application where modeling was taking the place of real-life testing, and I knew pharmaceutical companies were involved in computer modeling also. If we could wait long enough, all the rats and rabbits and pigs might be saved from our laboratories.

Lorna was still ranting.

"How do you think we got so smart about immunization against diseases like polio and diphtheria and all the childhood diseases like mumps and measles? Where do you think our sophisticated knowledge of insulin and chemotherapy comes from?"

I'd had enough. I caught Berger's eye. I shrugged my shoulders, meaning, *I'm not really of much use here.* I tapped my watch, meaning, *I have to pick up Matt.* He nodded and tilted his head toward the door. Perfect body language, I thought, glad I was able to communicate with more than one cop.

I HATED DAYS when I ran late for everything, and this was one. I didn't like the idea of Matt sitting in his room when he could be home, where I had brownies waiting. I decided to check my phone messages on the way to the hospital since I hadn't had time to access them before I left home for the police station. I hadn't even reconnected the phone by the bed. I punched in my number and then the code for the answering machine.

The computerized voice was frustratingly slow. "YOU HAVE THREE NEW MESSAGES." I tapped my fingers on the steering wheel, wishing I could fast-forward the machine. It wasn't as if I had anything else to do but sit in the traffic, I told myself. The pace of my life seemed to have picked up without my being aware of it. In California I seldom had more than one extracurricular activity a week, and fewer when Elaine Cody was starting a new relationship. I had no twenty-four/seven consulting jobs, no significant other.

"MESSAGE ONE. EIGHT TWENTY-TWO A.M."

The first message was from Rose, who should have known better than to call before nine, even on a good day.

"Still sleeping, I guess. Well, good. I told MC about Lorna so she wouldn't worry anymore. And of course whew, whew, whew, we're all so relieved. Looking forward to having Matt home. I'll bring a lasagna over, but I won't stay. I'll bet you made brownies last night."

"MESSAGE TWO. NINE THIRTY-FOUR A.M." I stopped at a light and dribbled moisturizer on my hands. Not to waste a few seconds.

"Oh, hi, Gloria. It's Andrea Cabrini. I haven't seen you so I thought I'd call and see how the case was going. I know there was another murder, but I guess no one at the lab was involved, huh? I hope everything's okay."

That one embarrassed me. Once again, I'd forgotten about Andrea. The fact that she thought she needed to give her last name told me what a poor friend I'd been to her, calling her for help, **and** seldom otherwise. I made a note to invite her to my engagement party. Rose would be delighted that I was thinking along those lines.

"MESSAGE THREE. NINE FIFTY-SIX A.M." The last one.

"Hi, Aunt G and Matt if you're home. Wayne Gallen wants to meet me, one last time he promises, so I'm going. If you're around...hello...are you screening your calls? Guess not. Well, anyway, I'll be meeting him in about an hour, so, like eleven o'clock, and if you can meet me there it would be great, but if not, no prob, okay?"

It took a few seconds to register. Wayne Gallen was in jail, wasn't he? I slammed my foot on the brake, pulled over to the curb and then into a supermarket parking lot. I caught my breath and tried to construct the timeline. What was the time on MC's message? I couldn't bear to listen to the first two messages again to find out. I knew it was this morning, after Andrea's, which was around nine-thirty. No matter—Berger had told me Wayne was pulled in in the middle of the night and would be held for twenty-four hours. So either Wayne Gallen had escaped, or someone else called MC.

I knew where Lorna Frederick was. Berger's voice rang in my mind. *The Houston PD can't find Simpson.* Then I heard MC's voice: *He did a pretty good Texas accent...*

Alex Simpson, the man who was so good at disguising his voice, had called MC, pretending to be Wayne Gallen. But where were they? I didn't think I heard a meeting place on MC's message. I bit my tongue and punched in all the numbers to listen to the messages again, this time as impatient as if someone's life depended on it. I played them through. "MESSAGE ONE… MESSAGE TWO…" I wished I'd read the instructions to my phone system more carefully. I was sure there was a way to skip to the third message, but this was not the moment to experiment. It had taken two tries to reach the messages at all this time. My fingers were slippery with moisturizer and my brain was searching for what to do next.

I punched in the number for the hospital and asked for Matt's extension.

I heard his cheery "Hi, I'm all set to go."

Like it or not, I was about to change his mood.

"MC is in trouble, Matt. Alex Simpson is in Revere and has managed to lure her…someplace."

"Hold on, hold on." A steady voice, that allowed me to tell Matt what I knew and what I didn't know.

"They could be anywhere," I said. "What does he want with her? It's over; there's nothing he can do now to avoid arrest."

"He might just want to get back at someone. Or he might have some hostage scheme in mind. That's not important right now."

"It *is* important. This probably means Lorna's telling the truth and Alex is the one behind the murders." I took a breath. "I'm sorry. I know what you mean."

"Let's work with this. MC wouldn't go anyplace that would be obviously too private or hidden."

"No, she wouldn't. She'd want to be in a public place." I tried not to be influenced by the fact that MC had done a number of not-so-sensible things in her life, like letting a man push her around. She was over that phase, I told myself.

"A public place, like a restaurant."

"Yes," I said, getting into the rhythm. The man who'd been having trouble staying conscious lately was helping me calm down. "But her message came just before ten o'clock. Too early for lunch, so a coffee shop. In fact her message said they were going for coffee. Why didn't I think of that sooner?"

"Now we're getting somewhere. What would be her favorite coffee shop, where she'd feel comfortable? Someplace you would know also, so she wouldn't have to give you directions or anything like that."

"You mean if she remembered to tell me where."

"Right."

In my mind I ran up and down the streets of Revere looking for a coffee shop. Then it came to me. "Tomasso's Coffee Annex. We had coffee there last week. It's not that far from where I am."

"Stay where you are, Gloria." I'd never heard his voice so firm. "I'm hanging up. If you want to do anything, try Berger's cell phone while I track the nearest cruiser."

I sat in my Cadillac and looked ahead of me. My eyes soared over the roofs of the cars in the parking lot, toward the roof of Tomasso's Coffee Annex, about a mile away, through city streets. I tasted blood from where I'd been chewing my lips.

The connection was broken, but I heard Matt's voice again. *Stay where you are.*

THIRTY-SEVEN

MC CHOSE A LARGE ARRANGEMENT of asters, mums, and some tiny purple stems only her mother and a florist would be able to name. She wrote out a thank-you message to Gloria and Matt on a small card and filled out forms to have the basket delivered to Fernwood Avenue.

The whole process took longer than MC thought it would— it must have been the pimply young clerk's first day, the way he kept going to the back of the shop for answers to questions. MC bounced from one foot to the other.

Not that she was eager to see Wayne Gallen, just anxious to get it over with.

She was, in fact, having second thoughts about the whole idea. What if she just didn't show up? Any normal guy would take it as a lost cause and head home, but Wayne wasn't your normal guy. She wouldn't put it past him to tear up his ticket until he had his last look at her. She pulled at her hair, wishing she hadn't washed it after her run. Maybe if she looked scraggly he'd bug off.

The kid clerk was in the back, probably getting a lesson in addition. MC was the only customer in the tiny shop, which smelled just like the parlors she passed every day on her way to and from her apartment. A light rainfall had started up again out-side, perfect for her dreary meeting.

She rolled her shoulders back. Okay, this was a good time to practice the mind/body breathing technique Rick at the health club had taught her. She stood still, focused on her stomach, and imagined a small balloon in that space. She breathed in, inflat-ing the balloon, counting off ten seconds. She heard Rick's voice.

Hold for ten seconds. Now gently deflate the balloon, exhaling through your mouth.

Good thing there's no one else in here, she thought. *This could look weird.*

MC left the store and got in her Nissan, silently cursing Wayne Gallen as she turned the key in the ignition. She looked at the empty cup holder and wished she could look forward to the upcoming espresso at Tomasso's. She felt like calling Matt, finding out if you could have people deported to their home states.

There I go, relying on someone else to solve my problems, she thought.

A little girl in lavender pants and pink sneakers crossed in front of her while MC was stopped at a light. A woman old enough to be the girl's mother held her hand until they reached the opposite sidewalk. Tears came to MC's eyes, matching the light mist on her windshield. *What's this all about? Don't tell me I wish I had a kid? Or that I were six years old again?*

When the light turned green, MC pulled over to the curb. A new decision came to her. She clenched her jaws and nodded, as if she were agreeing with herself. She flipped through the CD holder on the passenger seat and found an upbeat jazz disk Matt had given her. She shoved it into her player and turned the volume up. She moved forward, got into the left lane, and made a U-turn, heading toward Revere Beach. She imagined herself standing under one of the pavilion rooftops, her breathing slowing to the sound of the surf.

She made a firm resolution never again to have coffee with anyone unless she wanted to.

The best thing was she'd forgotten to say where she was meeting Wayne, so she didn't have to worry about Aunt G getting stuck with him.

THIRTY-EIGHT

STAY WHERE YOU are, Matt had said, surely the most sensible advice.

I started the car and rolled out of the parking lot. A right onto the street would take me to the hospital, a left to Tomasso's. *There's still time to be sensible.* I turned left, my windshield wipers going more slowly than my heartbeat.

I punched in Berger's cell phone number. When it rang through to his voice mail, I clicked off, not bothering to leave a message.

I made it to Tomasso's in record time, in spite of a new downpour, ignoring the speed limit as if I had a siren and flashing lights attached to my Caddie. I'd hoped to see six or seven cruisers crisscrossed in front of the restaurant, but the street was quiet. I didn't see MC's Nissan, either, but realized it didn't mean anything, since she might have walked.

I pulled up across the street from Tomasso's and studied the exterior of the squat yellowish building. The right side, the main dining room, was dark, but the Coffee Annex on the left seemed busy as usual. Through the long narrow window onto the street I could make out a few people at the drink counter, several occupied tables and chairs, and the long handles of baby strollers.

Once again I was on a kind of stakeout without a description of the person I was there for. I let out a loud sigh. *With any luck,* I thought, *Alex Simpson doesn't know what I look like, either.*

I checked my watch. Eleven-ten. MC had said she'd be here about eleven, but she tended to run late. Or, MC was across town in another coffee shop. That thought was too frightening to pursue.

I reviewed my options.

I could go into the restaurant and look for a Texan. I wondered what the chances were that Alex too had a handlebar mustache. I figured MC would have mentioned that at some point.

Be more specific, I told myself, *look for a man—did I know his age? He'd be old enough to run a major science program, and he'd be sitting alone. Looking like a killer.*

I got out of my car to the sound of *ding ding ding.* My keys. Not that I was nervous.

At the last minute I decided not to enter through the front door. What if Alex had a gun pointed and ready as soon as MC gave a sign that she recognized me? What if he was shooting everyone coming through the door? That theory was happily blown when an old man with a cane entered and I heard no shots or sounds of struggle.

There was a small alley around the side of the restaurant, along the left wall of the building, on the Coffee Annex side. In the old days of the bakery, I remembered, there was a delivery door there.

I got back in my car and drove up the block and around so that I was now one half a building past the restaurant, on the same side of the street. From this position, I could exit my car and walk around the front of it, and then down the alley without being seen by the people in the shop.

I got out again, this time remembering to take my keys.

Thanks to unpredictable weather the last few days, I was wearing my flat, black boots, comfortable and rubber-soled. Quiet, as the shoes of a scout should be. There was no window along the wall, no opening except the old delivery door with a new-looking storm door in front of it. A narrow overhang prevented me from getting soaked. I made my way down the alley, keeping my back against the wall. *Another jacket lost to the job,* I thought, as I heard the scraping of the rayon against the rough wood.

In front of me was the yard to the next house, raised off the sidewalk and surrounded by a chain-link fence. If anyone were looking out the top window, what would they think? The senior-citizen branch of the CIA let loose on the street? An inmate from the nearest asylum? I picked my way through orange peels and half-crushed soda cups and straws. And Styrofoam to-go containers, to remind me of Matt waiting for me at the hospital. I took the reminder as a signal to turn off my cell phone, in case he tried to call me. Wouldn't that make an amusing headline on the police blotter—RESCUE ATTEMPT FOILED WHEN CELL PHONE RINGS.

I could hear crowd noises from inside the shop, but not too loud, with background music that could have been classical jazz or some other instrumental strains. I pictured the interior of the restaurant just behind the door. I'd been inside enough times and had a clear memory of the rest rooms at the back, beyond the door, between the main dining room and the coffee shop. When I entered the door, I'd be not quite that far back, but in front of the kitchen area and directly behind the famous, enormous copper vat.

Only after I pulled the storm door toward me and felt the old wooden door give way at my gentle push did I realize I'd had no backup plan in case the doors were locked. *Better lucky than smart,* my father, Marco Lamerino, had often said.

I listened for police sirens, but heard none. I couldn't imagine what was taking them so long.

I slipped into the back of the restaurant. A couple of young men in kitchen-help outfits saw me and smiled, as if this were an everyday occurrence. I smiled back. I was prepared with an "I'm looking for the ladies' room" or "I just want to check the bulletin-board photos" defense, if questioned.

I smelled Tomasso's wonderful, strong coffee and realized I'd had nothing to eat or drink since a fingerful of brownie batter at two in the morning. Pretty soon I'd be back as a regular customer in the front of the shop, I told myself.

I positioned myself behind the copper vat. At my height, I was mostly hidden by the vat, and I could look through the space between the center urn and one of the smaller sections, over the largest spout. The eagle at the very top of the center section hovered over me.

I scanned the area.

The ORDER HERE and PICK-UP HERE counters on my left had no one in line at the moment. Several tables along the right were occupied by women and children in strollers or booster seats. The new daycare environment. A row of tables down the middle of the room held an old couple that included the man with the cane, a young Asian woman writing in a notebook with a textbook to her side, and...a man by himself, his back to me, on a black wrought-iron chair not more than four feet away. Average age, average size.

It was Alex Simpson. I knew because of his posture, his tight black jeans, his pointy maroon boots sticking out into the aisle. Nothing, really. Just that he was the only single man and I didn't like the looks of him, even from the back. The good news was MC was nowhere in sight.

The next moments rolled into one. Two RPD cruisers pulled up in front of Tomasso's. Through the front window, I could see four uniforms swagger toward the door, two abreast. As they entered the shop, the man in front of me, who I was convinced was Alex Simpson, stood up, reached his right arm back, and lifted his plaid jacket.

The silver butt of a gun stuck out from his belt.

I felt part of a naturally flowing drama and let my mind and body respond freely. I grabbed hold of the thin strap that secured the vat against a floor-to-ceiling beam. I slipped the strap from its loose knot and did a quick calculation. If the vat's center of mass was where I thought it should be from its external proportions, the vat would topple straight ahead, its towering center section hitting only the man and no one to either side of him.

I placed my hands squarely in the shiny vat, side by side, and pushed it over with all my might.

When the first section hit Alex's right shoulder he was bent slightly, his hand on the handle of his gun. He turned a few more degrees and I caught his expression. His tanned face was pinched, first in surprise, then in pain as the eagle landed on his head.

My calculation had been correct.

The RPD rushed toward Alex Simpson, trapped under Tomasso's vat, and arrested him.

THIRTY-NINE

IT'S ALWAYS LIKE THIS, I thought. A stormy week or so, and then a peaceful gathering of everyone I love. Matt was more than halfway through his radiation regime and was doing fine, better than in his pre-therapy stage, in fact.

Rose was pleased that Matt and I accepted her offer to throw an engagement party at the Galiganis' residence. Our only stipulation was no presents. As a result we got a variety of amusing items, including an enormous "police badge" for me, made of plaster of Paris, and an oversized blue ribbon with BEST COUPLE in gold letters.

I lingered for a while in a corner of the living room with Jean and her children—my in-laws to-be. Alysse had a large red mark on her cheek. At first I thought it was a teenage rash, but on closer look I saw that it was a giant letter S.

"It's for Stevie, my boyfriend," Alysse said.

Jean rolled her eyes. "It's what they do these days. Thank God it's not permanent ink. I'm sure Stevie isn't permanent."

Alysse's turn to roll her eyes.

I roamed the room listening to the spectrum of conversations, joining one now and then, but mostly thrilled to belong to this gathering.

My first stop was with MC and Daniel Endicott, standing by the fireplace, each leaning an arm on the mantel.

Daniel to MC: Maria Telkes's heating system used black sheet metal collectors to capture solar energy, then it was stored in these bins by the phase-change of a sodium compound.

MC to Daniel: I read about that. I think it was sodium sulphate decahydrate.

Daniel to MC: So would you like to see the traps we use for the coyotes? I have some in my garage. Then maybe grab some dinner?

MC to Daniel: Sure.

I smiled and wandered to the police conversation.

Matt on a chair, with Berger leaning over him: I guess he [Alex Simpson] thought he'd walk MC out the door with a gun held subtly to her back and…who knows? Make an issue of the fact that he wasn't going to surrender easily?

Berger to Matt: Gallen was an even stranger guy. I saw him after the D and D stint. He told me he considered himself a failure because he never got to kill anyone. He wanted to kill Forman at the Beach Lodge that night, before Forman could get to MC, but when he got there Forman was already dead. Of course, now we know that Simpson killed Forman. Gallen said he wanted to kill Powers, but Simpson beat him to that, too.

Matt to Berger: Can't arrest anyone for talking. So it looks like Simpson was in Revere for a week or so, not on his dude ranch.

Matt to Berger: Yeah, I guess he didn't completely trust his errand boy.

Elaine and my cousin Mary Ann were at the buffet table together, filling lovely china plates with salads and calzone from Rose's grandmother's recipe, which called for both pepperoni and sausage.

Mary Ann to Elaine: I'll be glad when they're married and not living…well, whatever they call it these days.

Elaine to Mary Ann [scooping polenta onto her plate]: They call it fun!

At the other end of the room, the two morticians talked shop.

Frank Galigani to his son and partner, Robert: The aspiration process has nothing to do with the flow, so I don't know what they're talking about.

Robert to Frank: I know, Pa, but this guy at the conference said aspirate for only five minutes unless the case is really bad, you know, if the bowels…

I left quickly.

Rose still had questions about MC's near miss at Tomasso's, and stopped at Matt's chair to inquire about the efficiency of the RPD.

Rose to Matt: Why did it take the police so long to get to the Coffee Annex? Gloria got there first and there must have been a police car closer, don't you think?

Matt to Rose: They were waiting for a fax from Houston PD with a photo of the guy they were looking for.

Matt sent a glance in my direction to remind me I was never one to let something like lack of description of a perp get in my way.

Andrea arrived early to help set the tables. Peter came later but behaved like her date, a pleasure to see.

Peter: I'm so happy for you and Matt, Gloria. Things always work out well in the end, don't they?

Me: They certainly seem to.

Andrea: [smiling hugely, sighing audibly, no words necessary]. Back to the funeral directors.

Robert to Frank: They found the guy's horse, you know. Farther up toward Saugus. I looked into what they do with them.

Frank to Robert: With what?

Robert to Frank: Dead horses.

Frank to Robert: Oh yeah? What?

Robert to Frank: They call it a tallow works factory. They process dead farm animals into byproducts.

Frank to Robert: Like what?

I left again.

Robert's wife, Karla, had picked up Mrs. Cataldo, who'd taught both MC and me chemistry, albeit in different decades. MC took pains to explain to Mrs. Cataldo that not all Texans were evil, that she'd made many wonderful friends there.

Mrs. Cataldo, on the couch, to MC and me, standing: Do you ever use your chemistry, dears?

MC: All the time, Mrs. Cataldo.

Me: Now and then, and when I do I think of you.

Mrs. Cataldo: Do you ever do that amazing trick with the banana and the liquid nitrogen?

Matt passed by just in time to hear Mrs. Cataldo's question. He looked at me. "Don't tell me. Nitrogen is after carbon on the periodic table."

I nodded and gave him my best smile, fiancée to fiancé.